PA...

"Appearance i... ...kes a
young lady desi... ...said
gently. "And ther... ...nds of appealing looks in
the world. Do not disparage yourself."

"My brother calls me his spotty little pixie," Pamela
said, a rueful tone in her voice. "I am so small, just a
dab chick, he says. And freckled. Freckles aren't fashionable."

"Your brother is teasing you because he loves you.
You are, as the French would say, *une petite fille
gamine*. Lively. Mischievous. But it doesn't diminish
how pretty you are."

"Do you really think me pretty?" Her tone was
breathless.

"Yes," he whispered. "You are very lovely."

"Do you think . . . am I pretty enough to fall in love
with, even if a gentleman had been in love with a
lovelier, more elegant lady before me?"

Warmth flooded his heart. It was almost a declaration, he thought, affection welling into his heart like
a healing balm. She was asking him if he could ever
love her after being in love with the elegant, perfect
Dorothea. He turned her on the bench and held her
shoulders, gazing at her pretty, upturned face.

He pulled her close and waited, but there was no
sign he was moving too quickly, no stiffening, no
pulling away. So he encircled her with his arms and
touched her lips briefly with his . . .

Books by Donna Simpson

LORD ST. CLAIRE'S ANGEL

LADY DELAFONT'S DILEMMA

LADY MAY'S FOLLY

MISS TRUELOVE BECKONS

BELLE OF THE BALL

A RAKE'S REDEMPTION

A COUNTRY COURTSHIP

A MATCHMAKER'S CHRISTMAS

PAMELA'S SECOND SEASON

Published by Zebra Books

PAMELA'S SECOND SEASON

Donna Simpson

ZEBRA BOOKS
Kensington Publishing Corp.
http://www.kensingtonbooks.com

One

"Pamela, you are not going out yet! We have just arrived in London, and we are not yet *au courant*. You must see the modiste and the hair stylist and the milliner, and . . ."

Pamela Neville shrugged, wishing desperately she could block out her mother's nattering voice. She had thought she could evade her by sneaking down the stairs and out the front door of Haven House, their London home, but her mother, Lady Haven, was in the gloomy, windowless hall surveying the load of baggage and trunks and ordering the servants around in her most harrying tone.

"Leave the girl alone, Lydia. No one will see her if she goes out with a maid for a walk."

Grand, as always, came to her rescue as she reentered the hall from her tiny ground-floor room. Not everyone's grandmother would be so supportive, but Pamela's mother and her grandmother saw eye to eye on nothing. Pamela flashed the elderly woman, who supported her still-upright figure on a cane, a grateful smile, and the woman dropped her a wink.

"If she goes out looking like a fright, she will damage our stock as a family worth taking seriously!"

And that, of course, was Rachel, her elegant, perfect, *poisonous* older sister. Pamela, still standing on the bottom step of the narrow staircase, gazed at her gloomily, absently rubbing the smooth wood of the newel post at the bottom of the banister. Rach used to be fun when they were children, but now, at twenty-three she was that most deadly of things, a dedicated husband-hunter. This was *her* season, she was convinced of it, and she had prosed on and on ever since the decision to come to London had been made, that they must make every moment count if they were going to catch decent husbands. Rachel's two previous seasons had been cut short by deaths in the family, but this one would see her triumph!

Not that Pamela cared about any of that. She was only there because Grand had promised to help her learn how to attract the attention of their long-time family friend, Sir Colin Varens. If only Colin wasn't stuck on Rachel. If only . . . but that was why she was there. Grand was convinced that his attention could be turned from Rachel to a more deserving object, namely, Pamela!

Resigning herself to staying in, Pamela bounced over to her sister-in-law to be, Miss Jane Dresden, who was sighing over her trunks and valises, baggage that had been sent to London to await their arrival from her invalid mother's home in Bath. "Do you need any help, Jane?"

"It's all right, Pammy," the young woman said, affectionately, ruffling the younger girl's curls. "This is all too familiar to me." She sighed and handed her traveling pelisse to a waiting maid and stripped her gloves off. "I shall have to sort all this folderol out sooner or later, I suppose. My mother doesn't have room in her home, now that she is married. I just didn't think she would send it all at once."

Her tone was sad, and Pamela knew it was because

Jane's mother, recently married to a man Jane despised, had made it clear she did not expect to hear from her only child for some time, and didn't intend to honor the marriage ceremony with her presence. She had all but severed the ties that bound them, now that her daughter was provided with a suitable husband-to-be.

And as Pamela's thoughts turned to that husband-to-be, her only brother, the viscount Lord Haven, bounded into the house from giving orders to the stableman and groom. He rubbed his hands together, and, maintaining a deliberately cheery tone, said, "Isn't this going to be wonderful, Jane?" He went to his fiancée and tenderly chucked her under the chin. "You and I can see the city at our leisure, while the girls hunt for husbands."

Pamela looked from one to the other uneasily, noting the young woman's stiff stance, though she was trying her best to look cheerful. This had not been Jane's idea. She and Gerry, as Geraint Neville, Viscount Haven was called by those who loved him, were supposed to be using this time to build their tiny cottage up home, in Yorkshire—it was the wedding promise and gift he was giving to his wife-to-be—and preparing for their wedding.

But this trip to London so soon after their betrothal was all Lady Haven's idea. She had accosted her son and upbraided him with his sad neglect of his sisters' future. Now that he had a suitable fiancée, how could he ignore the welfare and future happiness of his beloved siblings? And the only place for ladies of their caliber to find mates was in London. During the Season. Which had just started. She would leave it up to his conscience as the head of their family and the guardian of his sisters.

She was masterful at dispensing guilt, a talent she matched with an ability to bully people into doing what she wanted if guilt didn't work. But with her son, guilt was so effective she seldom had to resort to offensive tactics.

He had gone to Jane and told her his mother's proposal. They would only have to stay in London as long as it took to see Rachel well-launched, he promised. And it was an opportunity for Jane to shop for bride clothes and any other purchases for their marriage. Though everyone in the household knew Jane's opinion of London, the *ton*, and the artificial atmosphere of society in general, she had acquiesced.

Pamela could see through Jane's determined cheerfulness at this moment. The poor girl would rather be anywhere but here. Putting her arm through her sister-to-be's, she whispered, "We'll get through this and have a jolly time, you'll see."

Jane gave her a quick hug, and murmured, "You don't like this any better than I do, so don't try to cozen me, little sister."

Lady Haven and the dowager Lady Haven, affectionately known as Grand—it had become virtually a title over the years, for she was a very grand lady when she chose to be—bickered animatedly, Gerry tried to keep peace, Rachel whined and Jane and Pamela just tried to get through it all. The servants, most of them hired from a distance by letter and a few of them poorly trained, milled about with little idea what each was supposed to be doing. The house itself was gloomy and damp, with few windows, cramped passages and narrow chimneys that made the fireplaces smoke relentlessly. The next few months were going to seem like forever, Pamela thought, watching her mother reduce a maidservant to tears.

Forever.

It was only a week after their arrival, but the weather had dramatically improved. From as drizzly and chilly as April could sometimes be, it had turned to sunny and warm, and the trees had burgeoned, throwing off their shrouds to burst forth in tender, green leaves. The tiny pocket garden in the square opposite Haven House glittered wetly with dew, tulips and daffodils poking their cheery heads through greenery to greet the morning sun.

But Pamela's mood, as she sat glaring out the window in her small bedroom early one morning while the household slept, had gone from hopeful to miserable after a week of poking and prodding and endless hours standing for the modiste and submitting to Monsieur Harold, the hair-stylist. Her mother was never happy, especially with the dresses that Grand was demanding Pamela be provided with; not suitable for a girl in her first season, said Lady Haven. And not *for* a girl in her first season, Grand said, since it was, in truth, Pamela's second season.

It did not need to be restated that her first season had been an unmitigated disaster, with her penchant for the company of those to whom she should not even be speaking, her disastrous lack of any skill in dancing, her new love of stableman's cant, and her outrageous antics, the worst of which was dressing in breeches and sneaking into a boxing match.

If her Aunt Viola hadn't died just then, in late March of the previous year, sending the family into mourning and away from London, she would have been in disgrace.

But she had been only eighteen then, and nothing had prepared her for London and the Season. Her mother's attention had all been taken up with the beauteous Rachel and her chance at a glittering match, one to make the *ton* take notice. Pamela had had to scramble into whatever knowledge of proper behavior she could—or in truth, that she wanted to, for it wasn't important to her—and clearly her training had been wanting the year before. But since then she had paid more attention to the dancing master's stern tutelage, and had even had private etiquette lessons with Grand, who had been a most elegant London belle in her own right many, *many* years before. She was supposed to be mature, now, and she was trying, really she was. She did her best to be ladylike, to refrain from inappropriate language, be demure, eliminate the bounce from her step and the laughter from her voice.

So why did she feel not a jot different? Colin would never see her with Rachel around anyway, so why did it even matter?

In that dismal mood, feeling like she was going to burst if she spent another whole day inside, with chattering seamstresses, surrounded by mounds of delicate fabrics, only to be followed by an evening spent with dull, titled nincompoops at some arid ball or musicale, she knew she had to do something for herself, something to soothe the wild impulses that were becoming more difficult to ignore. If she didn't safely vent that valve, she thought—remembering a demonstration she had seen once of a steam engine that the inventor said would blow up if not properly vented— then she would burst out in some shocking speech or do something outrageous in public. Her mother would be furious if that occurred.

She bolted across the room and rummaged around in her trunk, pulling everything out and tossing it on her bed as she lifted out the false bottom that only she knew about. She stared down into the depths and sighed happily. There, at the bottom of the trunk, lay her sanity.

Ten minutes later she crept down the dark stairs. The household slept after another boring outing the night before, a ball, scantily attended and dismal. They were late getting to London for the Season, and it made their mother frantic, trying to catch up with all the other match-making mamas. And so it had been one introduction after another to yawning younger sons and boring barons, vacuous viscounts, and even a maudlin marquess. She had hated every moment of it, despising the men and disdaining the girls, who all looked ready to fall asleep, the appearance of elegant languor was so well inculcated.

Pamela was going to escape, at least for an hour. Maybe then she could stand the rest of the day, the intolerable morass of boredom her life had become. And so she slunk down the stairs, boots in hand, a disreputable cap jammed over her riotous curls, wearing breeches that even the maid she and Rachel shared didn't know she had brought to London. At the bottom of the staircase, she sat on the last step and pulled on her riding boots, then made her way down the long passage to the back of the house, down some stairs and out a service door that her sister probably didn't even know existed in their London residence, Haven House.

The walled-in garden was damp and dank, no sun reaching it this early in the morning. But Pamela's

spirits lifted, even as she noted the dew sparkling on
a straggly plum tree that was just beginning to blossom weakly in the unclean London air. She shivered,
not having anything but an old short jacket of her
brother's to wear over her disreputable costume, but
she trotted briskly through the gate and toward the
stable, knowing Tassie, her bay mare was waiting for
her. That was the one thing she held firm about; she
was going to have her own mount in London.

After some resistance from the stable groom, sur-
mounted when she put on her most haughty air and
told him he would be sacked if he did not obey the
viscount's favorite sister, Pamela was free, free at last.
She wouldn't think of doing this at the fashionable
hour—she knew how it would ruin her family's reputation if the daughter of the house was seen this
way—but it was so *very* early. The park would likely
have only grooms exercising their master's mounts
and other servants cutting through on errands for
their employers. Surely she would be taken for one
of the grooms, with her slight, boyish frame and
short cropped hair tucked up under the cap.

Mounted astride, using a groom's saddle, she trotted south to Curzon Street, past costermongers and
drays delivering produce and coal, and thence to the
park, entering at a canter, her anxious mount seeing
green space ahead. She leaned over Tassie's shoulder and whispered, "And now, my lovely, for a good
gallop!"

It was a heavenly half hour. The landscape
whipped past, and she jumped hillocks and raced
over sloping green swards. It wasn't as good as Yorkshire, but it was better than nothing at all. Her
courage and confidence waxed. If she could just do
this every couple of days, perhaps she could get

through the awful season, and get home to Colin, to show him how changed she was, and how mature. With any luck, Rachel would be married and he would learn to forget her and come to realize his best chance at happiness lay with his old friend, Pamela.

Then they could marry and she could move to Corleigh, his estate near Haven Court, and live in jolly happily-ever-afterdom with Colin and his delightfully eccentric sister, Andromeda. Lost in her daydream, she was completely taken by surprise by someone on a galloping mount who whizzed past her, shrieking.

"Hey!" Pamela shouted. "Didn't anyone ever teach you not to ride so close to . . ." Realizing that the rider was slipping sideways, Pamela shut her mouth and bolted after the rider, who was clearly in grave danger.

It was neck and neck, and then she was close enough to see that the rider was a frightened girl who was clinging to the horse's whipping mane. She had her eyes closed and her mouth open, and tears streamed down her pale face. Pamela urged Tassie closer and grasped the fluttering reins, pulling the mare to a stop slowly, and calming the great heaving beast who still shied and rolled its eyes. Her own perfectly steady mare's demeanor finally calmed the other beast, and Pamela, out of breath, was just opening her mouth to speak to the girl when another rider pelted over the hill just after them.

But he was clearly not out of control. In fact he was probably one of the best natural riders she had ever seen, Pamela thought, admiring his seat, just before the fellow reined to a halt and commenced to roar, in a stentorian tone, "Belinda Amie de Launcey, what the hell do you think you are doing, taking off like that! This was supposed to be a riding lesson, not a galloping spree!"

The pale, quivering girl burst into great, heaving sobs, fresh tears rolling down her cheeks to her pointed chin.

"Do not shout at her like that! She has just had a horrendous experience, and then you go and dress her down like she is an infantry soldier." Pamela leaped down from her mount and moved around to help the girl down from her own heaving, shivering steed.

The fellow leaped down too, and took two long strides. He grasped the sobbing girl by the shoulders and stooped, looking into her eyes. "Belinda, stop crying. You are clearly not injured." He straightened and turned to Pamela.

She gazed at him with frank interest. Nice-looking, though not by any means an Adonis, he was a strongly-built gentleman of medium height, with very dark brown hair and light brown eyes. He was dressed in casual riding gear, and carried a crop that he was tapping against his Hessian boot. He looked like a country gentleman, not a London beau, and she thought him very handsome when he wasn't yelling.

"I took you for a stable lad," he said, shock in his voice. "But you're a girl."

"A lady," she said, drawing herself up to her full, if unimposing, height.

"Pardon me, a lady," he said, with a rusty laugh.

The girl's sobs had subsided, and she gazed back and forth between her two elders.

"I must thank you for your bravery in helping my wayward niece," he said. He put his arm around the girl's shoulders, but the child stayed stiff and separate from her uncle. "Belinda, introduce yourself properly and thank your rescuer."

Feeling awkward, Pamela said, "Oh, she doesn't have to thank me . . ."

"Yes, she does," the man said, steel in his voice. "A little gratitude will not harm her."

"I am Belinda de Launcey, miss, and I thank you." The girl gave a bob that was supposed to be a curtsey.

The man rolled his eyes. "I am Strongwycke," he said, stepping forward and putting out his hand. "Sorry for such an informal introduction, but it seems to suit the surroundings."

"Pamela Neville," she said, taking his gloved hand in her own and shaking.

"*Miss* Pamela Neville?"

She nodded.

"And you are in London . . . ?" He stopped and raised his brows.

"I am in London for the Season with my brother, Lord Haven, and his fiancée. They are here to prepare for their wedding in a few months. And my sister and mother and grandmother; we are all together."

"Sounds like quite the family party. May I call on you and thank you properly, Miss Neville?"

Alarmed, Pamela shook her head. "No! I mean . . ." She paused and considered how to word the next part. She took a step back toward Tassie and twisted the reins around in her hand. "If you don't mind, sir, I would rather this morning meeting remain just between us."

He smiled, and it turned into a grin. He looked her over, from her boots, to her breeches to the dirty hat jammed on her curls. Shaking his head, he glanced down at his niece, and said, "Like clings to like. It seems that you and Belinda have something in common, perhaps a liking for early morning gallops? But you, evidently, are more skilled than my troublesome niece."

Pamela saw the hurt in Belinda's eyes at her uncle's description. His opinion mattered to her, and it no doubt was painful to be described as troublesome. Pamela felt a kinship for the girl.

"I wouldn't have lost control if the stupid horse had not shied at a groundhog." The girl kicked at a rock. "Lucky, my own mare, would never have been so idiotic."

"That's enough, Belinda!"

He could be quite intimidating, Pamela thought, shooting the girl a sympathetic look. Tears stood in her dark eyes, and, heart hurting for her, Pamela said, "Would you like to go for a proper ride later, Belinda? One of those calm, boring ones but . . ." She glanced around in an exaggerated manner and lowered her voice. "If you can see the park sedately, you can tell where to gallop and where *not* to gallop next time. Familiarity is *everything*. I have been here already this spring and walked over the green, you see."

The girl's tears dissipated. "Could we, sir?" she asked, looking up at her uncle.

Strongwycke hesitated, but then said, "Only if I may be allowed to accompany you two ladies." He saw the looks on both of their faces. "I am sorry my presence will be such a damper, but Belinda is my responsibility, and at least for the first time, I will accompany you. Like it or not."

Pamela, noting the inflexibility of his tone and admitting to herself it was not an unreasonable demand, agreed for both of them. "Later then, sir. Shall I meet you at the Curzon Street entrance at three this afternoon?"

Agreement made, Pamela departed as the other two rode off in the opposite direction. For the first time, with acquaintance of her own, she could look forward to the afternoon without dread.

TWO

"What do you mean you are going riding? We are promised to Lady Marrowby's for a literary reading!" Lady Haven, arrested in mid-movement as she repositioned a vase on a table in the cramped and unpleasant drawing room, stared at her youngest child.

Pamela stared back at her mother in dismay. How could she explain about Strongwycke without revealing her early morning gallop? And without explaining Strongwycke, how could she say how important this afternoon ride was, that it was an engagement, not just a whimsy on her own part?

"If she wants to go riding, she should go riding." Haven, lounging in a chair by the window, threw her a wink.

Pamela sighed in relief. Her brother was going to come down on her side. It was hard to tell with him, sometimes, for he generally let their mother have her way in matters pertaining to what he called his sisters' "social schedule." He was as harried and hectored by their mother as Pamela, so he tried to avoid conflict as often as possible.

"But she cannot go riding alone," their mother pointed out, straightening and glaring at his lounging pose. She was not a tall woman, but her posture was erect and her mien forbidding. She was always perfectly dressed and coifed, and she expected no less from her children. "And we are all going to Lady Marrowby's, I assure you. There is no sense in riding in London anyway, until she has some acquaintance to meet at the park, some *eligible* acquaintance!"

"But Mother," Haven began, sitting up straighter.

"No!" The woman held up her hand, her word final. "Pamela must meet eligible beaux if she is ever to contract a desirable marriage. It is all very well for you, Haven; you are betrothed, *and* to the young lady I picked out, may I remind you. But your sisters are not getting any younger. Would you have them alone and unhappy after I am gone? What are you thinking?"

"Rachel and Pamela will never be alone, Mother; they will always have me," he said, his voice hard.

"Do you truly want your sisters to grow old and ridiculous like Andromeda Varens?"

It was a final blow and Pamela could see in her brother's eyes that it was a telling one. Andromeda Varens, Colin's older sister, was a spinster of what was politely referred to as "a certain age," meaning she was over thirty. Where Pamela saw Andromeda's distinct quirks as interesting and amusing, others just saw her as an aging spinster, firmly on-the-shelf and pitiful. Haven had become increasingly uncomfortable in Andromeda's presence before his recent engagement, since the woman had fixated on him as her only possible beau, and had made a couple of clumsy attempts to entrap him into a marriage proposal.

"Pamela," he said, with a gusty sigh, "perhaps it is best if you go to Lady Marlby . . ."

"Marrowby," his mother corrected. She went back to her vase, pushing it a fraction of an inch closer to the center of the table, than standing back to see the effect of the alteration.

". . . Marrowby's this afternoon. You can go riding tomorrow." He shook out his newspaper, threw himself back in the chair and was lost in the agricultural news.

"But . . ." Pamela looked from her brother to her mother, but there was no aid in any quarter.

"No 'buts,' Pamela," Lady Haven said, crossing the room and looking her daughter over. "Get dressed for an afternoon out. That new light green, I think. I wish your grandmother had not interfered. I thought the pink was much more becoming, and in the design I favored, but she *would* have her say."

Lady Marrowby's town house was everything Haven house was not; it was gracious and airy, bright and beautifully furnished. Light streamed through floor-to-ceiling windows, and white paneling expanded the sunshine throughout the room. And the woman had excellent taste in company. The cream of society was there, well-fed, well-fêted, most of them happily regarding each other in self-congratulatory bliss.

The dowager renewed very old acquaintances, while Jane renewed a few not-so-very-old ones from her previous seasons. Rachel, in her element, made conquests, and their mother made connections. Pamela just made faces.

The reading was poetry, and she despised poetry. But she would have gone through the afternoon much better if she didn't keep looking at the mantel clock, counting the hours as they chimed and knowing that Strongwycke and Belinda were just arriving at Hyde Park . . . had waited for her . . . had given her up . . . were riding . . . and now were likely on their way home, exchanging bitter views on the flighty and irresponsible Miss Pamela Neville.

"Is something wrong, Pammy?" Jane, elegant in pale blue silk cut low, displaying her plump bosom and shoulders, put her arm around Pamela and squeezed.

"Nothing that anyone can help me with," she replied, sighing. She shifted awkwardly, finding even the light stays considered appropriate for her uncomfortable. The lively green color of her dress, trimmed with an embroidered pattern of ivy leaves, was well enough, she supposed, compared to the gaudy pink fright her mother had wanted made for her. It was one of the very rare occasions when Lady Haven did not prevail, and Pamela was grateful for her grandmother's exquisite taste. Her mother, for some reason, though she had impeccable taste for her own clothing, had no idea how to dress her youngest child. Gloomily, she said, "Why must mother control everything so?"

Jane followed Pamela's gaze to Lady Haven, who was monopolizing their hostess; Lady Marrowby, a sweet, motherly woman, had no idea how to escape the older woman's clutches.

"I think it is likely," Jane said, "that she has always felt second-best to Grand."

Pamela, startled, met her future sister-in-law's gaze. "Do you think so?"

"It has occurred to me." Jane threaded her arm through Pamela's. They stood at the back of a few rows of chairs facing the fireplace, while a young man, pacing back and forth by the mantel, nervously shook out a long sheet of paper, clearing his throat preparatory to his oration. "Your grandmother is a formidable force of nature. I can only imagine what it must have been like when your mother married your father and moved into Haven Court."

Pamela chewed her lip. "I've never thought of it that way. You've only known them a few weeks. How did you figure that out?"

"I didn't; I am just guessing. But I don't have a lifetime of being accustomed to their quarrels to blind me." Jane smiled and squeezed the younger girl's arm again, then released her. "I love Grand, but she would be hard to take on as a mother-in-law. I would be terrified. In a way, I admire your mother for always being willing to confront her. It can't have been easy."

Pamela thought about it for a moment. "You're right. No one opposes Grand except Mother." She watched her mother for a moment, how she held Lady Marrowby's arm in an iron grip while that lady desperately looked around the company for a savior.

"That doesn't solve your problem though, does it, whatever it is?" Jane said.

Hesitantly, Pamela confided her dilemma; she confessed her early morning ride, in breeches, and her memorable encounter with the gentleman, Strongwycke, and his niece. "And they will have gone home now, and think I am a complete flibbertigibbet."

"And that matters to you?" Jane's soft voice was barely audible over the droning tones of the reader, who was torturing an epic poem of his own creation, entitled *Ode To A Prince*. It appeared that the long sheet was only the first stanza, for a young woman seated nearby handed him a second page.

"Yes, it does. If you could have seen that poor girl's

face, how it lit up at the idea of an afternoon ride, and how her uncle shouted at her so . . ." Pamela shook her head. "And I *promised!* I never break my word."

Jane examined her face, and then said, "And what was the gentleman's name again?"

"He introduced himself only as Strongwycke," Pamela said, all the misery of her forced abandonment of her new friends suffocating her again, as she thought of Belinda and her uncle and what they must now think of her. "I don't know what else he is called."

Jane elicited a description, and then parted from her young sister-in-law-to-be. Pamela was her favorite, as she was Haven's. And just as Grand did, Jane worried that Pamela's unrequited love for Sir Colin Varens would blind her to any other man who might show an interest in her. But here was a man in whom Pamela seemed—even if she didn't know it herself—to be interested.

Crossing the room to where the elegantly-gowned Grand sat in state, in the most comfortable chair available, Jane knelt by her and whispered, and then asked a question. The old woman frowned and thought for a moment. Then her blue eyes, so like her grandson's, blazed with interest.

"Strongwycke?" she murmured. "There is . . . let me think." She tapped one crooked finger against the chair arm. "Yes, there is a Lord Strongwycke, Malcolm Bercombe. He is the sixth Earl of Strongwycke, a Cumbrian title, I believe. I wonder if this is the same one? There cannot be more than one Strongwycke, can there?"

"I don't imagine. Can you mine your acquaintances and find out?" Jane glanced across the room at Pamela; the girl looked so alone and bereft. "There was something in her tone of voice that I found revealing. I can't say for certain, and I am sure she is not aware of it herself yet, but I think she was attracted by Lord Strongwycke. If he should be of the right age and eligible . . ." She didn't need to finish her statement.

The dowager nodded. "Good work, child. Let me do some gossiping and I shall find out more."

"Good. Now I suppose I must go forth and socialize."

"Do not make it sound like it is such a chore, child." The old lady's blue eyes twinkled with amusement. She had revived with the energizing London atmosphere of afternoon visits and balls and company. The city had changed in the many years since she had last graced its drawing rooms and parlors, but people, for all the different fashion of clothing they now wore, were still people. She was finding endless amusement in their vanities and scandals.

Jane sighed as she stood and straightened, patting out the wrinkles in her blue silk. "It *is* a chore." She didn't share the dowager's enjoyment of human intrigue and frailty. Perhaps it was just that she had spent far too much of her life in drawing rooms, listening to gossip. From London to Brighton to Bath, she knew this life only too well, and despised it. Life in Yorkshire had all the novelty of newness, as well as suiting her temperament better. She had always longed to live a simpler life in a cottage in the country, and Haven had promised her a cottage of her own as a wedding present. All of her eager anticipation was dwindling, though, in the unhealthy London atmosphere, to a suspicious doubt of it ever actually happening. Or at least in the way she so fer-

vently desired, marriage in the Lesleydale chapel
and a fortnight in their private cottage, shut away
from his interfering family.

London, as far as Jane was concerned, was no fit
place for humans. But while she was immured in
the awful old town, she would do what good she
could. She made her way across the room to their
hostess, intent on rescuing her from Lady Haven's
single-minded absorption. Delicately, skillfully, she
detached the younger lady from the older, pointed
Lady Haven in the direction of another acquaintance, and chatted to the grateful Lady Marrowby.

But all the while she was mulling over her own
unhappiness.

It had all happened so quickly, and she supposed
that was the problem. There was a brief, delirious happiness when she and Haven had become engaged,
and then suddenly, before she had time to come to
terms with her new status as a bride-to-be, she was
thrust back into a milieu she knew too well and de-
tested, the artificial world of "society," with all that
implied. Idle chit-chat, poseurs, frauds, and gossip.

If only she could summon up even a modicum of
enthusiasm for the Season. But all Jane knew was
that only three weeks after coming to an understanding with her intended husband, a man she had
thought to despise on sight, and finding that not
only was he the perfect husband for her, they were
also in agreement on so many things, including their
preference for country life over city, she was
plumped back down in the middle of everything she
disdained.

And she was so very lonely.

Even as she chatted with her hostess, smiled and
greeted others, listened with what she hoped was an

intelligent look on her face, she was lonely. And she resented that loneliness. Now that they were in London, Gerry was busy all the time, having decided to make the most of the London trip with meetings and purchasing trips and a thousand other incomprehensible business ventures. She was still deeply in love with him, but wondered if he was ever going to defy his mother and put his wife-to-be first. Was this a portent of their life together? Would she always come second?

She braced herself with a stern inner resolve. She was a lucky woman, and somehow, everything would turn out for the best. She would find a way to manage her fiancé, would return to Yorkshire in time to get married and be happy again. In the meantime, if she could act as a cupid for her favorite sister-in-law-to-be, Pamela, then at least the weeks in London would be put to good use.

In the meantime there was this recitation to be gotten through, and then an evening's entertainment at the theater. One more long London day.

Evening was closing in. As his valet pulled the curtains of his bedchamber closed against the deep purple of twilight, Strongwycke straightened his cravat and gazed at himself in the mirror, not to admire his valet's work, but to make sure he was correct in every way, not a fold out of place, nor a stray hair. One's position in society very much depended on presenting to the world a correct face, it seemed to him, emotionless and proper. He had been young and carefree once—was that only a couple of years ago?—but now knew that life was a grim and sober affair. The only pleasure lay in doing one's duty and doing it well.

This evening's theater engagement did not promise to give any pleasure, but the gentleman who had given the invitation was a valuable government ally, so Strongwycke knew he must present his best face. He must be charming but not too forward, agreeable but not obsequious, relaxed but not informal. He well knew the drill.

But even as he asked his valet to fetch his greatcoat and hat and stick, his mind kept wandering back to the afternoon ride with his niece.

And the disappointment on Belinda's face when she realized that her new friend was going to disappoint them. He could have told her Miss Neville wouldn't remember their engagement. The girl was clearly flighty at best, wild at worst; totally unsuitable for any kind of acquaintance, especially with his impressionable niece.

So why had he agreed to her invitation to ride? Had it only been the look on Belinda's face as she talked with Miss Neville, the first time he had seen her eyes shine since her parents had died almost a year before in that dreadful coaching accident?

Or had it also been something gallant and adorable in the young Miss Neville's expression?

Not that she attracted him. She was clearly too young, looking not even sixteen with her cropped locks and slender frame. And that outfit! He shuddered, hoping Belinda didn't get any ideas about riding in breeches.

He tapped on the door of her sitting room and opened it. Miss Linton, the governess he had hired, was sitting with Belinda by the fire and reading from a history book, but his niece was clearly not listening.

She had been staring gloomily at the fire, and dully looked up, meeting his gaze with a listless apathy that tore at his heart.

He entered and crouched by her chair. "I'm off now," he said.

"To the play?"

He nodded. "Would you like to go to the theater sometime?"

"I suppose," she said. "But it doesn't matter."

He sighed and longed to reach out, to touch her unruly drift of dark hair, but they were not on those terms. If he could find anything she would look forward to, anything that would make her happy—but there was nothing. She spiraled daily between this dreadful apathy and bitter anger, with little ground in between. He stood and nodded to the governess.

"I must be off, then. I'll see you at breakfast tomorrow morning, Belinda. Shall we go riding again, another lesson?"

"If you like," she said, and then turned her gaze back to the fire.

He departed without another word. There was nothing left to say. That morning he had seen that brief—oh, so very brief—flare of interest during the encounter with Miss Neville, and her disappointment that afternoon when the flighty young woman hadn't the decency to show up at the park had been devastating.

Even his distracting train of thought had not stopped him from leaving the house, mounting his elegant coach and rapping on the roof to signal his readiness to his driver. If this theater invitation had not been extended to him as a very great favor, he would much rather have stayed by his own fireplace in his comfortable study. But as it was, he must suffer a play he had seen before and disliked, and then consume a late dinner at his mentor's home.

Lord Fingal, who had offered the invitation, considered him young; Strongwycke knew that. At just barely thirty, many of the older men thought he needed more seasoning. But the marquess was impressed by Strongwycke's oration in the House and had hinted that the future belonged to such men as the youthful earl. If he wanted that future. He leaned his head back against the cushions, longing suddenly for the green valleys and tumbling hills of his Cumbrian home, Shadow Manor.

When had he left behind the love of his home, the devotion to his people and his land? Was it when Euphemia and her husband died, leaving him the caretaker of their headstrong daughter? Or was it even before that, when Dorothea, the love of his life and his fiancée, had abandoned him for a better catch? And was he making the grave error of staying in the very place that could never soothe the pain of all that tragedy?

He straightened as the coach slowed. They were close to the entrance of the theater, and he must assume the correct attitude and demeanor of a gentleman worthy of Lord Fingal's regard, which meant none of his turbulent emotions must show on his face. He must put aside all his worry and deny his grief. He had become proficient at that, at the very least.

He entered the theater and made his way to Lord Fingal's box.

"Ah, here is the last of our party," Fingal said, greeting him with a smile and an outstretched hand.

Strongwycke moved into the box and greeted the other gentlemen, all selected for their promise as the next wave of power in the Whig party. As the favored son of the moment, he sat by Lord Fingal, an elderly man with an irascible temper and declining mental powers.

The play was a comedy, but Strongwycke found nothing new to laugh at in the antics of the lovers, as sorry a pair as he thought he had ever seen. It hadn't been amusing the first time he had seen it; a second viewing couldn't improve it. And so his attention wandered to the other boxes, lit individually by lamps that glowed softly, shining on the beautiful fabrics of the ladies' garb and swallowed by the dark clothing of the gentlemen. In the not-so-distant past gentlemen had been as gorgeously arrayed as the ladies, but in a relatively short period styles had changed so much, and now proper men's wear was mostly a sober color like dark green or blue, or the most elegant of all, black. Thank the good Lord above, he thought. He couldn't see himself in blue embroidered silk and holding a fan, his face painted and patched.

He recognized most of those in the other boxes. As usual, few made even a show of watching the play, but rather chattered and visited, flirted and gossiped.

His gaze rested on one box where he thought he knew none of the spectators. Perhaps they were new to London. There was a very grand old lady with white hair piled high and dressed with jewels. She was flanked by a lady some years younger than her—Strongwycke raised his glass—yes, she had a dissatisfied air and a peevish mouth. There was a gentleman by her, a bluff, country-looking gentleman with an open, honest countenance. Strongwycke frowned, thinking he might have seen that fellow's face before. The young woman by his side was lovely, in a placid, buxom way.

And then there were two younger ladies in the box, one extraordinarily beautiful. He took in a deep shaking breath. She looked very much like Dorothea, and it hurt just below his ribcage to see her, looking so familiar, and flirting with two gentleman who had clearly just entered the box, seeking an introduction.

And then there was a girl in the corner, dressed in lovely clothes but looking forlorn. His heart went out to her. She seemed so lost and unhappy. Where had he seen those large eyes before? What color would they be?

He picked up his opera glass again and focused, with some difficulty, on the young lady's face. Curling brown hair, slight figure, and yes, lovely, large eyes. Eyes he had seen before. . . .

In the park, looking up at him with a smile. It was Miss Pamela Neville. He snapped his opera glass closed and tossed it down on the empty seat beside him. He turned his attention back to the stage, and for the rest of the act kept it there.

Three

Face white, lip raw from being bitten, Pamela stared across the theater at the box. *The* box. Strongwycke was there, and she had caught sight of him just as he snapped his glasses shut and threw them down with a quick, angry gesture. Had he seen her? He *must* have seen her. Surely there could not be two people in the theater with whom he had reason to be so angry.

She longed to leave their box and race down to tell him it wasn't her fault. She would have been in the park if she could have, sent him a message if she couldn't, but. . . .

She felt rather than saw someone sit down in the seat next to hers.

"Pammy, what is wrong, dear?"

It was Jane, and Pamela turned gratefully to her. "Do you see that box—five boxes over?" Her finger came up to point out the box in question, but Jane patted her hand down. Reminded it was impolite to point, Pamela clenched her satin-gloved hands together and explained more thoroughly. "Five boxes to our right, and on the same level. Do you see a gentleman there, a good-looking gentleman with brown hair and a strong profile? He is staring at the stage intently?"

Jane counted and found the box—with the arc of the theater seating she could see the inhabitants of that box seat reasonably well—but said, her words concealed from the others by the loudly declaiming actors on stage, "Pam, there are five or six gentlemen, and at least two have brown hair."

"But there is only one good-looking one."

"No, both brown-haired men are quite presentable."

Pam frowned and gazed over. How could Jane think the other gentleman held a candle to Strongwycke? Really, was she blind? "The one closest to us!"

"Ah!" Jane smiled. "Is that a gentleman you find interesting?"

"No! I mean . . . that is Strongwycke! Oh, I wish I could go down and tell him . . . apologize for not keeping our engagement this afternoon." Pamela rose, thinking that if she could just make her way there with no one noticing. . . .

Jane put out a restraining hand. "Pamela, *think*, my dear. You must learn to think before taking action on your impulses. You know you can't do that. No lady can just wander into a gentleman's box, especially when she hasn't even been properly introduced to him. People would mistake you for . . . well, they would misunderstand."

Flushing, Pamela didn't need a hod of bricks to fall on her to understand Jane's concern. Her impetuous behavior was what had caused trouble for her in her first season. It seemed that she wasn't completely cured of her rashness, then, though she thought she had learned circumspection. She took a deep breath and pressed one hand against her stomach, which was oddly fluttery. "Does that mean there is no way to tell him?"

"I didn't say that. Just sit and wait, my dear." Jane

rose, swept her elegant gold skirts behind her and
went over to hold a whispered conversation with
Grand.

Pamela saw her grandmother slew her gaze
around to the box in question, and raise her opera
glasses. The two women conversed, and then Haven
himself, stiffly formal in black evening wear, was
brought into the discussion. He used his grandmother's glasses, frowned thoughtfully, and then his
face lit in a broad smile. He nodded enthusiastically,
and then went back to watching the play.

And then nothing. Pamela fiddled with her fan,
slapping it open and shut and tapping it against her
thigh. Their box was full, Rachel's "court," as Pamela
thought of it, the two young gentlemen who had arrived, having never left after an introduction was
effected. They flirted and gossiped together,
Rachel's rippling laughter silky and soft, perfectly
modulated as always.

The second act was over, and still, nothing had
been said. Were they all just teasing her? Was no one
going to do anything? Pamela felt like she was going
to jump out of her skin, and the urge to race down
and tell Strongwycke what had happened that afternoon got the better of her. She would find a way to
get his attention and call him out of the box. Maybe
one of the theater serving staff would help her, take
in a message or something. Surely that would be acceptable.

She rose, quietly, and started back to the back of
the box, when a strong hand closed over her wrist.

"Little sister, sit down like a lady and wait!"

Haven so rarely spoke in that tone that Pamela sat
back down abruptly.

"I have heard the tale of your escapade, and we

will solve your dilemma, I promise," he said, more kindly. "But if you had confided to me *why* you wanted to go riding in the park this afternoon, we could have avoided this imbroglio."

Rachel and her two beaux left the box to walk and find refreshments, and Lady Haven had spied some of her acquaintance and was leaving the box to confront them about something. Haven, with Jane on his arm, left the box, too. Pamela and Grand remained alone.

"Try to cultivate some air of tranquillity, my dear child," the old lady said, dryly, rearranging the folds of her spectacular ice-blue silk gown.

"What?"

"And do not say 'what' in that stupid tone." The dowager, exasperated, shook her head. "You should say, 'I beg your pardon?' And you wonder why Sir Colin prefers Rachel to you! At least Rachel behaves like a lady!"

Pamela, her feelings wounded, folded her hands together on her lap and bit her lip, mortified tears welling up. What was wrong with her? It wasn't like her to take Grand's sharp words to heart, nor to fuss so just because someone had gotten a mistaken impression of her. But all afternoon and even through dinner she had been pondering what Strongwycke and his niece must be thinking of her, and then he was there, so close. She could apologize, explain! She hated the thought that they would despise her for her ill-manners.

Was it so wrong to want not to appear like an ignorant featherbrain?

But somehow that put her in the wrong with everyone. No one understood, not even Jane, in whom she had confided. She wished she had never left

Yorkshire. At least there she could ride and visit Corleigh and play with the dogs. Here she was just a nuisance to everyone, even Grand and Jane and Haven.

She took a deep, steadying breath.

And now she was being just as childish as everyone accused her of being, petulant and self-pitying. Grand was right. If she wanted to attract Colin's notice, she must learn to behave in a ladylike and quiet manner, to become demure even, as Rachel appeared, even though Rachel was far from demure in truth. And there was no time like the present to practice. Pamela straightened and sat, taking in a deep breath and letting it out slowly, trying her best to look serene.

The dowager chuckled, then, and clucked her tongue. "You look, child, for all the world like some martyr about to be sent in to face the lions. Relax your expression. Empty your eyes. Your face tells a thousand tales, child, and that is not the London way."

"I know," Pamela said, ruefully. "I will do my best, Grand."

"That is all I ask."

Strongwycke was listening to Lord Fingal expound about some abstruse political theory that he could not, in truth, give a damn about, but in which he must appear interested. He was almost cross-eyed with boredom. The other gentlemen had left the box in the break to stretch their legs, they said. In reality it was to get away from the sound of Fingal's monotonous voice.

There was a tap at the door in the back of the box, and a couple entered.

Strongwycke stood.

The gentleman came forward and stuck out his hand. "Strongwycke, am I right? I am Gerry Haven; we met at Lord Langley's three years ago at that gathering where we were discussing sheep!"

Strongwycke frowned for a moment and then an involuntary smile came to his lips. "Yes! I remember! You and I stayed up all of one night discussing the new breeding experiments over a bottle of Langley's best brandy! By the end of it, we made very little sense at all. I seem to recall we had decided that Napoleon's idea of a tunnel to the mainland was a jolly good idea, for then the drovers could take flocks over to the continent to graze, once all the grasslands in England were exhausted!"

Both men laughed, and Haven pulled the young woman at his side forward. Strongwycke heard the softness in the other man's voice as he gazed down at her and said, "This is my fiancée, Miss Jane Dresden. We are in London to buy bride clothes and get ready for our marriage."

After congratulations, Haven glanced at Lord Fingal, and then said, "Strongwycke, could you come back to my box so I may introduce you to my family?"

Guiltily realizing he would like nothing better than to escape Fingal's political theorizing, Strongwycke said, "Certainly." He introduced the couple to his mentor, and then said, "If you will excuse me, my lord?"

The old man grumpily released his captive with an ill-tempered nod.

It was not until Strongwycke was on his way down to their box that he realized that he had seen Haven and his wife-to-be, and they were in the same box as Miss Neville. But it was too late to avoid the contact. He was already there, and Haven was introducing first his grandmother, the regal looking lady with the white hair piled high.

"My mother is out gossiping, and my oldest sister is around somewhere, but may I introduce you to my youngest sister, Miss Pamela Neville? Pamela, this is the Earl of Strongwycke."

His sister! Strongwycke, stiffening, bowed low, and said, "Your servant, Miss Neville." But when he looked up, it was directly into her large, speaking eyes, gray-green, he noted, and fringed with brown lashes. There was an appealing scattering of freckles over her pert nose, though someone had applied powder to try to make them disappear.

"L-lord Strongwycke?" She rose and curtseyed, then dropped back into her chair.

"Will you join us, my lord, for the third act?"

That was the dowager Lady Haven, the viscount's grandmother, and her question was put in such a way that it sounded like a command. But he was not one to be commanded, not by anyone, not even an elderly lady. "I must return to my box. I am with Lord Fingal's party, and we have a late dinner to attend afterward."

"He will not mind if you sit with us for one act," she said, reaching out for his arm as the lights in the theater dimmed and there was a bustle at the back of the box. Some people entered, presumably Haven's other sister and beaux, and the elderly lady had a firm grip. It would have been the height of rudeness to pull away from her abruptly.

When he was finally released from her grasp, he found himself shifted to a seat near Miss Neville, he wasn't sure how. He turned to make his excuses and leave, but the young lady's eyes were fastened on him, and he sat back down.

"Sir," she whispered. "I have been so worried all day. I *so* wanted to come this afternoon for our ride in the park, but my mother had made other plans, and then I could not. . . ."

She was interrupted by the strident tones of the subject of their speech, the other peevish-looking woman he had noted from his box.

"Jemima Lindsey has gotten positively fat. Her chins—there are more than one—wiggle when she talks. I swear I could not keep my eyes from them, but if she is offended it is her own fault. She should start slimming. Who is this?" She eyed Strongwycke.

Haven made the introductions. The more she talked—and she talked through the entire third act—the more Strongwycke sympathized with Miss Pamela. By the end of the play, he was quite in charity with her. There was nothing the child could have done if her mother had chosen to command her time.

As the lights came up at the break before the juggler was to perform, he rose, though. "I must return to my party, as we aren't staying for the last performer." He bowed and thanked them for their hospitality.

The dowager took his hand when he was making his obeisance to her. "Are you alone in London, sir?"

"I am presently with my niece, for whom I have engaged a governess."

"But you have no wife or . . . anyone?"

"No," he said, shortly, thinking bitterly of Dorothea. They would have been married six months or so by now.

"Then would you attend, with your niece, of

course, a very informal dinner party for my grand-daughter's birthday?"

Lady Haven squawked, "Dinner party? For what?"

"For Pamela's birthday, of course."

Miss Dresden glanced at Pamela, and then at Lord Strongwycke. "What a lovely idea, Grand. A party for Pamela's twentieth birthday. It isn't every day a girl turns *twenty!*"

Strongwycke, taken by surprise, glanced over at Pamela Neville, whose cheeks had turned crimson under the scrutiny of all in the box. "I . . . Belinda and I would be delighted," he said, not recognizing his own voice, it sounded so strangled. Twenty? He had taken her for fifteen. Though he should have known differently by her manner and apparel this night. She was gowned in a lovely embroidered silk dress, the color of old ivory and trimmed in green silk ribbon roses. It clung to slender curves, expos-ing her white arms and fragile, lovely bone structure. Twenty. He would have to be circumspect, for if he was not mistaken, there was some degree of match-making in the air, and he had no intention of being tied for life to anyone just then, least of all a young scatterbrain like Miss Pamela Neville.

Yes, he would have to be very, *very* careful.

Four

The sideboard was heavily laden with all manner of breakfast food, from toast and eggs to curried herring and a selection of cheeses. Pamela greeted Jane, who already sat at the table, grabbed a plate and glanced over what was available.

"Why, suddenly, does Grand want to have a dinner party for my birthday?" Pamela shoveled eggs onto her plate and took three pieces of toast. She and Jane were the only ones in the dining room, since Haven had already breakfasted and left the house and Grand, Lady Haven, and Rachel would all be abed for hours yet. She sat down by Jane and nodded when the footman came forward with the coffee pot.

"Perhaps she has taken a liking to Lord Strong-wycke." Listlessly, Jane took a sip of her coffee, but pushed her breakfast away untouched. "You know your grandmother; no one ever questions her motives. She does what she wants."

Pamela glanced down the table at her friend and sister-to-be. Jane didn't look well. Her eyes were puffy and she was pale. Perhaps London didn't agree with her. She knew, having heard the long, whispered quarrels, that Jane hadn't wanted to come to London. She had put up as much resistance as was consistent with her placid character, but then had given way when Haven had given her a certain "look" that Pamela had never seen before. On anyone else she would have called it "sheep's eyes," but Haven had too much natural dignity to be accused of that.

"Bosh," Pamela said, chewing on a piece of toast. She took a gulp of coffee to wash it down and stabbed the air with her fork in Jane's direction. "You told Grand I met Strongwycke in the park, didn't you?"

"Yes, I did. I wondered who he was, and Grand knows everyone and everything. And we decided to ask Gerry about Strongwycke; it is just coincidence that he knows the earl."

"Earl!" Shaking her head, Pamela let out a long, low whistle. "I never suspected he was an earl." Remembering his country clothing and bluff manner when he was riding in the park, it was still hard to reconcile the two, the lofty title and the rather ordinary gentleman to whom it was attached. She pushed her eggs around on her plate and stared absently at the resultant mess. Not at all toplofty, Strongwycke, even if he was a bit surly.

"Yes," Jane replied. She pulled her plate back, took a bit of her toast and chewed. "An earl." She glanced at Pamela, then went on. "And so very good-looking; I have seldom seen such an appealing gentleman. Apparently he is from the north, too. Last night when Gerry and I were, uh, talking, he told me that Lord Strongwycke's estate is in the Lakes District. Not that far from Haven Court, really, just over the Pennines."

Jane was watching her, Pamela realized. She shrugged. What was she supposed to say? "I appreciated the chance to tell him why I missed our ride in the afternoon, Jane. Thank you. You . . . you didn't *really* tell Haven about that part, did you? That I met Strongwycke on a morning ride I'm not supposed to be taking?"

"I did. Pammy, you know he wouldn't forbid you. All we ask is that you be discreet. It wouldn't do to have you caught at it by anyone who would tattle."

"I know that. I have learned something in the last year, you know. Strongwycke won't tell anyone."

"How do you know?" Jane asked, with a quizzical smile lifting her lips in one corner.

Shrugging, Pamela said, "I don't know for sure, I just feel it." She downed her coffee in one last gulp. "I think he is an honorable sort. But temper! Y'know, he seems pleasant enough on first meeting him, but his poor niece! He barks at her so, it is no wonder the girl looks miserable."

"It cannot be easy for either of them. He isn't married and has no children; he likely never expected to be raising a young girl."

"I wonder why he *is* looking after her?"

Jane played with the ring on her slender finger and slowly said, "I wondered that, too. Gerry says that he saw a notice in the paper about a year ago. Maybe less, he is not quite sure. He hadn't remembered it until now, and only noticed it at all because he had met Lord Strongwycke a year or so before that, and his name was included in the story." She shook her head, her gray eyes filled with gentle sorrow. "Gerry says that Strongwycke's sister and brother-in-law were killed in a carriage accident. That must have been Belinda's parents, and he must have been left her guardian. What a difficult time for both of them, Lord Strongwycke and his niece."

"Are you speaking of that very handsome gentleman who came to our box last night?" Rachel, up hours before anyone could have expected her, floated into the dining room clad in a rose morning gown. She frowned over the sideboard, and picked up one piece of dry toast, nodding to the footman for a cup of coffee, which she drank black.

"Lord Strongwycke," Jane said. "Yes. He is very handsome, isn't he, Pamela?"

She shrugged. Handsome? To be honest, she had thought so immediately, but why anyone would think it had bearing on anything, she still did not know. "I suppose," she said, reluctantly.

"Why Grand invited him to some fictional birthday party for Pamela, I do not understand," Rachel said. "Unless . . ." She smiled slyly, arrested in mid-movement as she picked up her coffee cup. "I wonder if he has taken notice of me? That *must* be it. Perhaps Lord Strongwycke noticed me across the theater and begged an introduction." She sat up straight, her eyes sparkling as she concocted the romantic tale. That it ignored any factual evidence to the contrary she disregarded. "I will thank Grand in that case, for finding a way to bring us together. An earl! He is a very fit *parti* for me, I think."

Pamela and Jane exchanged a look, both restraining giggles. Grand's reaction would be interesting to watch. Pamela was sorely tempted to burst her sister's bubble, to claim prior knowledge of the gentleman, but firmly shut her mouth. Her morning rides were no one's business, and telling Rachel was as good as telling their mother.

"Why are you up so early?" Jane asked, mildly.

Pamela was relieved to see that she was looking a little better for their idle chatter. Maybe she was just missing Haven; her brother was so busy, he rarely found time for his new fiancée. And it was not the done thing in London society for betrothed couples to sit in each other's pockets, even *she* knew that. But still, they had been affianced for such a short time!

"I have an appointment with the modiste," Rachel said. "If I am finally to be presented, my court dress must be ready."

Pamela shuddered. "I am to undergo the same torture. It is an 'honor' to which I do not aspire, but must endure."

Jane silently agreed with Pamela's assessment of the occasion. She had been presented to the Queen, of course, in her long-ago first season, and only remembered it as a hot, stuffy, costly, brief, troublesome affair. But Rachel had ambitions, and being presented was the beginning of her planned conquest of all of London society. They were late coming to the Season, and so she would have to rush things through, which explained her early appearance at the breakfast table. Most ladies had been planning their court dresses, sumptuous old-fashioned monstrosities, for months, or had already been presented. Rachel had missed her presentation other years because of the brevity of her Season. The Neville family had had the bad luck to have a couple of relatives die with extremely poor timing, a fact Rachel had been heard to bemoan most earnestly. That people timed their demises badly was a constant refrain of hers, and she seemed to take it as a personal insult.

It occurred to Jane in that moment that as a newly betrothed lady she could be expected to make her curtsey to the queen again, an ordeal that often accompanied a lady's change in status, as well as her first entrance to society. She shuddered. She would just keep very, very quiet about that possibility.

"When will you and Gerry go back up north to be married?" Pamela asked.

Jane's train of thought interrupted, she shrugged, her mood plummeting. When, indeed? When he stopped pandering to his mother's tyrannical nature? When his love for her, as great as he said it was, won over Lady Haven's determined harping and nagging? Jane hadn't wanted to come to London in the first place, but she knew that it greatly enhanced Pamela and Rachel's consequence to finally have a proper Season with their brother as sponsor, and so she knew, in her more rational mind, that it was necessary, though she hated everything about London: its artificial manners, its required busyness, its emphasis on titles and position rather than goodness of heart.

And so she would do this, for their sake. She fiddled with her china coffee cup and stared off toward the oak sideboard. It wouldn't be so bad if she could get some assurance from her husband-to-be that once the Season was over, they would return to Yorkshire and Haven Court. But now Lady Haven was beginning to hint about a London wedding for the Viscount Haven and his bride, and how it would be the social event of the year, and would so greatly elevate their stature among "those who mattered," whomever they were. Even Grand, as sympathetic as she was, was not averse to the wedding taking place in London.

But Gerry had made promises to her, promises she was not so sure he would keep now. Their courtship had been confusing and strange. On her way to meet the lofty stranger, Viscount Haven, of whom she had nothing but bad reports—he was said to be grim and dour—she had run away and sheltered at a local widow's cottage in the moors of Yorkshire. There, in Mary Cooper's home, she had met a handsome farmer, Gerry Neville, who was everything she had ever imagined a suitor could be, charming, gentle, truly engaging. She had presented herself as Jenny, a lady's maid and relation of Mary's, and over the course of a few short days they had fallen in love, though neither was aware of the other's true identity. It was like a kind of hazy dream to her now, those first days when the thrilling opiate of love had confused her senses and fogged her brain.

Then the cold hard light of truth had shone over their clandestine relationship. They had discovered that they were really Miss Jane Dresden, runaway bride, and the viscount Lord Haven, master of Haven Court.

The mutual revelation of their true identities had been shocking, but they found they still loved each other, and wanted so many of the same things; their home, a family, and country quiet. They still called each other Gerry and Jenny in their increasingly rare private moments. They had been betrothed a scant four weeks now, this very day, but already the pressures around them made them feel more like strangers than they had the first moment they met.

The intimacy was gone, and their arguments came with increasing frequency. It was frightening, because like it or not she was committed to marrying this man, though she was beginning to forget what it felt like to kiss him, even, or hold him.

"Jane?" Pamela, a furrow between her eyebrows, said, "Are you all right? You don't look well at all. I asked, when do you and Haven expect to get married? And go back north?"

"I don't know, Pammy," Jane said, taking a spoonful of sugar and adding it to her coffee. She stirred, concentrating fiercely to keep from getting weepy. She hated weepy females, however. . . .

"Why would anyone be in a hurry to leave London?" Rachel said, her eyes sparkling. "This Season is going to be unforgettable. Just last night I had *two* gentleman soliciting my hand for the next ball. And do you know what I heard? I heard that Lord. . . ."

As Rachel prattled on and Pamela teased her sister, Jane took a deep breath, calming herself. She believed in Haven's love, truly and deeply. She must hold on to that conviction that they were meant for each other. And so she would wait. And renew her determination to at least do some good while in London. If she could help Pamela, who was clearly interested in Lord Strongwycke, even if she didn't realize it herself yet, then her time in London wouldn't be a complete waste.

Just hold on, she told herself.

What little sun there was to cut through the foggy miasma of London could not pierce the gloom of the narrow street lined by townhouses; the city residence of the Havens numbered just one of many tall, compressed townhouses, most with only windows on the front and back walls, contributing to a gloom inside so profound candles were required even at midday. Even in the front drawing room in mid-afternoon, little light peeked through the curtained windows.

Age was a cruel joke of nature, the dowager Lady

Haven decided, shifting in her position on a hard chair in the ugly drawing room. She sat at a tall, ornately carved escritoire, but found that the only chair tall enough to enable her to write on the surface, was very hard on her back.

She sighed wearily and straightened, shifting the candle to shed just a little more light on her paper. Damned gloomy house!

Even at eighty, she still found life endlessly fascinating, from her grandchildren's lives right down to the love affair between the chambermaid and the footman, but everything had become so much more of an effort, now. At Haven Court she knew where everything was and each of the maids and footmen by the sound of their footsteps. But here in London they had only a few of the Court staff; the rest were hired in London. They were insolent—though never more than once to her—and lazy, and if it were up to her she would dismiss the whole lot of them and start over.

And the house! She had not been here for many years and had forgotten how dreary and depressing it was, and how poorly designed. Her room, off the hallway, was as small as a closet, and she could not bear to be in it for more than sleeping. The passageways were cramped, the light poor, and the windows inadequate. It needed a complete redecoration to brighten it up, but that was no longer her affair. She supposed her daughter-in-law could do it, but she would not trust Lydia.

Jane had the taste and sensibility, likely, but she would never prevail over her mother-in-law to be. The girl, as much as the dowager liked her, lacked intestinal fortitude. She was too mild and meek.

Needed some of Pamela's spunk, or even Rachel's bossiness.

She wrote some more, but was soon forced to stop. Her hand was cramped and her eyesight was failing as she made out the invitation list for Pamela's birthday party. The light was dwindling, that was the problem, even with the aid of the candle. But if she was to get up herself to draw back the curtains, it would take her ten minutes, even if she could find her cane.

Old age. She snorted in disgust.

Light footsteps in the narrow hallway outside the door signaled someone coming, and the dowager called out, "Hey, whoever is there! I want these curtains drawn back, if you please."

"All right, Grand," Pamela said as she danced into the room. "There was a time you would know it was me, just by the footsteps in the hall!"

That was true; were all of her faculties failing, then? Depressing thought.

Pamela jerked back the curtains and leaned on the sill looking out. Whirling around and examining her grandmother, she said, finally, "What are you doing?"

"I am making up a guest list for your birthday party, three weeks from now. Your birthday is a Friday, and I think that an auspicious day for a dinner party."

"When are we going to continue my lessons, Grand?"

"Lessons? What are you talking about, child?"

Pamela came and stood by the desk, watching her grandmother's crabbed hand crawl across the page. "You can't have forgotten," she said, with a petulant sigh. "You promised me that if I came to London and behaved myself, you would give me lessons on how to comport myself so Colin will want to marry me. You said it could be done! We started at Haven Court, but then with all the fuss and bother of coming to London, we haven't progressed any further."

The dowager sighed and laid down her pen. "You will hold me to that, will you?" She took her granddaughter's hand in her own. Why was the child so stuck on marrying the man who was wildly in love with her older sister, Rachel? Sir Colin Varens was, she supposed, all very well, but she could not see what anyone would admire in him. He was plain and countrified and blunt, not a gentleman of the caliber of, say, Lord Strongwycke. Rachel was quite sensible really, placing her own charms and value above the baronet and his modest Yorkshire estate.

But Pamela thought he was a god, and openly talked of marrying him and moving to Corleigh. The dowager could not help but think that it was simply because, as isolated as they were, the girl had no one with whom to compare Varens. And marrying the baronet would keep her in Yorkshire and close to her beloved home, while removing her from the uneasy company of her mother. Pamela and her mother did not get along.

The dowager's hope was that, presented with a decent man like Strongwycke, the child would soon lose her infatuation.

The dowager had agreed to the lessons for two reasons, though, and both were still valid. First, it made Pamela agree willingly to leave Yorkshire behind and go to London for the Season with her brother and sister. And too, if the girl could just learn to talk and walk and act like a lady, she might find a husband who would outshine Varens.

Again, someone like Lord Strongwycke.

Already Pamela had made strides in that direction. She no longer objected to proper dress, and even seemed to take some pleasure in looking pretty. She tried in company to join the conversations, too, instead of awkwardly holding back, or boldly monopolizing the flow. She was getting better at the give and take of idle talk. And so, with a gentleman like Lord Strongwycke as a possible suitor, she must make the rest of the transformation.

"We will start this afternoon, my child. Now, go get into something suitable for tea, and that is how we will begin. Until then, let me finish with this list."

Pamela skipped up the stairs as her grandmother bent back over her spidery script. She would change into the ivory tea gown Grand had demanded she be provided with, Pamela thought, and she would learn how to serve tea correctly. She had watched it done a thousand times, but never yet had she performed the ritual. By the end of the Season she was determined to go back to Yorkshire as proper and correct as even Colin could want.

She stopped midway to the top and put one hand on the smooth banister. Colin. She frowned. She had only been in London for a week, but already he seemed so removed from her life. That could not be! He *was* her life, or would be when they were married. He was kind and good-natured and smart, and would make an exemplary husband for a horse-mad girl like herself. He loved horses and riding almost as much as she did, and his home Corleigh was snug and pretty, much nicer than Haven Court.

Running the rest of the way up the stairs, she raced into her room and directly over to her small jewel case. Carrying it to the bed, she opened it, spilled out the contents on the white bedspread, and picked up two cherry-colored ribbons, the only feminine gift Colin had ever given her, on her eighth birthday. She caressed them, running their faded silkiness through her fingers. Colin. Ah, yes, now his face was coming back to her. She sighed with relief. It had just been a momentary aberration, that inability to see him, to remember his dear, homely face.

She lay back on the embroidered counterpane and closed her eyes. Colin. One day she would stand before the vicar, and he would lift her veil and she would gaze into his light brown eyes. . . .

Sitting up, she frowned into the dimness of her chamber. Light brown eyes? What color *were* Colin's eyes? Were they not green? Or gray? Whose eyes had she been picturing then? Disgusted with herself, she decided then and there that she wasn't cut out for romantic day dreams if she couldn't even remember the color of her beloved's eyes. Colin would likely be glad. He had only ever spouted romantic nonsense at Rachel and would be happy to have a sensible girl to wed who didn't need that kind of idiocy.

She called the maid she and Rachel shared, and rummaged through her clothes. Where was that tea gown? She had a lesson to learn, a lesson in how to catch the man of her dreams.

Five

It was at times like this that Strongwycke missed the feminine companionship he would have had if Dorothea had kept to her word and married him. She would have known what to say to Belinda, how to make her mind, to obey . . . what the girl *wanted* from him! But women were fickle, and Dorothea was now Lady Dalhousie, wife of an earl. An earl with an older lineage and more acreage than he had.

"Belinda," he repeated, sitting in a chair in her bedchamber and clasping his hands together. "You *must* agree to go back to school."

They had had this argument many times before, and every time he came out the loser. How was it that a man who had hundreds of people at his command, who managed vast acreage, and was an important voice in Parliament, could not command a thirteen-year-old girl? It was idiotic, and he would no longer dally. She *would* go back to school.

"To make your life easier?" The girl glared at him from under dark, thick brows. She was lying across her bed on her stomach, her chin on her folded hands, staring at him, her dark eyes the color of coffee beans.

"Not to make my life easier. This is for your own __d!"

"For my own good," she mimicked, ferociously. "Fustian!" She buried her face in the covers and refused to look at him.

What was he going to do with her? He had already sent her back to school twice. The first time she had run away, and he had been hard put to conceal that awful fact. If it got about it could spoil whatever chance for a decent match she would ever have in the future. But more than that, more than any future consideration of her reputation, he remembered the sick horror in his stomach when he found out she had disappeared from her school, and no one knew where. He had searched for three days, finally finding her working as a scullery maid at an inn near Shadow Manor.

She had made her way almost all the way back to what was her only home now, *his* home. He had never considered that in an encouraging light before, he supposed. Had she wanted to be caught? He didn't suppose he would ever know, for she would certainly never tell him. He was all she had, for his parents were both dead, and her father's mother was living on the continent.

Belinda had courage, he had to give her that. How many gently raised thirteen-year-old girls would have done so, gone so far, and then found employment? But he had been ill with worry; her punishment— not severe unless one knew what it would cost her—had been that she would not ride for a month.

The second school she went to had sent her back to him within a month with a note, warning him that she was incorrigible, and he was never to ask them to take her again. He didn't even want to know the whole story behind that episode. Coward though he knew himself to be, he was afraid the truth would be too awful.

But now he had found another school that would accept her, if she would only go. It was stricter, and he refused to think of their disciplinary methods, for they promised she wouldn't escape them. They had experience, they said, with fractious children. But he was at his wit's end to know what else to do. He couldn't keep her home with him. What did he know about raising a girl like her?

"Admit it," she said, finally looking up, her dark eyes snapping with anger. "Your only concern is to make your own life easier."

"It is not my only concern!" he said, though it soon would be. They seemed to always be working at cross-purposes. They could not understand each other, or perhaps, *would* not was more accurate. He struggled to find the words that would convince her it was for her own good. "It truly is for your *own* sake. Someday you will be married. . . ."

She snorted.

"Now, see, *that* is an unladylike expression. Totally unsuitable for a girl who is destined. . . ."

"Destined for what?" She propped herself up on her elbows. "Marrying some egg-headed nobleman's brat and bearing him a nursery full of thin-blooded, smelly infants? I don't want to!"

Strongwycke felt the rage build up within him. He clasped his hands so tight they turned white at the knuckles, and yet she didn't heed the warning signs.

"You can't make me do anything, for I will just run away again, and this time I will . . . I will pretend to be a boy and sign on to go to sea, or . . . or something."

"Go ahead!" he exploded. "You have no idea what

you are saying." Strongwycke stood and paced in front of his niece, his boot heels clumping solidly on the wooden floor. "If you did that, and succeeded in fooling them, they would whip you raw for insolence by the end of a week! Then you would find out what discipline is all about. You think being a girl is hard?" He stopped before her and stared down. His next words he dropped like buckshot, pelting them at his niece. "My father regularly whipped me, just on the principle that it took a hard man to make it in the world. I have the scars to prove it, scars from bloody welts for insolence less atrocious than yours. Girls have an easy life, so don't think you are so hard done by."

Belinda sat up, an ugly, pouting expression on her face. "That was in the old days, when *you* were young!"

She said it as if his youth was back in the time of the Druids. Disgusted and bewildered, Strongwycke threw up his hands. "I don't know what to say to you." He blew out a long breath and passed one hand over his face. So far, since she had been in his London home, she had sneaked out once at night and ended up in a nearby tavern, wrought havoc in the house with mischievous love letters among the serving staff, and locked the housekeeper in her pantry for two hours. The hoaxes had stopped, for the time being, and an uneasy peace reigned, but he still didn't trust her. "I am going out this evening. If you don't listen to Miss Linton and do exactly as she says," he said, speaking of her temporary governess, "then . . . then I shall be forced to have you confined to your room. And I do mean locked, *bolted!* I will do it, Belinda, so do not try my patience."

He strode from the room, startling a maid who was lingering in the hallway, listening, no doubt. Behind him he could hear his niece burst into a torrent of tears, meant, no doubt, for him to hear. He trudged down the stairs, trying not to listen.

But it hurt. Oh, how it hurt to be the cause of her tears.

What was he going to do with her?

Completely at sea trying to deal with Belinda as he was, he knew he couldn't give up. What else was there but to keep trying to get through to her? All he wanted was for her to behave herself, go to school, and then, when the time was right, he would launch her on her own London Season, as elaborate and costly a one as any girl could want.

What else was there?

She had to learn to curb her impulsive behavior though, before then, or she would become notorious, like Lady Caroline Lamb. He shuddered, thinking of that lady's notorious behavior and how it had damned her in society's eyes. He *must* find a way to get through to Belinda!

Pamela sighed as they waited in the carriage to pull up to the door of the house at which they were to attend a ball that evening, and patted the folds of her lovely silver and white dress, thinking that it was the most beautiful thing she had ever owned. It glowed even in the dim light of the carriage and was much too pretty for her.

But Rachel's was finer, of gold and rose, with silk rosebuds adorning it. Pamela had to admit that her sister was the most beautiful girl she had yet seen at any London party. There was something about her, from the coil of glossy dark hair on her neck to the perfection of features that assembled to create an image of a flower of womanhood in full blossom.

She sighed once more. If Rachel was a flower, she was certainly the weed in the garden. Where her older sister was curvaceous, she was slight, almost non-existent. Where Rachel was pale and lovely, she was freckled and inclined to burn in the sun, to which she exposed herself far too often.

"Stop fidgeting Pammy," Rachel said. "You will ruin my dress. And your own."

"I'm not fidgeting. But why don't we just get out and walk up to the door? Why must we wait to go . . ." She leaned out of the window. "Lord, it is only fifty feet to the gate. I am getting out!" She reached for the door latch, but Grand's knobby hand clutched her thin wrist.

"Do not do that. You will remember what we spoke of this afternoon and conduct yourself correctly."

Forced to think, Pamela stopped, reciting the lessons she had learned over tea. *A lady is patient. A lady allows others to help her. A lady . . .* Pamela sighed again. She did that a lot lately, it seemed; sighing. It was no good. She supposed it was just that she was far too old to be learning these lessons now, when her bad habits were so deeply ingrained, but for years she had done exactly as she pleased, indulged by her older brother and ignored by her mother. Grand had tried, often, to teach her manners, but Pamela had merely avoided her when the old woman was on a tear, and so years had passed, years in which she should have been learning to modulate her behavior to something more approaching acceptable.

The truth was, one wouldn't learn something until it became important. And with her advancing age, it had become important to her to find a way to get through to Colin, to show him that she was a better match for him than Rachel. Perfect Rachel, to whom proper behavior was as natural as breathing in and breathing out. Whereas for herself, it seemed that every instinct in her warred with the dictates of society, and it was a struggle. Why must she quell every natural urge just to suit Colin's taste? He seemed to like her well enough, but his love was reserved for pale, lovely, *ladylike* Rachel.

Ladylike.

Taking a deep, steadying breath, Pamela sat back against the cushioned seat and waited until they arrived at the gates, and allowed herself to be helped from the carriage instead of leaping down the two steps as was her natural urge. She, Rachel, and Grand were in the first carriage, while their mother, Jane, and Haven followed in a second. Together they all entered, their maids disposed of their wraps, and they were guided down a passage, behind a multitude of other arrivals, and herded to the head of a set of stairs.

And Pamela's breath was taken away. Here was the grand scene she had been told about by Rachel, who had a first Season before Pamela. No ball she had attended so far had prepared her for this magnificent spectacle.

"Didn't I tell you, Pammy?" Rachel squeezed her hand briefly, before they descended the steps into the magnificent room. "I told you when we finally attended a truly grand affair, you would know it."

"You did," Pamela whispered, squeezing back. "But I couldn't have imagined."

The ballroom glittered; there was no other word for the light of a thousand candles sparkling and

gleaming from crystal chandeliers and gilt cande-
labra. Gauzy, diaphanous curtains dressed the
windows, and greenery created bowers along the
outer edge of the room, which was really three or
four rooms thrown into each other, the pocket doors
pushed open.

And the company! Milling about were hundreds
of gorgeously gowned ladies and black-clad gentlemen, jewels and fans and plumes adorning them all.
It was, from above, like a rich tapestry, woven with
glittering precious threads and feathers and—

Or like a stained glass window, with the gentlemen
in black like the dark lead between the glorious, col-
orful glass panes—

"Pammy, do not stand gawking! Move forward! We
are holding others back." Rachel gave her a shove.

She stumbled down the first step, only righting
herself by leaping down the stairs to the bottom,
where she slammed into a gentleman's black-clad
back.

"Do not disgrace us, young lady," her mother
hissed, moving swiftly down to grab her arm. "Or I
swear I shall disown you."

"Leave the girl alone, Lydia," Grand said.

"Ladies," Haven said. "Let us all try to get along
for one evening."

First they had to find the dowager a good seat and
so Haven, stocky and strong, parted the crowd and
guided his family group to a bank of chairs flanked
by potted palms. They were approached by a number of gentlemen seeking to reserve dances with
Rachel, who prettily thanked each and every one.

"What a coincidence," Grand said, airily, nodding
toward the doorway. "There is Lord Strongwycke,
Haven. Do say hello to him."

Pamela followed her grandmother's gaze. It *was* Strongwycke! How nice that they had happened to be at the same ball, for she knew that they had invitations to a number of functions that very evening. What a coincidence that they were at the same one as the earl! He was, so far, the only acquaintance she had in London, besides a number of youthful gentlemen who remembered her from the previous Season and expected her to be up to some larks. She had promised Grand that she would, as much as possible, ignore them if they insisted on treating her in an overly familiar manner.

Haven approached Strongwycke and they clasped hands. Haven indicated his family group, and the other man nodded and followed the viscount back. He bowed before them. "Ladies, Miss Neville, Miss Pamela, how nice to see you all again."

Rachel smiled prettily and curtseyed, but Strongwycke only looked pained, for some reason. Or perhaps he just had a spot of indigestion, for Pamela couldn't imagine anyone seeing her sister and not falling instantly in love.

But instead he turned to *her* and said, "Miss Pamela, is your dance card full yet? Might I beg a polonaise or country dance?"

The music started at that moment and Rachel was claimed for her first dance, but her expression was one of puzzled pique. Twice she glanced back over her shoulder as her partner led her to the floor.

Pamela, embarrassed by how very empty her card was, stammered, but then, as Grand caught her eye, took a deep breath, lifted her chin regally and said, "I believe I have a polonaise free, Lord Strongwycke, the second dance, as a matter of fact." One of her youthful acquaintance, a lad named Dexter, had reserved this first dance, and finally came to claim her, carelessly. When he saw the earl, his face colored and he bowed deeply, behaving himself with much more dignity than before.

As she was escorted away, she caught a look between Grand and Jane that she could not interpret. Her grandmother nodded, and Jane smiled, secretively.

The first dance was soon over, and her partner, chastened, it seemed, into good behavior by the illustrious company of the earl, returned her to her grandmother and mother. Strongwycke arrived punctually, bowed before the ladies and took Pamela's arm.

People watched as they moved toward the floor, and she wondered why for a moment, until she thought that perhaps it was just that Strongwycke was so very good-looking. He truly was a marvel, with crisply curling brown hair, brilliant brown eyes, and immaculate dress. She thought at first that she might be coming down with something, for she felt flushed, all hot and strange. But Strongwycke smiled as they formed lines of couples, and oddly, she felt a little better.

"You look lovely tonight, Miss Pamela. I did not at first recognize you at the theater, the other night, I must say."

Stung, Pamela replied, "I don't always wear breeches, my lord."

He chuckled. "I am sorry if I have offended you. You are entitled, though; that was rude of me. I should have left it that you truly do look lovely."

"Th-thank you."

They moved silently through the slow polonaise. She felt his gaze on her, and looked sideways at him. "What is it? You look as though you would ask me something."

"I was wondering if we could make up our missed riding engagement, tomorrow perhaps, this time with your mother's knowledge and approval?"

"I would be delighted. And it would give me the opportunity to apologize to Belinda. I felt so terrible about missing our engagement."

"Wonderful. She was very disappointed. She had so looked forward to it, and she rarely anticipates anything these days, it seems to me. And an afternoon ride will show her the transformation in you, for I rather doubt you will appear in breeches at the fashionable hour!"

She chuckled. "You are terrible, sir, for saying such a thing. But I do believe I have a proper riding habit somewhere."

He looked bemused, and his gaze took in her tissue-fine gown and elegant hair-style. "I look forward to it. I would like Belinda to see that a lady doesn't have to be all prunes and prisms. The example of someone as natural and charming as yourself may disabuse her of some of her more wild imaginings."

Pamela was startled but not displeased by his words. He thought her "natural and charming," when it was he who had put her at her ease by his mild teasing. Well, perhaps that meant that she didn't need to be haughty and flirtatious, like Rachel, or lisping and babyish, as she had seen some young ladies behave. She had been at a loss as to how she should behave, simply because none of her natural instincts led her in the right direction, or so she had thought.

But she had changed, she knew. She had left behind the stableman's cant that she had found so amusing in her first Season, realizing that all it did was alienate those around her and give a mistaken impression of who she was. The words sounded foolish coming from her anyway, and made her mother screech with annoyance, though Haven had secretly laughed at her when their mother wasn't around.

Once she had decided to leave behind some of her more deliberately wild behaviors and relaxed, she found she could, on occasion, enjoy good company. Not all of the *ton* was silly and affected. Just look at Strongwycke! He was rather pleasant, away from his bullying manner toward his niece. And he was so kind to her!

"I look forward to getting to know Belinda more," she said, finally, to break their silence. "She reminds me of myself at that age, I must say."

"Now that you are so much older?" he teased, smiling down at her, his light brown eyes lively with amber light.

She lost her train of thought for a moment. What splendid eyes he had! "I . . . well, the difference between thirteen and twenty is vast for a young lady, sir. Those years are the most difficult, for everyone is telling you who you should be, how you should behave, how to talk, walk, laugh. What to do, what not to do. Especially what *not* to do!"

He met her eyes and nodded. "I see. I think that is where I am having trouble with Belinda right now. I suppose I thunder at her, and she reacts, and then we argue. I only want what is best for her, but that is difficult when she continually defies me." He sighed deeply. "She has been in such trouble . . . but I won't burden you with those stories. Yet."

Pamela squeezed his hand. "It may be frustrating for you, but it is for her, too."

"I guess I hadn't thought of it that way," he said, ruefully. "I have been so caught up in how this affects me, that I hadn't really considered what she must be feeling. She was such a sweet child before . . . before her mother passed on. But lately . . ." He sighed and shook his head, guiding Pamela through one of the more intricate moves of the dance in silence for a moment.

They parted, and came back together in the figures of the dance. "Would you . . . if you can, that is, I don't want to take away your time during the Season."

"You haven't told me what you are asking yet, sir," she said, smiling up at him as they moved toward each other and apart, her skirts swaying around her slender limbs.

"You have lovely eyes," he said, with a sudden smile. "Has anyone ever told you that before? I am sure some young man must have. They are a beautiful color, and so large."

Embarrassed by the compliment, she brushed it aside with just a murmured "Thank you." She regained her composure, and then was able to meet his gaze again. "But you haven't told me what I may do for you yet, Lord Strongwycke."

"Would you talk to Belinda?" he said, his tone serious once again. "Whenever *we* talk, we argue. Perhaps someone closer to her own age . . ."

"I am almost twenty, not . . ."

"I know, I know." He took her hand as they promenaded in the steps of the dance. "But you are closer to her age than I, and you are a young lady, too. I am just her uncle. And . . . and I believe she misses her mother fiercely."

Pamela heard the pain in his voice. He missed his sister, too.

"I think a lady . . . a young woman," he continued, "may be able to say things to her that I cannot."

"I would be happy to try, but it will be up to her to talk to me. I won't pry confidences out of her."

"She is tighter than a clamshell, believe me. You *could* not pry anything from her that she was unwilling to divulge. We will call for you tomorrow, if that is all right with your mother," he said, as the music ended and he walked her back to Lady Haven and Grand.

Permission secured, he bowed and smiled. "Good evening, ladies. I have another function to attend, so I will be leaving now. I will see you tomorrow, Miss Pamela," he said, and kissed her hand, just as Rachel was returned by her partner.

Grand, looking for all the world like a grinning cat that has found the dairymaid's soft spot, said, loud enough for her other granddaughter to hear, "My goodness, Lydia, Lord Strongwycke is leaving. He only danced once. With Pamela. How very peculiar."

Six

Bouncing into the drawing room, Pamela surprised Jane and Haven with their arms wound tightly around each other and their hands. . . .

Face flaming, her eyes covered with her slim fingers, she said, "Sorry, you two, but if you are going to do that, at least you should lock the door!" She was about to exit, but her brother called her back.

"Come back, Pammy."

Reluctantly she turned, to find them quite respectably a few feet apart, and if Jane's face was a deep pink, the coloring suited her. Pamela examined them with searching eyes. "You two really do love each other, don't you?" she said, her gaze darting from her brother to her sister-to-be.

"We do," Haven said, glancing at his fiancée. "I am a lucky man." He passed one hand over his thick, sandy hair and took in a deep breath, releasing it slowly.

Jane said, softly, "And I am the most fortunate woman alive." She moved back to the shelter of his arms and he held her close.

Pamela felt a warm little trickle in her heart and swooped across the room to hug them both. She had felt some tension in the household lately, and just knowing that Jane and Haven were as much in love as they had been before London made her feel warm and safe inside.

Laughing together in a group embrace, they didn't hear the door and turned as one when a voice behind them said, "Haven, you seem to be in a fortunate position, with an embarrassment of ladies who adore you. Would that I had your skill."

Pamela giggled as her brother's hearty chuckle vibrated through his chest. He moved away from his sister and fiancée and held his hand out. "Strongwycke, good to see you again. I take it you have come to take Pammy riding?"

The earl nodded. "My niece is waiting impatiently. I think Miss Pamela has promised to help her defeat my strict injunction against galloping in public."

Coloring, Pamela pulled her gloves on. "As if I would do such a hoydenish thing, sir!"

They all laughed at her.

A groom had brought Tassie around to the front, and she was already saddled with the sidesaddle made of fine, soft leather. Pamela accepted Strongwycke's aid to mount, and walked Tassie to Belinda's side, greeting the girl with a cheery smile.

"Did your uncle explain about the other day?" Pamela asked. A carriage passed and Tassie shied, but was calmed by a single word from her rider.

The girl nodded. Her eyes sparkled, and she whispered, "Do you always escape like that from the house, like the other morning? When no one is looking? I didn't have the opportunity to ask you then."

"I need a good gallop sometimes, yes. But my brother knows about it," she said, with a mental apology for what was almost a lie. She hadn't been the one to tell Haven, but he did know. "And I am very careful. And I am twenty. Almost."

"Oh."

Strongwycke joined them, and they started down the street.

"You are riding a different horse today," Pamela said, looking Belinda's chestnut mount over. "Looks like she has good wind, strong legs. Let us see how she does on London streets."

The ride to the park was done with great circumspection, as traffic was particularly bad; phaetons and carriages competed for space on the narrow streets with tradesmen's drays and barrows. Pamela observed Belinda's seat on her mare, and how she guided her. When they got to the park, she led them to the shade of a tree.

"You hate sidesaddle," she announced, staring with a challenging look at her young companion. "And so you take it out on the horse. You will ruin her that way, and she will be unfit for riding. If you keep it up, she will have a hard mouth in no time."

Belinda bridled. "She's not my horse! Lucky is back at Shadow Manor. This is just a stable hack."

"All the more reason to be gentle! If you take your pique out on that poor creature, you are not fit to ride."

Belinda slumped untidily. "I don't like this horse, I hate sidesaddle, and I don't like riding in London."

"Then don't ride at all!"

Strongwycke sat back and watched. Pamela was happy he had evidently made the decision not to interfere. His trust in her judgment was deeply satisfying.

Belinda had not replied, and her expression was edging toward petulance.

"It isn't fair to blame your mount, and you will be

sorry for it," Pamela went on, more gently. "It isn't your mare's fault that you must ride sidesaddle."

"Why do we have to? You were riding astride the other morning."

"I prefer it," Pamela admitted. "I always ride thus in the country. And if the rules were changed tomorrow, I would ride astride always, in London as well. I think sidesaddle is idiotic and unnatural, and all the old arguments for it make not one bit of sense to me. But if the choice is between sidesaddle and not riding at all, I will ride sidesaddle, and I will not take my pique out on Tassie," she finished, patting her horse's neck.

Belinda sat up straighter, her thick hair ruffled by the breeze that swept through the trees. "All right," she said. "I can do that. I can learn to ride sidesaddle properly, and I can treat my animal better. What else?"

Strongwycke had to admit himself impressed that afternoon, not only with Pamela but with his niece. He saw a side of her that he had never seen before. Belinda was intelligent and, when not being petulant, could be charming and funny. They rode as much as they could, cantering over hillocks and across the green, but as the park became busier, they walked their mounts and talked.

He hung back a little, not wanting to stifle their conversation with his presence. He watched from a distance; a lad of about nineteen, one of Pamela's youthful friends, had met them, and they stood their mounts in the shade and talked pleasantly. Belinda was animated, her round face wreathed in smiles.

Smiles. He swallowed hard and whispered a prayer of gratitude. This was the most the girl had smiled in almost a year, ever since . . . since the tragedy. There was something about Miss Pamela Neville that she responded to, some connection.

As the group broke up, he rejoined them. "One of your admirers, Miss Pamela?"

"Dexter? Good Lord, no, he is just a child."

He laughed out loud, and that felt good, too.

They finished the afternoon with pastries at a tea shop, and he found himself once more watching his niece and her new friend. How unusual Miss Pamela Neville was! Even the evening before, dressed in silver and white, carrying a fan, with glowing pearls on her slender throat, she had stood out like a fresh daisy among a grouping of hothouse orchids.

After being unceremoniously released from their engagement by the love of his life, Dorothea, now Lady Dalhousie, he had gone through a period of extreme cynicism about the distaff members of society, but he wasn't such an idiot as to think that all women were cast in that mold. And Pamela seemed as far removed from Dorothea as any young woman could be.

He must be circumspect, though. Her grandmother was clearly on the lookout for a suitable match, and he had made himself conspicuous by his attention to her. But he would also not ignore the joy he felt in her presence. He wanted to marry someday, have children. He had mourned for Dorothea long enough, it seemed. Was he ready to move on and find love with someone as unlike Dorothea as one could find? Or was that the danger? For it didn't follow that because one hothouse orchid had disappointed him, that he must perforce prefer a daisy his whole life.

He watched Pamela laughingly wipe cream from Belinda's cheek. And it could well be that he was just experiencing an excess of gratitude for her treatment of Belinda. He loved his niece, even if she did make him feel that he was going to lose his mind, and he hadn't seen her so happy in a very long time.

So until he knew which way his emotions were heading, he must remain as prudent and wary as he had always been. Mere gratitude or true preference; only time would tell.

"Strongwycke," Pamela said, turning to him. "We have a scheme in mind. Belinda wants a good gallop, and so do I. I say a party into the country—Richmond, perhaps—would be capital. What say you?"

Looking into a pair of sparkling gray-green eyes, he found his lips turning up and his mouth twitching. "I say it sounds 'capital.'"

The two girls gave a cheer.

"Thank you, Uncle," Belinda said, prettily, after catching a look from Pamela.

Stunned at such pleasant behavior, Strongwycke said, "You are certainly most welcome, Belinda. We shall plan it for a week hence, considering the weather. Miss Pamela, if there is anyone else you would like to include, anyone who won't keep you and my fractious niece from galloping, feel free to do so."

"Thank you, sir, I already have people in mind."

"Jenny, my love, how I wish we were already married." Haven pulled his fiancée against him hungrily and kissed her lips.

"Gerry, oh, Gerry!"

Silence for a while. They were in the library, a room no one in the household voluntarily entered, since it was gloomy and damp, with just one small, dark window overlooking an alley.

Haven lowered Jane down onto a settee and they twined themselves together passionately, making the most of their stolen moment, one of the very few they had managed so far. Feeling the hunger build, the blood pounding through his body, and the heat mount, he ran his hands over Jane's lush body. He would go mad. At this rate, and with the strictures she had placed on him—not to marry until they returned to Yorkshire and he built for her a cottage of their own as a retreat—they wouldn't be married until autumn, if then.

How much easier it would be if. . . .

Pausing to breathe, he looked down at his love lying beneath him on the velvet settee. "I think I shall go quite mad with wanting you," he said, his voice husky and strained in the dimness.

Her gray eyes dreamy, her breath coming in short puffs, she luxuriously moved against him, and said, "All the more reason to find husbands for your sisters so we can go back to Yorkshire."

He groaned. "Do we have to wait, Jenny?"

She chuckled and threaded her fingers through his hair and pulled his face down to hers for another long, lingering kiss. "Not . . . not if you don't want to, my love." Her voice was soft, shy.

"You mean you'll marry me now? Here in London?"

"Marry?" she gasped. "I thought you were asking for something . . . something else."

The full implications of her words sunk in and he felt an urgency pounding through his veins. If only he could . . . but he wanted their first time as lovers to be perfect, not some furtive, stolen hour.

He took a deep shaky breath and let it out, feeling his heartbeat slow. Firmly, he said, "I meant marriage, my love, so we can use the master suite upstairs and be well on our way to heaven before the fortnight is through."

Jane pushed him away and sat up, patting at her mussed hair. "No. No, no, *no!* I want to marry in Yorkshire. I want our first night as man and wife to be in our cottage, away from . . . the family."

She meant away from his mother, he knew that.

"But you were ready to make love with me here . . . now," he said, pressing his advantage.

"A moment of weakness," she said, forcing her tone to be light. She stood and paced to the window and pushed back the faded crimson draperies. The small, grimy window, cracked in one corner, looked over the arched alleyway through which the carriages passed to get to the stables behind, and was dark and dreary, just like most of this house. She shivered and rubbed her arms. "I . . . I have this superstitious dread that if I don't keep to my wishes, if we don't return to Yorkshire to be married, that we will never leave London."

"That is utterly ridiculous," he said, rising and pacing, trying to quell his arousal. He was going mad seeing Jane every day, smelling her, touching her, wanting her. "Work has already started on the cottage; you know that."

"I know that," she said.

Before they had left Yorkshire to come to London, the plans had been set, the site selected, and the materials chosen for their own little cottage in a grove of trees deep in the Haven property, nestled between two moors. It was to be their retreat from the rest of the family, his wedding gift to his wife.

"So what is wrong with marrying here? If we have to be here anyway, we might as well be married and able to enjoy ourselves thoroughly," he said, softening his brusque tone and approaching her. He pulled her to him and she settled in his arms, resting her cheek against his chest.

"It might not be so long," Jane said, her fingers tracing the outline of his waistcoat. "Rachel is determined to catch a husband, and if Pamela and Strongwycke should marry . . ."

"Strongwycke and Pamela? Are you out of your mind? The man is almost as old as I am."

"Haven," Jane said, pulling away from him. "Grand has discovered all of the details. The earl is just thirty, and Pamela turning twenty. That is not an uneven match at all. I have seen younger girls married to older men."

"But not girls like Pammy! She is so innocent, naïve . . ."

"Haven! She likes him, I can tell. And he is very eligible. If he should like her too, I don't see why you are in such a taking?"

"So you and Grand have decided it between you, have you? You are going to sell off that innocent girl to that . . . good God, there is ten years between them! And all so you can return to Yorkshire more quickly!" He paced angrily away.

Quivering, Jane said, "How could you say that? How *could* you? You know how I feel about Pamela!"

"But you have only known her a month. She is *my* sister. I have told her she need never marry."

"So you would keep her with you forever? Haven, she deserves her own life, her own home, a family . . ."

"Don't tell me what she needs!"

"Gerry . . . Haven . . ."

He stormed toward the door and flung it open just as the butler opened the front door to the returning riders. Haven struggled to control his anger as Pamela, a wide smile on her pixie face, bounced in, followed by Strongwycke and a younger girl.

"Ah, Haven," the earl said, coming forward, hand outstretched. "I have returned your sister to you, but she insisted we come in so that my niece could meet your family. I hope we have not come at a bad time?"

Jane pushed past him and graciously moved forward, taking the outstretched hand herself. "Lord Strongwycke, how nice to see you again. And this must be Belinda?"

Haven frowned, but joined the company as they moved to the gloomy drawing room. When had he lost control over the situation? He was Pamela's guardian, and he supposed he had known she might marry sometime. But in the back of his mind he had always thought she would marry Sir Colin Varens, their nearest neighbor in Yorkshire.

But Colin had always treated her with a kind of amused tolerance, as if she was *his little* sister, too. Adoration he reserved for Rachel, who had refused him often enough that it had become something of a joke.

Haven had tried, subtly, to make him see Pamela's love for him. They would make a good couple, both country folk, both loving horses and riding and Yorkshire. They would make the perfect couple. And Pamela wouldn't have to leave Yorkshire. He knew her, and knowing how she felt about her home, didn't think she could be happy going somewhere else to live.

Pamela was chattering with young Belinda and Jane as Strongwycke looked on, an expression of amusement on his handsome face. Dammit, the man *was* handsome, much more so than homely Colin. But Pamela wasn't frivolous, not one to be swayed by a handsome face, nor a handsome purse or title, for that matter.

And how could Strongwycke see her as anything but a child? She was only six years older than his niece. He examined the man, and thought that was all there was to it, likely. She amused him, in a sisterly fashion, and she got along with his niece. That would be the end of it.

She was laughing gaily, and she reached out to touch the earl's hand to emphasize some point she was making. As Haven watched, he saw an expression, fleeting but unmistakably there, of question on Strongwycke's face. The man paused and glanced down at the hand she had touched and covered it with his other hand, and then looked up at Pamela earnestly, though she had gone back to her conversation. Good God, would the man decide after all that Pamela was marriageable?

And what would he do if Strongwycke asked permission to court her?

Seven

Alone in the small sitting room on the second floor, the dowager sat in a deep chair by a smoldering fire and relished her privacy, the silence that enclosed her like a woolen blanket. She was enjoying the Season thus far, but at eighty, it required vast resources of energy that she must summon from the depths of her soul, and to replenish those resources took time alone, silent, in thought.

Everything was proceeding just as it ought. She had insisted on coming to London with the rest—even though the journey had been arduous at best and torturous at worst—for one reason. She did not trust anyone but herself to oversee the acquisition of a suitable husband for her favorite and youngest grandchild, Pamela. Lydia was careless and guided by greed more than motherly concern, Jane did not know Pamela well and was far too complaisant, and Haven! Haven was hopelessly prejudiced in favor of Colin Varens. Only *she* was willing to carefully guide the girl to a marriage that would be a joy to her forever.

She knew what she wanted for her favorite grandchild.

The favored suitor must be titled. Strongwycke was

an earl; one could not expect to do better than that, certainly.

He must be mature, and not the type to keep high-fliers, for she would not see Pamela's heart broken. The child, for all her wildness, was a romantic. The dowager had closely, though subtly, inquired into the earl's habits. If he kept a mistress, no one knew about her, and he was thought by those who should know to be an abstemious and ambitious young man with no vicious habits.

And lastly, but most important of all, he must be fond of her. A girl of Pamela's sensitive nature would need much love and care, and it appeared to Grand that Strongwycke was not only capable of that kind of caring, but perhaps well on the way to loving the girl. She judged him to be a young man of powerful feelings, neither capricious nor changeable in the slightest.

Everything was moving along nicely; now if she could manage to convince Jane to marry Haven right away, here in London, instead of waiting for some ridiculous cottage to be built, she would be perfectly happy.

The creak of a door hinge warned her first that she would not be alone for much longer. The door opened, and Rachel slumped in listlessly. Bother! She and Rachel had very little use for each other, but she was still her granddaughter. She examined the girl's pale face and red-rimmed eyes. "What is wrong with you, girl?"

"I beg your pardon, Grandmother?"

Rachel was the only one of the three who called her "grandmother," not "Grand." "I asked what is wrong with you? You are slumping. You never slump. And you look listless. Are you getting ill?"

"Nothing is wrong with me," Rachel snapped. She straightened and her head went up, the hauteur that was her least attractive characteristic settling back down over her like a veil.

"Yes there is," the dowager said, examining her in the weak light. "Now, what is it?"

"I am perfectly fine. I just came to see if you would like tea downstairs with the rest of us, or will stay up here alone?"

"Bosh, you didn't even know I was here." Grand felt her blood stirring. Nothing like a good screaming match to get things going. "What's wrong? Pining for Pamela's beau?"

Ah yes, that pinched at the superior young lady's self worth.

"What? Lord Strongwycke? You must be joking! He is no more her beau than . . . than Haven is. Don't be ridiculous."

"Oh, but he is. Or will be. I have every expectation of bringing him to heel with a marriage proposal before the end of the Season. What think you of that?"

"I wish her luck of him. He seems gloomy." Rachel paced back to the door. "Well?" she said, over her shoulder. "Do you want to come downstairs or not?"

Satisfied to have nettled Rachel back into her normal behavior, the dowager settled back in her chair. "I don't think so. I think I shall just take a nap." And yet, when her granddaughter left, she did not sleep, but frowned into the guttering grate. Everyone, including herself, had assumed that Rachel was well-nigh heartless and in complete control of her own life. She certainly gave every appearance of being emotionless. And yet . . . she would have to think on it. Perhaps there was more to Rachel than met the eye. To be ruthlessly honest with herself,

Rachel was, of all her grandchildren, the one most like herself.

Yes, she would have to think more deeply on the complex subject of Rachel, her wants and needs.

Downstairs, Lady Haven muttered over a letter in her hand as the tea tray was carried in by a footman. Haven was sitting by the window reading his paper and Pamela and Jane were huddled together looking over a new book of fashion plates.

As Rachel entered, her mother said, "Rachel, my dear, I think you are going to have a proposal!"

"I am?" Rachel frowned and joined her mother at the small round table.

Jane looked up eagerly. The minute both girls were betrothed, she intended to pressure Haven into returning north to wed. No matter what anyone said, she was going to hold firm this once. And yet she was dreadfully afraid that she would crumble in the face of opposition yet again. It was owing to pressure from her mother and Aunt Mortimer that she had even traveled north to meet Haven. She could not now be sorry that she had allowed herself to be bullied into it, but if she hadn't run away, and if she and Haven hadn't met under the circumstances they did, she didn't know how their relationship would have progressed, because neither was predisposed to like the proposed spouse they were being forced to meet.

And so this time she would stand steady, even if all were against her. She had a right to want the wedding to be where she wanted it. She must keep repeating that to herself.

"Who is this beau?" she asked, keeping her tone even and detached.

Lady Haven eagerly held up the letter. "It is Major Sir Henry Waring. He writes to ask permission to pay his respects on the morrow. Is that not exciting?"

Jane watched Rachel get up and pace to the window. She and Rachel didn't see eye to eye on most things, but in this instance she sympathized. "Is he not to your liking, Rachel? I know he is very handsome."

"And he is heir to old Lord Poston," Lady Haven said. She did a quick calculation in her head. "Poston is seventy if he is a day, and rheumatic, if I remember right. And without children of his own. Young Waring will step into the viscount's shoes soon enough."

"But do you *like* him, Rachel?" Jane insisted.

Haven put down his paper and listened, watching his sister closely.

Rachel shrugged. "He . . . he *seems* very pleasant."

"But?" Jane stood and joined the younger woman at the window, searching the smooth, expressionless face. "Rachel, do you love him?"

"No, of course not. How does one come to love someone?"

She sounded irritable and out of sorts, and Jane exchanged a look with Haven. He shrugged. Rachel was a closed book to both of them. She had seemed perfectly happy planning to marry whatever beau promised to be the best—meaning most prosperous—husband. But now she sounded hesitant. Was it just nerves, or was there more to it?

"You spend time with him, you talk and ask questions and . . ." Jane stopped. No, that wasn't it.

Lady Haven was looking on with barely concealed impatience. "Of all the . . . Rachel, do you think to attach someone of greater property, or more wealth?"

Jane ignored that lady and searched for the right words. She took Rachel's arm and drew her to a seat apart from the company. Lady Haven snorted and went back to the letter, pulling her writing materials toward her to pen an affirmative, no doubt.

"Forget what I just said. When you care for someone—I don't know what you want from marriage, but don't settle for less than at least that—you will know it. And it *is* important to care for your future husband. Let no one press you into marriage before you are ready." Least of all herself, Jane thought, ashamed of how she had been numbering the weeks until she could count on Rachel being safely betrothed.

Rachel looked away and brushed something out of her eye. "I thought it would be so easy," she said, her voice low. "So easy. But I am becoming less sure every day. I don't know what to do. Why do I feel this way? It is supposed to be a simple matter; important, but simple. But I am just not sure what to do, how to know."

"Don't hurry. There is no rush."

"But I may never have another chance!" Panic welled into her melodious voice. "This is *the* Season, the one I have been waiting for. I am at the height of my beauty." The manner in which it was said was without conceit, a mere statement of facts. "Another year or so and I will begin to decline, and then no one will want me! I must choose now!"

Appalled, Jane gasped. "Who told you such absolute rubbish? Decline? You are a young woman."

"But it is common knowledge." Rachel rubbed her hands together, and sat anxiously on the edge of her seat. "The ballrooms are full of girls who didn't snatch their chance when they could, and now are considered old maids. Some of them will *never* marry, and even if they do, it won't be to one of the most eligible beaux, the true 'catches' of the Season."

"Rachel, you act as though your beauty is the only thing you have to recommend you," Jane said. "And does it matter if your husband isn't what society deems one of the Season's 'catches'?"

The young woman looked aghast, her pale eyes, a washed out version of her brother's, wide with disbelief. "Of *course* it matters, Jane. Else, why would everyone be in such a pother about the best catches?

"Who is everyone?"

"Why, the other girls, the mothers . . ."

"The girls who have been taught the same things and the mothers who have been reared in the same manner and are ambitious now for their daughters."

"Well, yes. Of course."

Jane realized she was getting nowhere. Though inculcated with the same beliefs as a girl, she had never been able to work up any enthusiasm for the system. It seemed a monumental shame, to her, the artificiality of the "Season," though it had worked, after a fashion, for a long time, she supposed. It was a place for young gentlemen and ladies to meet and assess one another. But what did they often end up with? Marriages where the two most deeply involved found, after the initial novelty had worn off, that they had little in common besides any children they had borne.

She looked at Haven, who appeared to be deep in thought, his bluff face turned toward the window, his startling blue eyes hooded. She had fallen in love, she thought, with a country gentleman, a farmer, only to find out that he was a viscount, powerful, commanding and . . . completely under the thumb of his mother.

Perhaps she was ill-equipped to be giving advice on marriage and choosing a mate to anyone, least of all a young lady who had seemed, up to now, to know exactly what she wanted. Sighing, she turned back to Rachel. She put her hand over the younger woman's, knowing that some advice, at least, was solid. "Make no rash decisions. Take your time. If this Major does not stir you, then say *no*. Refuse to be rushed. You are a beautiful girl, and will have plenty of time to find the right man."

Rachel threw her a grateful glance, the first of its kind. "You are kind. I didn't know you would be. You seemed to like Pamela better and . . ." She broke off in confusion.

"We are only just getting to know each other," Jane said, thinking that she really must make more of an effort to know Rachel. "Sometimes that takes longer than with others."

"I suppose." She seemed lost in thought for a moment. "It is just that I thought this season would find me with so many beaux, the choice would be made easy. I must do what I think best, I suppose. And there is still some time to find a suitor with more of what I am looking for in a gentleman. Mother," Rachel said, standing and moving to the table. "I will be telling the Major tomorrow that I do not feel we know each other well enough yet to make a commitment."

Then, head held high, she sailed imperiously from the room.

Jane wasn't quite sure that Rachel had truly taken

her advice in the spirit in which it had been intended.

Another ball, another musical afternoon, a literary tea. A Venetian breakfast, *al fresco*. The Season moved on; another week passed. Pamela and Rachel had their court presentations, which the older sister found invigorating and the younger awesome but fatiguing. Lady Haven airily suggested that since Jane and Haven were betrothed, perhaps it was time for a second court presentation for Jane. It would be the correct procedure to introduce Jane to London society as the next Viscountess Haven.

For once, Haven stood up to his mother and supported Jane's refusal, but only after a furious argument between the engaged couple. Jane was becoming more and more unhappy and worried, her dislike of London and London society more pronounced.

But Pamela had discovered that there was much to enjoy in London, if one made the effort. With Belinda and Strongwycke's company, rides in the park became bearable, even though they could not, of course, gallop, and she must ride sidesaddle. She even took pride in her young friend's increasing ability, mastering that difficult skill. She and Belinda talked, often, and she found in the girl a surprising friend, and a maturity that was startling in one so young. Though headstrong and resistant to her uncle's command, Belinda could be philosophical at times, and had deeper thoughts than many twice her age.

It became evident to Pamela that much of Belinda's difficult behavior was an attempt to get her uncle's attention. When she behaved herself, he became lost in his work and books. But when she caused trouble, he spent a lot more time with her. It was important that she see that there were other ways to get her uncle's attention.

As they all spent more time together, she became less fractious, more malleable. Once or twice she and Strongwycke even laughed together. It warmed Pamela's heart.

And she found herself, as the days passed, that Strongwycke was surprisingly easy to talk to, for a gentleman so highly thought of in government circles. Far from stuffy, he was relaxed, and occasionally even genial, though there lingered a solemnity that must be habitual, she decided. It was not an unpleasant trait, but he did need occasional teasing to keep him from being too stodgy. Left to his own devices, she thought, he would become old before his time.

At a ball one evening they spoke about Yorkshire and Haven Court, and then about Shadow Manor, his home in Cumberland, east of Penrith. He told her about its ancient halls, with armor guarding the front door and the Strongwycke coat of arms, an eagle with arrows clutched in each talon, adorning every surface.

"It is haunted, you know," he said, watching her face, his expression not giving away whether he was making a jest or was in earnest.

"Really?" They were seated together on a settee in the corner, and she felt unaccountably happy, having someone who sought her company, rather than being miserably alone, as she had anticipated would happen this Season.

"Really. The ghost is said to be—isn't this always the way?—the spirit of a young woman who was disappointed in her lover and threw herself from the top rampart one gloomy November day."

"How silly. Why did she do that?"

Strongwycke shrugged. "He married another. Is that not enough?"

"I should say if he was that inconstant, then she had a lucky escape. Just think what that signals about one's character, to be so changeable."

Pamela felt his eyes upon her. They were sitting out a dance together, and she tapped her fan on her knee in time to the music.

"Do you really feel that way?"

His tone was earnest and she smiled up at him. "Of course I do. It is just logical. If a gentleman abandons you, then it is best that it happen *before* marriage. Marriage is forever; his capriciousness wouldn't signal a good future husband, isn't that true? Or it could just be that he found the one he was *truly* meant to be with. In either case, it was best to happen before the marriage took place." She sighed. "That is so difficult, isn't it? To find the one you are truly meant to be with?"

"Yes," he said.

He seemed distracted. She gazed at him for a moment, but he was staring off into the distance, so she let him be. She felt completely comfortable with him, the kind of comfort that comes when friendship has truly taken root, and so she felt no need to fill every moment with chatter. She only did that when she was nervous with someone.

The music was ending. Her next dance partner, her friend Dexter, was approaching. She leaped to her feet.

Strongwycke stood and touched her arm. "Miss

Pamela, would you save me a dance? Are you . . . have you been given permission to waltz?"

"No," she said, shaking her head regretfully. "Not yet. Countess Lieven is supposed to be at the next ball, though, and Mother says she is going to seek permission. Rachel can waltz, though, and she has the next one free, I believe."

"I don't want to dance with your sister," he said abruptly.

"I say, Miss Pammy, all set to jar our bones out on the dance floor? It is a *contredanse;* lots of jolly bouncing." That was Dexter, buoyant and eager, like a spaniel puppy.

Pamela allowed him to lead her out on the floor, but she watched Strongwycke for a time after that, even as she and her friend moved through the complicated maneuvers of the dance. Dexter wasn't too sure of himself on the dance floor yet, and concentrated on the steps, but Pamela was a much better dancer than she had been the year before, and had time to contemplate.

What was it about Rachel that Strongwycke didn't like? They hadn't spoken two words to each other, and yet she sensed an antipathy toward her sister that seemed unwonted in so sensible a gentleman as the earl.

At any rate, she hoped it didn't spoil her plans for their outing. Their day trip to Richmond had been set for the Friday of this week, and she had, thinking of Belinda, invited Dexter—he was a jolly sort and didn't stand on his dignity like some of the young gentlemen—and her family, along with Rachel's current beau, a Lord Yarnell. She hadn't been going to include Yarnell, whom she couldn't find appealing, but her mother had taken charge at the last minute and had insisted. Lord Yarnell was a marquess; very highly placed and said to be looking for a wife this Season. There was no resisting once Lady Haven had her mind set on something. But the stuffy fellow would just have to look the other way, because she and Belinda were going to have a good gallop across the green swards of Richmond Park.

When she and Dexter had finished their dance, Strongwycke was standing with her family group as he returned her.

"I was just telling your brother, Miss Pamela, that I shall be busy for the next couple of days, with business, but that my groom is available, if you and Belinda would like to ride."

Gratefully, she put one hand on his arm and said, "You are so considerate. I think I can speak for Belinda when I say thank you, we would be delighted."

Strongwycke smiled down at her and covered her small, gloved hand with his own. "Until Friday, then, and our picnic to Richmond." He bowed to the company, Haven, Jane, and Lady Haven, and left.

Pamela followed him with her gaze, but when she looked back, it was to find Haven glaring at her. "What is wrong with you?" she said. Haven was, in the normal course of things, the most equable of men but he looked positively ferocious just then.

"Nothing is wrong with him," Jane said, taking his arm and squeezing it. "Strongwycke is such a delight, is he not?" she said, with a smile up at her fiancé.

He merely grunted, but Pamela said, enthusiastically, "He is wonderful! So thoughtful and obliging. I am hoping in time that Belinda will see all of his good qualities. I think she already has started to improve her opinion of him, which is good. He really does care for her; I know it from things he has said to me. I thought him solemn at first, but he is just quiet."

Rachel, escorted by her beau, Lord Yarnell, joined them at that moment. Of course, from that moment on Lady Haven dominated the conversation, doing her best to draw out the staid and dour marquess, and Pamela was glad to be claimed by another of her youthful gentleman friends.

The Season that she had so dreaded was turning out to have moments of great joy, she reflected later, as they returned to their townhouse, all thoroughly exhausted. As much as she had expected to dislike balls, she found that dancing was enjoyable exercise. And just when she thought another literary afternoon or musicale would bore her to flinders, there was a morning gallop with Belinda or an afternoon ride with her young friend and Lord Strongwycke.

In truth, he was responsible for most of her moments of true enjoyment. People thought him stuffy, but in her presence he smiled on occasion, and even laughed out loud. She liked to hear him laugh. She rested her head back and closed her eyes, his dear face floating before her. His eyes were his best feature, she decided, for they were warm, the color of caramel. Not that the rest of him was unhandsome; even his detractors had to admit that he was a fine-looking man.

She had never been one to measure a man by his face or figure, though. There was a subdued warmth within him that only needed a kind word to bring out. He had seemed hesitant to relax at first, but as the days passed, he had become truly a dear friend.

A very dear and *cherished* friend.

Eight

Pamela's only anxiety had been that the weather would not cooperate with their plans. With single-minded ferocity she prayed for decent weather every night. When Friday arrived, it turned out to be glorious; sunshine, a balmy breeze . . . though of course the full merit of the day wasn't felt until they were well and truly out of London. The amorphous fogs of London made one day very much like another; it wasn't until one got away from the odorous influence of coal fires and river effluvium that one could smell grass and trees and see the cerulean blue of the sky or guinea gold of the sun.

They traveled through Chelsea, the ladies who intended to ride mounted as well as the gentlemen, and the rest in carriages. Over the Battersea Bridge they trundled and thence out of the city, where the air freshened, the trees and wildflowers and fields gladdening Pamela's heart and giving her many new objects to gaze at and wonder over. Belinda, as eager as she and twice as energetic, let her mount canter, but when Pamela called her back she restrained her urge to gallop and returned to her new friend's side.

"How do you do that?" Strongwycke asked, as Belinda moved to trot along side Dexter on his hack.

"Do what?" Pamela batted away from her eyes the

silly plume on her elegant shako. Grand had insisted on one new riding habit, and she had to admit, she felt graceful and attractive in the green velvet.

"Make her behave. We are friendlier than we were, but still are at daggers drawn on too many occasions, and I just cannot seem to move to that affable footing as you did immediately."

"But it was easier for me," Pamela said. She frowned into the distance, finding it hard to put into words what she instinctively understood about Belinda and her complicated feelings toward her uncle. "We have talked often—she doesn't realize how much she divulges about her feelings when she speaks unguardedly to me on occasion—and I think it is going to take some time and some patience on your part. Being her guardian . . . she knows it wouldn't have been your choice, you see."

"Good God," Strongwycke said, aghast. "I hope she doesn't feel that I don't want her, or. . . ."

"No, Strongwycke, listen." She put out a hand and touched him to gain his attention and warn him to keep his tone light. The sound of the carriage wheels and horses's hooves disguised their words, but his unguardedly passionate tone had attracted notice. "She lost her mother and her father. I cannot imagine what that was like for her. I know I miss my papa, and if I had lost both parents, and at her age. . . . I think she feels . . . abandoned right now. Adrift. And school isn't the answer; she will only feel more . . . oh, *isolated!* That is the word I was looking for. Isolated. She feels alone. Don't try to send her to school for a while; she sees that as you trying to get rid of her, you see."

The earl frowned and played with his reins. His gelding sidled and Strongwycke stopped fussing and relaxed his arms at his sides. "I just do not know how to get through to her, and then she continually defies me, and I become angry."

"If *you* feel the frustration of not being able to communicate with her, think how much worse it is for *her*. You are both struggling with . . . with your sorrow." Pamela felt as though a cloud passed over his face in that moment. She saw the pain, and honored the love he had had for his sister. "But you will get better at it. I can see that you care for her, and in time she will know it, too. She isn't so much stubborn as sad and bewildered right now. But she is intelligent, and I believe she is working through all of the pain. Give her a little time. And don't give up on her. Perhaps it would be best if you just relaxed for now, and didn't try to enforce quite so many rules."

"So you don't think it will get any better immediately? Should I . . . ?" He hesitated and glanced around at the countryside. They rode on in silence for a moment, but then he said, "Should I perhaps marry, bring a lady into the house to help ease her pain?"

Pamela shook her head. "Worst thing you could do right now. You are all Belinda has, Strongwycke. She would only feel then that she had to compete for your time and attention with your wife. I would not do it. Let your relationship with her become more comfortable first." She hesitated, but couldn't help asking. "Why? Do you . . . do you have a lady in mind?"

He cast her a curious look; almost thoughtful, considering, Pamela thought. What it meant, she could not guess.

"Not seriously. No."

"Good," she said, relieved. "Give yourself plenty of time." Pamela chuckled and shook her head. "Listen to me! Child-rearing and marital advice from a girl who always thought she was a harum-scarum infant!"

"Actually, you are remarkably sensible. And I am not Belinda's only friend." He laid his gloved hand over hers, clasped around her reins, and smiled warmly. "She has you, too. Thank you for that."

Pamela felt a giddy kind of warmth flood her heart, an unexpected spurt of elation, pleasure in the day and the weather and her companions. "We are almost there!" she cried. "I can smell the open green spaces of Richmond!"

Strongwycke laughed at her joyous announcement and trotted after her and Belinda and young Dexter. They had a good canter, then, far outpacing the carriages and the constraints placed on them by the nagging of Lady Haven.

Richmond Park, that grassy paradise just far enough from London to feel like the country, sprawled out before them like an emerald blanket. Haven lay with his head in Jane's lap and stared up at the sky while she threaded her fingers through his hair. He wasn't manipulative by nature, but he had reached the point where he thought almost anything was preferable to this prolonged agony of wanting to be with his sensuous wife-to-be in the most intimate ways, and not being able to. He was even conniving with his mother and grandmother to cajole her into an early marriage. The thoughts came often; what ploy would make her break her unusual stubbornness?

They had spoken since their clash over that desire of his, that they marry immediately. They couldn't seem to stay angry at each other, and he was grateful for that. His mother had a resentful temper and he had dreaded finding that same peculiarity in his wife.

But though she didn't stay angry, neither was she inclined to give an inch. She had submitted, she said, to his will in coming to London for the Season to present his sisters and buy bride clothes, even though she didn't need any more clothes, but she wouldn't compromise the dearest desire of her heart, and that was to marry in Lesleydale's chapel and spend their first night together as man and wife in their new cottage.

He nestled his head in her warm lap and closed his eyes. He felt her lips on his forehead and he wanted nothing more than to pull her down to lie with him in the grass. But there were people all around; Belinda, Dexter, and Pamela were playing at some kind of mad game that involved a great deal of running, some tickling and much laughter. Rachel and her beau were walking by the small lake, and Strongwycke sat with Lady Haven, talking. The man seemed bored, but that wasn't Haven's problem. He wished them all to Jericho at that moment, for he would have been sorely tempted to take Jane up on her fleeting offer of pre-connubial bliss.

The heat of the sun, her full breasts brushing against him when she moved, and his own lascivious thoughts were having an uncomfortable effect on him. And when Jane's small hand rested on his chest, and then moved down to his stomach, he could not breathe. He opened his eyes and gazed up at her. "I love you, Miss Jane Dresden, but your contumacy is causing me great suffering."

She smiled knowingly. "Shall I bathe your fevered brow with ice water?"

"Damn the ice water. If you truly loved me, you would go with me for a walk in the woods," he said, with a sly wink.

She giggled. "You, sir, are a rogue and a rascal, and a young lady's virtue is certainly not safe in your presence."

"Every lady but you can go to the devil this instant," he said. Turning over on his side, he cradled his head on his arm and curled around her. Determinedly closing his eyes, he let the warm sun lull him to sleep.

Lady Haven having abandoned him to superintend the servants, who were laying out lunch, Strongwycke watched the easy interchange between Haven and his lady, and then the way he curled about her protectively as she caressed him. What must it be like to be so relaxed in each other's presence, to be in love and know that love was returned? Had he ever felt that way with Dorothea? He certainly had never laid his head in her lap, nor had she ever caressed him so intimately. Their betrothal had been formal, though friendly. He had asked for her hand in the presence of her mother, and had been demurely accepted, after which he was given a half hour with her alone. They had shared kisses, but nothing as intimate and . . . well, *naked* as the longing looks between Haven and Miss Dresden.

Even a stranger could read in their eyes their love and desire for one another; it felt, sometimes, like invading their privacy, to see them together, their yearning was so evident and exposed.

Disturbed by the envy he felt, he turned away to watch instead his niece and the two others gamboling like lambs in the spring sunshine. Miss Pamela Neville was a puzzle, part woman, part child. Or mostly woman? Why did he call that playfulness in her "childish"? It was possible that she would remain delightfully frolicsome even after marriage. Lucky man, her husband would be, to smile and laugh all day and be able to love her all night.

And he didn't doubt she would be married by autumn. She was almost twenty, and though it remained unsaid, she was clearly in London to find a husband. Everyone in the family was trying to push them together, from Lady Haven to the dowager and Miss Dresden. No, not everyone. Haven seemed oblivious or hostile to any suggestion that he spend time with Miss Pamela. Likely just didn't want to lose his little sister. He treated her very much as a child, Strongwycke had observed, failing to see the lovely young woman struggling to break free from the chrysalis of childhood.

Yet, she didn't flirt with him, nor did she even understand his hints. When he had mentioned marriage on the ride to Richmond, she had been completely unconscious of it having any connection with her. Any other lady to whom he had paid such particular attention would have at least some thought toward matrimony. It had certainly occurred to Lady Haven and Miss Dresden, and to the grandmother, too, whose crocodilian gaze he had caught fixed on him more than once as he sipped tea in their parlor. The dowager—she had stayed home this day, not deigning to eat "in the wild" as she called it—was, he thought, intent on manoeuvering him into a proposal for her youngest grandchild, patiently and steadily guiding every conversation to marital prospects.

He wasn't ready to make any declaration, though.

It was too soon and he was unsure of his feelings for Miss Pamela, nor did he feel that he knew her well enough. He would be circumspect, cautious this time, for he had been hurt deeply by a rapacious woman whose only intent was to secure a husband before her charms faded. Dorothea had never cared for him. He doubted if she could care for anyone. She had been merely biding her time until a more eligible gentleman blundered into her path.

And as he thought of rapacious females, who should appear but Miss Neville and her supercilious beau.

Yarnell, yawning, took a seat beside Strongwycke on the folding wooden chairs that had been brought for those members of the party too stiff or too dignified to sit on blankets on the ground. "Lovely weather for a picnic," he said.

Rachel demurely took the chair between the two men and fanned her face languidly. "It is truly lovely. How delightful of you to think of this day, Lord Strongwycke, and to be kind enough to include us."

He felt the hairs on the back of his neck bristling; even her well-bred, perfectly modulated voice reminded him of Dorothea. "It was Miss Pamela's idea," he said, frostily.

"Ah, but the planning, Strongwycke, I would wager you did not leave that up to the children," Yarnell said, raising his glass and watching as Dexter, Pamela, and Belinda collapsed, exhausted, on the grass.

The earl rose and bowed, excusing himself from the couple's company with a muttered word about talking to his niece. What he really wanted was to get away from Miss Haven and Yarnell. Those two deserved each other, he thought, as he strode across the turf and joined the three, who sat on the grass and watched him approach. Vain, emotionless, absorbed in the world of society, Yarnell and Rachel would be perfect foils for each other.

"So," he said, as he approached the younger people. "Have you tired yourselves out too much? I was going to offer after lunch to teach the ladies cricket, Dexter, but if everyone is feeling too lazy . . ."

Belinda leaped to her feet and raced to her uncle's side. Her dark eyes, so like her father's, glowed with enthusiasm. "Will you really, Uncle?" She grasped his arm and turned back to Pamela. "Wouldn't you like to learn, Miss Pamela?"

"I've played before, but if Strongwycke wants to have a go, I'm game," she said, laying back on the grass and putting her arms behind her head.

Her lithe, green-clad frame blended with the verdant carpet, and she reminded Strongwycke of a wood sprite or meadow pixie. And never had he had a more fanciful thought, he mused.

"That would be capital," Dexter said, with enthusiasm. "I shall go scout out some level ground." He raced off.

"Uncle was the best bowler in his class, weren't you?" Belinda said, looking from Pamela up to her uncle. "Mama said . . ." She stopped and blinked, swallowing. Without warning a deep wrenching sob shook her. "Mama said . . ." Tears started into her fine, dark eyes.

Pamela leaped to her feet, but Strongwycke shook his head slightly, and took his niece in his arms. "Would you walk with me, Belinda?" he gently asked, stroking her dark, glossy curls.

Leaning against his chest, she nodded, sobbing, and the pair moved off toward the woods.

"Don't wait lunch for us," he said, over his shoulder, catching Pamela's eye.

She nodded and called out, "We'll save something for you."

Nine

"He should send her back to school and take no more of her nonsense. He coddles that girl, and that is the truth." Lady Haven, seated regally in one of the wooden folding chairs nodded to a footman, who poured another glass of barley water and lemon for her.

Pamela, sitting cross-legged—it was only her family and Dexter around, after all, and what did she care for Lord Yarnell's shocked expression?—was about to open her mouth to come to her friends' defense, but it was Rachel who spoke up first.

"Mother, the girl lost *both* parents. Do you not think she is entitled to some coddling?"

Her mouth gaping open, Pamela stared up at her sister, she who always agreed with their mother about *everything!*

"But that was almost a year ago." Lady Haven's tone was pettish, as it always was when someone disagreed with her.

"A year must not seem very long for such a loss," Rachel said, nibbling on a grape. "I was about the same age as Belinda when Papa died, and I wasn't myself for much longer than just a year, I think."

"I quite agree with your mother, Miss Neville." Lord Yarnell raised a glass and nodded to Lady

Haven approvingly. "It does not do to pamper children; they only turn out spoiled and overindulged."

Rachel was silent.

"This isn't a case of too much sweets," Pamela said. "She was deeply hurt by her parents' death."

"Yarnell, my mother may talk of not coddling Miss de Launcey, but this is the same woman who wouldn't see any of her children sent off to school, away from Haven Court," said Haven, taking another serving of chicken, and smiling. "Her philosophy now may be the result of not following that advice herself. I find people giving child-rearing advice usually do give the opposite of that which they followed themselves."

Lady Haven bridled. "You were all delicate children, not fit for the rigors of school, but that girl . . ."

"Oh, yes, as you can see, I am a delicate fellow," Haven said, indicating his broad, powerful frame.

Jane, sitting next to him on the soft woolen blanket, poked his stomach. "You are barely clinging to life, Gerry. Better finish that chicken."

The company laughed, all except for Yarnell and Lady Haven; the latter looked fretful and affronted.

"Lord Strongwycke is doing the right thing, I think," Pamela said. "He is truly trying to do what is best for his niece, and I honor him for it." She tossed an apple core across the green to some curious geese that were parading the grounds. "Earlier, he asked what I thought of marriage for him, and I told him I wouldn't advise it for now, for Belinda needs him while she works through her sadness."

Silence greeted her statement, and she looked around at the others.

Only Haven nodded approvingly. "I quite agree. Marriage would only complicate his life right now."

"On the contrary," Jane said, with a significant look. "I think the *right* wife would be an immeasurable comfort to both Lord Strongwycke and Belinda."

"But it isn't fair to the young lady who would wed him to present her with a thirteen-year-old in the household when the marriage is new." Haven wiped his hands on a cloth and took a drink of ale. "No new bride should have to think of such things. Much better for him to wait a few years."

"I agree that it would have to be an exceptional bride," Jane said. "But then I think Lord Strongwycke would know that."

"Nevertheless," Pamela said, watching the two with a frown, and wondering what this stilted conversation was truly about. "Strongwycke quite agreed with me."

There was nothing else to say on that topic, especially as the two subjects of the conversation rejoined the company just then, and sat down to eat their lunch. Belinda looked calmer, though her fine dark eyes were red-rimmed.

"Come and sit," Pamela said, rising and making room for Strongwycke and his niece on the blanket. "Have some lemonade," she said, gently, to the girl.

Conversation became general, and the group broke up, with Lady Haven, still nursing a grudge for being defied by her favorite daughter, muttering that she was going to sit in the carriage for a while. Everyone knew it was a fiction; she was going to nap, but no one said so.

After the two latecomers had eaten and rested, they all played cricket, with much laughter and blundering. Pamela was glad to see that Belinda had recovered her poise. Whatever Strongwycke had said on their walk seemed to help.

As they consulted about some point of rule,

Pamela said to Strongwycke, "She seems better. Were you able to talk to her?"

He nodded, and said, "I feel as if we made some progress. Our pain over Euphemia's and her husband's deaths is something we can both agree on, at least. She told me things . . . said things to me she has never said before. And she cried. Somehow, when I saw that, it was easier to reach out to her, something I haven't been able to do until now. She has never wept in front of me before. I told her that she need not go back to school until she feels ready."

"Bully for you!" she said, buffeting him on the arm.

He gazed across the field at his niece, who was pretending to fence with Dexter with the cricket bat. "I felt her thaw toward me just a little. Me! I have never dealt with a child, especially a girl-child, before. I was afraid the whole time I would say the wrong thing. What do I know about children?"

"Strongwycke, you are too hard on yourself!" Rubbing his shoulder, she added, "All you need to do is follow your heart. You will be a splendid father whenever you decide to marry and have a family."

He gave her a peculiar, intense look and glanced down at her small naked hand. "Follow my heart. Do you really think so?"

Taken aback by his earnest tone, she said, "Of course! You are a fine person, and . . ."

"Are you lot going to stand around jabbering all day?"

Dexter's plaintive wail made Pamela smile. "Of course not, idiot," she said, and dashed across the grass to her position. The game continued.

Just as Dexter made a hit, Belinda cheering madly for him even though they were supposed to be opponents, Pamela happened to glance over to the sidelines to see Rachel leap to her feet and cheer, and Yarnell remonstrate with her. She sat back down quietly and folded her hands together on her lap.

Pamela frowned, and skipped over to her sister and Lord Yarnell. "Why don't you two join us?" she asked, breathlessly, leaning on her knees. "We could use some extra help out there; Strongwycke and Dexter are just too good. Rach, you were once pretty good. You could join the girl's team!"

Rachel glanced at her elegant beau, and noting his disdainful expression, she said, "We will be content to watch you all play."

"But . . ."

"Run along," Yarnell said, waving his hand languidly.

"But Rach . . ."

"Your sister is rather like a pesky gnat, isn't she?" Yarnell said, turning to Rachel. "How does one get rid of a gnat?"

Rachel flushed, but remained silent and Pamela returned to the cricketers.

"What was that all about?" Strongwycke said, panting from the unaccustomed exertion. The day had turned out warm and he mopped his brow with his wilted cravat.

Dexter, who had removed his jacket to reveal perspiration stains, collapsed on the grass and teased Belinda, telling her jocularly that she was not bad "for a girl."

"I just thought Rach might want to play. She looked like she did for just a moment." She gazed back at Lord Yarnell and her sister, sitting on folded chairs and talking idly.

"Her type would not dream of soiling her gloves or mussing her hair," Strongwycke said, his tone bitter.

There was that antipathy again. Pamela was about to ask him why he disliked Rachel, but Haven and Jane approached, her brother with his pocket watch out.

"If we are to make it back to London before dark, we should begin. The servants have finished packing the carriages."

Strongwycke turned and called out, "Belinda, Dexter, we must be off."

And as quickly as that, the day ended. Pamela spent the ride home trying to figure out Strongwycke's distaste for Rachel. He didn't even truly know her, and she hadn't thought him unfair in any way, so his behavior was even more puzzling. True, Rachel could be a pain sometimes, with her prissy ways, but Pamela knew that underneath it all was still the same sister that used to run and play and tumble with her when they were children. Was it just that he didn't know her as Pamela did? The riding group was too closely gathered, though, for her to ask him, and she was left once again puzzled.

Soon she would have to find out; it was too great a mystery to leave alone.

Ten

May was a glorious month, Pamela thought, watching in the mirror her maid's skillful hands twist and curl her cropped hair. The Season was truly at its height now, and she found that though she missed the country, she didn't mind the balls so much, for now she had her own beaux, and since her court comprised of Dexter, a couple of his jolly friends and Strongwycke, it was very pleasant. She danced many of the dances, found she rather liked the bold sweeping movements of the waltz, and refused to stifle her laughter, as Grand would have had her do. "Beaux" to her surprise, were really mostly just friends. Perhaps that wasn't true for other girls, but it was so for her.

What had changed from the previous Season? Mostly her attitude toward the whole adventure, she thought. Where the year before she had resented the necessity of a London Season and so had gone out of her way to shock folks, her family included, this year she had made a determined effort to enjoy herself, and, surprise! She was enjoying herself! And with every passing day, she was gaining confidence that perhaps there was nothing so very wrong with her, as she had always assumed from Colin's disapproval. She wasn't Rachel, but maybe that was all right. Others certainly seemed to think so.

Maybe Colin could be brought to see that, too, in time.

Grand's deportment lessons continued, but she rarely mentioned Colin anymore. Pamela occasionally pictured the moment when she and Colin would first see each other after her amazing transformation into a lady. He would start and stare, and then he would say, *"Pammy . . . Miss Pamela, you are so lovely, so breathtaking . . ."*

Her imaginings usually ended there. Perhaps it was idiotic to think he would treat her thus, but when she looked in the mirror, *she* could see the difference. She carried herself erect, with no slumped shoulders or shuffling walk to diminish her already insignificant height; as a result, she looked taller, more elegant. Not as tall as her older sister, but she couldn't help that. And she had found a hairstyle to suit her. It wasn't completely modish, as Rachel's was. The bunches of little curls at the sides of the head that Rachel favored only made Pamela look dimwitted. But her close cropped "do," with a Grecian bandeau suited her well. The maid patted the last curl in place, and Pamela rose, with a "thank you" for the girl, and decided on the gauzy green shawl to go with her gold tissue gown.

She looked herself over in the mirror. From the hoyden of the previous Season to the modish young lady of this, it was a sea change. And yet. . . .

For all Grand's lessons, she found she couldn't absorb some of the more senseless advice. She couldn't appear bored, though she could see that many young ladies looked almost sleepy, they were so languid and graceful. Neither could she keep from stating her opinion, though she knew that young ladies were always supposed to defer to their male partners. She sighed often over her failures, but her hopeful disposition wouldn't let her feel anything but confident of success where Colin was concerned.

Over the last few days it had become clear that Lord Yarnell had defeated the competition and was the favored suitor, and daily Lady Haven was waiting for his proposal. Rachel *seemed* happy enough, or at least satisfied, but Pamela couldn't be sure. Yarnell was certainly one of the premier "catches" of the Season—Pamela often pictured him as a gaping flounder with a hook in his mouth and had to stifle her laughter around him—and he seemed intent on Rachel, paying no other lady nearly the same amount of attention.

And yet still, the much awaited, much pondered proposal didn't come. Trying to picture him as her brother-in-law at family gatherings and house parties, Pamela hoped that it never would.

And so another evening, and another ball. Pamela felt truly elegant in her gold tissue gown, a new one created just for this night, for Lady Haven was overwhelmed by the honor of the invitation, which was much-sought after, this being one of the premiere events of the Season. She was convinced the honor was due to Lord Yarnell's influence, and saw it as a good omen for the future. The trip there was silent, for Jane and Haven seemed to be quarreling again—Pam surreptitiously peeked at Jane's face, and could see it pinched into an unusual frown—and Rachel was absorbed in untangling the fringe of her Kashmir shawl.

Finally at the ball, a rather large one that promised to be a tight squeeze, they all stood by the windows, which gave out onto the terrace. She and Strongwycke had just been promenading around the

room, so he still held her arm on his. If that hadn't
been so, she might not have noticed his sudden jolt,
and the fixed stare he directed toward the entrance
of the ballroom.

A couple had just come in with a party of other
people, of whom they were clearly the foremost. The
gentleman wasn't handsome, though his face was
pleasant. But it was the woman on whose features
Strongwycke's gaze lingered. And when Pamela saw
her, she almost gasped out loud, for the woman had
such a resemblance to Rachel as to be a twin.

"Who is that?" Pamela said urgently, clutching
Strongwycke's arm.

"Who?"

"The lady at whom you are staring so intently."

"She is . . . I believe her married title is Lady Dalhousie."

"And how do you know her?"

Strongwycke shifted awkwardly and stayed silent.

"Strongwycke?" She stared up at him, waiting.

His voice strained, he said, "I was engaged to her
a year ago."

"Oh," she said. It wasn't what she had expected to
hear, and was unwelcome information.

The couple, greeted by other friends, promenaded, and it was soon clear that their path would
cross directly in front of the Haven group.

Strongwycke stiffened. "Will you walk with me,
Miss Pamela?"

"I . . . certainly," she said, at a look from her
mother. For some reason Lady Haven was often in-
sistent that Pamela spend much time in the earl's
company. Pamela didn't object, it was just strange,
since her mother generally took little notice of her
companions. He guided her to the terrace windows

and they walked through, the twilight brightening the sky in the west.

A breeze riffled through the ash trees, and Strongwycke guided her to the wall of the terrace, close to two other couples who were enjoying the evening air. They stood in silence for a few minutes. He stared off into the distance, and she examined his face. She knew him well enough to see the powerful emotions that creased his brow and muddied his brown eyes.

"How did your engagement break up?"

Strongwycke's face tightened as though she had just prodded a wound. He gestured with his hand back toward the ballroom. "As you can see, the lady prefers another gentleman."

Pamela put her hands on her hips. "You can tell me to go to the devil if it is none of my business, Strongwycke, but there has to be more to it than that."

He gave her a weak smile. "Really, there is little more to say." He shrugged. "She found a gentleman with more money and an older title, and told me very coolly that she was sorry, but she was ending our engagement. Weeks later my sister and brother-in-law died. It was a horrible time for me."

"I'm so sorry, Strongwycke." Pamela put her hand on his arm and rested her cheek against his sleeve.

He touched her hair, gently. "It was a bleak time, but as a very wise person once told me, it was better I find out how inconstant she was *before* we wed."

"You mean me, don't you?" His oblique reference pleased her. She had never had anyone take her seriously before, listen to her counsel and take it to heart. It was touching and sweet.

"Yes, I mean you." He caressed her cheek.

Pamela smiled and hopped up to sit on the terrace wall. "Oh, blast," she said, slipping back off. "I felt something catch. I hope I haven't torn my gown; I just received it this very morning and it is the most beautiful I have ever owned. I am so clumsy!" She checked, but her skirt seemed unharmed. "Now that is something Rachel never needs to worry about . . . Rachel!" A thought had occurred to her, and she regarded Strongwycke's handsome face in the dimming light. "Lady Dalhousie resembles my sister greatly. Is that why you dislike Rach so much?"

"I had hoped it was not obvious," he said, ruefully.

"It wouldn't likely be to others," she admitted. "You are accounted to have a cool demeanor in general, so your behavior toward her wouldn't be remarked upon. I am just so accustomed to being second-best to her, that when you didn't instantly abandon me for her, it surprised me into watching more closely how you behave in her presence. But Strongwycke, that is so unlike you to be unfair! Rach can't help looking like Lady Dalhousie."

"It is more than her looks," he said, his tone hardening. "It is that flirtatious way she has with her eyes, and how she *expects* every gentleman to pay her court. They are alike in more ways than one. And even her voice, the way she speaks. There are too many similarities for my comfort."

"But what you have said is just how ladies are taught to act, and how they are expected to. Grand says that flirtation is an art, and that I am never going to be better than indifferent at it."

"Don't change," he said, fervently, taking her hand and kissing it. "You are perfect just the way you are, and don't think that you must be like the others to be valued."

Pamela decided enough had been said. She was beginning to think he appreciated her most because of how unlike Lady Dalhousie and Rachel she was. That was an unwelcome thought, for some reason she didn't care to explore. "The music is starting. Do you think we ought to return?"

"Yes." But before they went in, he stopped and turned her to face him. "Will you save me the supper dance?"

Determinedly taking a lighthearted view of his solemn mood, she said, "Certainly, sir," and curtseyed playfully. "My vast court will be disappointed, but, ah, well!"

They re-entered and approached her family group, too late realizing that Lord and Lady Dalhousie had stopped to talk to Grand, who had made a rare appearance with them.

"Strongwycke," the old lady said, reaching out one knobby hand and grasping his arm in a firm grip. "Do you know Lord and Lady Dalhousie?"

"We are acquainted," Strongwycke said, stiffly.

"Lord Dalhousie's great uncle is my father's second cousin," she said, chuckling. "S'pose that makes us family, somehow."

Pamela examined the couple avidly as she was introduced to them and shook hands. The gentleman was of medium height, and as she had noticed, rather ordinary, certainly not as good looking as the earl. And yet there was something . . . yes, something handsome about his expression. When she looked toward the lady, it was to find her frankly examining her, and then her gaze fixed on one spot on her dress.

"Miss Pamela, there is a tiny tear on that lovely gown," Lady Dalhousie said. "Shall we retire to the lady's withdrawing room to repair it?"

Pamela hesitated, but the temptation to further know the lady whom Strongwycke had loved—perhaps *still* loved—was too great. Avoiding the earl's eyes, she nodded, and arm in arm they departed toward the far side of the ballroom.

In the quietness of the lovely rose-papered room set aside for ladies and their needs, Lady Dalhousie and the skillful maid stationed there helped Pamela, and in short order the tear was unnoticeable.

Before they returned to the ballroom, though, Pamela blurted out, "Strongwycke told me that you two were once engaged."

The older woman nodded, a smile on her lovely face. "Malcolm is a dear, *dear* man."

It took Pamela a moment to realize that the other lady still spoke of Strongwycke, until she remembered that his given name was Malcolm.

"I was heartbroken after our engagement was over to hear about his brother-in-law and sister," Lady Dalhousie continued. "Euphemia was such a lovely woman, and very kind to me." She sat down on a sofa and patted the seat next to her.

"So why did you break off your engagement, if Malcolm is such a dear, *dear* man?" Pamela was surprised to hear the savage edge to her tone and wondered at it, but it was too late to undo how it must sound. She plunked down on the seat next to the elegant woman.

To her credit, Lady Dalhousie didn't look surprised. She smiled, but there was embarrassment there and a hint of sadness. "I . . . quite frankly, I fell head over ears in love with Ian, my husband."

"Like you were in love with Strongwycke?"

Her words echoed in the dim chamber, and the little maid across the room stared at them, curiosity in her pebble-sharp eyes.

"I was never in love with Malcolm," the lady said, her voice hushed. "And, stupidly, I was not truly aware that he was in love with me until I actually broke our engagement. I was so startled by his reaction—I could see that he was deeply hurt, and, idiot that I was, I was stupefied—I think I left things on rather a bad footing. I had thought he liked me as I liked him, as a good friend."

There was no hint of evasion or insincerity in the lady's tone. Pamela said, "But if that is true, then why did you agree to marry him at all?"

She shrugged. "He asked. And I liked him very much. I had been taught to think that was enough. It was no different than most of the other ladies I knew were doing."

"But it isn't enough?"

Lady Dalhousie shook her head. "No, not for me, anyway."

"How did you know? That it wouldn't do, I mean, to marry Strongwycke?" Pamela was on the edge of the sofa, her hands clasped together.

"How does any woman know? I suppose I had known all along, if I would have just listened to my heart. When we parted—it was late May of last year; I can't believe so little time has passed and yet so much has changed—it was with the understanding that we would visit each other's families, and then decide on a wedding date. He was going to join me in Kent, and then we were going to travel up to Cumbria, to Shadow Manor, with my mother. I was in no hurry to marry. But Dalhousie was at my home when I returned, visiting my older brother, and . . . and I fell in love with him. It happened so quickly. I didn't mean it to happen, it just did. I wrote to Malcolm, asking him to come immediately to Kent, and I told him that I didn't think it best to continue with the engagement. Dalhousie and I were married by August."

Her hand was resting on her stomach as she spoke, and Pamela looked down, noting the lovely ring on her finger and the way her stomach protruded. She looked up into Lady Dalhousie's eyes, questioning.

"Yes, we are going to have a child. I am so happy." Tears thickened her voice and her dark eyes gleamed.

Pamela struggled against it, but she couldn't help but like the lady. In truth, she had done the honorable thing, after all. Would it have been better to go through with the wedding, having fallen in love with another man? What would she say if the lady were Rachel, and she and Yarnell became engaged; if Rach then found someone she preferred, someone she could truly love, would Pamela advise her to go through with her engagement simply to avoid trouble? No, she would definitely want her sister to find happiness with the man she loved.

"Are you . . ." Lady Dalhousie hesitated, but then plunged ahead. "Are you and Strongwycke engaged?"

"Me and the earl? Good Lord, no! Whatever gave you that idea?"

"I am sorry! I thought I saw . . . but never mind. I was mistaken."

"No, we are just friends, mostly because of Belinda, his niece." That was stretching the truth somewhat, for even if there was no Belinda, she would still want to be Strongwycke's friend.

"I hope he finds someone to love," she said, gently, touching her stomach and looking toward the door. "I remember our time together fondly, for he is the gentlest of men, but I can't help where my heart would go. Strongwycke was a good friend, but Dalhousie . . . I will always love him," she said, simply, standing.

Pamela followed suit and the two ladies walked toward the door together.

"He has . . . recovered, has he not? From our broken engagement?"

Pamela, remembering the fierceness of Strongwycke's tone when speaking of her and his unreasonable dislike of Rachel simply for a resemblance, couldn't answer.

"I am sure he must have. He looks marvelous, as handsome as always. I know he will make *someone* a superb husband." Lady Dalhousie smiled down at Pamela, but then a grimace crossed her calm face. She stopped and put her hand to her forehead. "I'm not feeling quite the thing," she said. "Could you perhaps send my husband? I think I should like to go home."

The Dalhousies departed and the evening progressed, but even though she talked and danced and walked, Pamela's mind kept reverting to her conversation with Strongwycke's former fiancée. The supper dance arrived, and Strongwycke claimed her.

She couldn't talk while waltzing; the movement was too intoxicating, and Strongwycke was an excellent partner. When they were finished, though, and he would have walked her to the supper room, she touched his hand. "May we go out for some fresh air instead?"

The darkness had closed in, and now the terrace was full of enticing shadows. They strolled, but

Pamela felt a tension in him. She stopped and sat on a low stone bench that lined one end. "Strong-wycke," she said, gazing up at him, the sharp angles of his face limned with moonlight, "are you still in love with Lady Dalhousie?"

Eleven

"I beg your pardon?"

"Are you still in love with Lady Dalhousie?"

"Of course not!" he snapped. "She stamped out whatever tender feelings I had for her with her dainty little feet. All that is left is dislike."

"I had thought you were a reasonable man," Pamela said, watching his face in the dim light from the ballroom, the hard planes twisted in a pained expression. "She fell in love," she added, more gently. "It isn't a crime!"

"This from the girl who told me an inconstant beau was best forgotten as a bad character!" He paced away, his footsteps hard and uncompromising on the flagstone terrace, and stared out over the garden.

Pamela frowned into the darkness and tried to formulate her feelings. "This is different. When I spoke, it was about someone who knowingly and unfeelingly leads one astray, and then abandons one. But she didn't know how you felt. She honestly believed there was only friendship between you, and that when she fell in love, it wouldn't be hurting you greatly to release you from your engagement."

He turned and gazed at her with a cynical glint in his eyes. "And I suppose you learned all this in the few minutes you were together in the ladies' with-drawing room?"

There was an audible sneer in his voice and Pamela approached him and touched his sleeve. It hurt to think that he still mourned for his lost love. "I was only judging by the sincerity of her voice. She was greatly saddened to learn of your sister and brother-in-law's death so soon after the break-up of your engagement."

"She wrote me a note of condolence after they died," he admitted.

"Did you answer it?"

He was silent. What could he say that would not paint him as a resentful character in this giving and trusting girl's naïve eyes? How could he say that he had torn it up and threw it into the fire? He couldn't now even remember what Dorothea had said in the letter. Looking back on his actions, he was ashamed. Dorothea and Euphemia had liked each other in-stantly, and had been forging the beginning links of a bond of friendship when the engagement was bro-ken off. Dorothea would certainly have been saddened by his sister's death.

Strongwycke turned away and stood staring bleakly out to the garden. His sister. Euphemia had been older than him by three years, and he had loved her fiercely. They had never fought as other siblings did, and he had never looked down on her as a "mere" girl, as some of the boys at his school did their sisters. She was, to some extent, responsible for the man he was, for he had come to believe in femi-nine intelligence and courage from her example, and to honor women for their pivotal role in a gen-tleman's development by seeing how important she was in his own life.

When Dorothea broke their engagement he had been wounded deeply, for though he was not demonstrative by nature, he had thought their love was deep and eternal. But her way of terminating their engagement had been so cool, almost brusque! It had made him doubt everything he had come to believe about her. Euphemia, when he went to her home to tell her his sorrow, had listened for long hours as he poured out his heart, and sympathized profoundly.

But then she had advised that he look deep into his heart and really examine what his love for Dorothea had consisted in. He couldn't now recall what conclusions he had come to, or even if he had. By then his sister had only weeks to live, but neither of them knew it. He had been about to return to London—he had taken her advice and decided it was not a good idea to immure himself north in his Cumbrian estate—when the de Launceys met their fate.

Was that when the bitterness started? He didn't think he was so full of festering anger toward Dorothea before that, but just wounded and saddened.

He had paced away in his agitation, the need for a moment of solitude overtaking him as it often did. Pamela, though, approached him unheard and touched his arm. He steeled himself, refusing to push her away. It seemed to him that he had spent the last year pushing away people and feelings.

"Strongwycke, would you really have preferred that she ignore her love for Lord Dalhousie and married you anyway?"

He turned to her and looked down into her face in the moonlight. So young, and so unexpectedly wise. And yet she would be twenty in just two weeks.

Twenty wasn't so young, perhaps, after all. Dorothea had just reached her twentieth birthday when he had proposed to her.

"Strongwycke," Pamela said, hesitantly. "If what I said was wrong . . ."

"No," he said, his tone deliberately light. Now was not the time for his reflections, but he felt he had some thinking to do, the thinking that had been abbreviated by his grief when his sister died. "No, Miss Pamela, in fact I think, in the grand tradition of ladies in my life, you have perhaps forced me to face a great truth."

She blinked. "I only say what I think."

"I know, and that is a gift I appreciate. Would you like to walk in the gardens for a moment?"

She took his arm and hugged it. "I have been breathing deeply the glorious scents out there and wondering if we might. Is it proper, do you think?"

"I won't keep you long."

They walked leisurely, along the paths trodden by other guests. The perfume of crushed herbs filled the air, and soft laughter erupted occasionally. Murmuring voices whispered words of love. English summer was about to begin, the sweetest months of the year, when life and love seemed good.

And he was happy. He was whole.

It came to him as a surprise, because he still was not sure of all of his feelings, but he did know this one thing. He wasn't heartbroken anymore, not over Dorothea, anyway. The pain of Euphemia's death would linger, but he would always remember her with love that sorrow could not taint.

He paused in a lovely little summerhouse concealed by a grove of budding fruit trees. "Would you like to sit for a moment? We can still hear the music from here." When she nodded, he guided her to a bench.

It was darker within the summerhouse. Perhaps this wasn't a good idea, for he had sworn to himself to be circumspect. And yet . . . he turned on the bench and discerned Pamela's features in the dimness.

"Are you enjoying your Season?" he asked.

"Oh, yes! Much more than I had thought I would." She leaned against him. "And a great deal of that is because of you, Strongwycke."

"Really? How?"

There was silence for a moment. "I have been used to thinking of myself as . . . wrong, somehow. I don't act like the other young ladies, and I say the wrong things and *do* the wrong things, but you make me feel that I am all right just as I am."

He put his arm around her shoulders and squeezed. He had only made the friendship for Belinda's sake, but now he wondered if Miss Pamela Neville would be his own angel, his saving grace. "You are *perfect* just as you are."

"But other ladies are so elegant, so graceful. Like Lady Dalhousie; I can see why you fell in love with her. She is so perfectly lovely."

"Appearance is only a small part of what makes a young lady desirable, you know," he said gently. "And there are all kinds of appealing looks in the world. Do not disparage yourself."

"My brother calls me his 'spotty little pixie,'" she said, a rueful tone in her voice. "I am so small, just a dab chick, he says. And freckled. Freckles aren't fashionable. I have been trying to bleach them with lemon, but . . ."

He felt her shrug, and chuckled at her chagrin. "Your brother is teasing you because he loves you. I used to call Euphemia 'Snowflake' when we were children because her hair was quite white and her skin so pale, almost translucent. Of course that made no sense at all when her hair turned darker, and yet still, to the day she died I called her Snowflake." It almost felt good to talk of his sister to Pamela. He wished that they could meet, for Euphemia would have adored the gallant waif at his side. "You are," he said, "as the French would say, *'une petite fille gamine.'* Lively. Mischievous. But it doesn't diminish how pretty you are."

"Do you really think me pretty?" Her tone was breathless.

"Yes," he whispered. "You are very lovely."

"Oh. Do you think . . . am I pretty enough to fall in love with, even if a gentleman had been in love with a lovelier, more elegant lady before me?"

Warmth flooded his heart. It was almost a declaration, he thought, affection welling into his heart like a healing balm. She was asking him if he could ever love her after being in love with the elegant, perfect Dorothea. He turned her on the bench and held her shoulders, gazing at her pretty, upturned face. Was there hope shining in those large, luminous gray-green eyes?

He pulled her close and waited, but there was no sign he was moving too quickly, no stiffening, no pulling away. So he encircled her with his arms and touched her lips briefly with his, feeling her warm breath on his mouth, before releasing her. She was startled, her mouth a round "o" of surprise.

He chuckled, throatily, and pulled her close again, lingering longer with this kiss, feeling her small body tremble in his arms, warmth stealing through him at the delicate touch of her tongue in answer to his.

It was all he needed to know. He stood and pulled her to her feet. "I think we ought to go back to the ballroom, for people will be missing us."

She nodded, mutely.

As they walked up the path and she still had not said a word, he asked, anxiously, "I didn't frighten or offend you, did I?"

"No," she said. "Not at all. I was . . . surprised."

He smiled in the darkness. "So was I. I must tell you that I did not lure you out there with the intention of kissing you, but I'm not sorry."

They entered the ballroom. Her party was just entering from the other direction, the supper room. Strongwycke noted the frown on the viscount's handsome, bluff features. Well, he couldn't say he blamed him. But he would make it right.

He guided Pamela back to her family party, Miss Neville, Miss Dresden, Lady Haven, and the viscount himself. The grandmother had expressed her intention of going home at the supper break, so she was absent. "Lord Haven," he said, bowing before Pamela's brother. "May I make an appointment to see you tomorrow afternoon?"

Almost grudgingly, it seemed from his tone, Haven said, "I shall be available between four and five in the afternoon, sir, if there is anything you wish to speak to me about."

"There is," he said, casting Pamela a significant look. Her face was blank of expectation, but she smiled prettily. It was all the encouragement he could expect before declaring himself to her guardian. "There is something, and it is of the utmost importance."

"Then I shall await your visit."

The party broke up somewhat as the ladies were

claimed by their after-supper dance partners. Strongwycke drifted in a happy daze through the rest of the evening. In one short period it seemed he had discovered, first, that his heart was healed of Dorothea's wound, though he hadn't admitted it until that very night. And he had found that the physician was a pert young lady who had stolen into his affections without him being aware.

He even smiled at Rachel, for the sight of her no longer tore at his heart.

She smiled back. Lord Yarnell was standing up with the hostess, and Miss Neville was unaccompanied for once, so he thought, if he was going to be a part of the family, he should certainly mend his fences where the older sister was concerned.

He bowed before Lady Haven and her eldest daughter. "Miss Neville, would you do me the very great honor of allowing me to walk with you around the room once or twice?"

She curtseyed prettily, splaying her lovely rose-colored skirts around her as she dipped. "Certainly, sir."

They were silent at first, her arm resting lightly on his, pale against the black of his jacket. He didn't know her, so it was difficult to think of any but the most mundane topics, and then he realized that it would be good to start with those. So they spoke of the ballroom, and the weather, the progress of the Season, and some mutual acquaintances.

She was well-mannered, and, he was relieved to note, didn't seem inclined to flirt with him, as she had at first. She would be his sister, soon. He gazed down at her. She was truly lovely, the most beautiful girl in the room, but he wondered what went on behind the pale blue eyes and under the masses of glossy hair.

"Did you enjoy our visit to Richmond?" he asked, speaking of the picnic.

"Certainly, sir, it was a lovely day."

There was no emotion to their voice. She might just as well have been saying "I like ham." " I have never been so exhausted as I was at the end of it," he said. "I have not played cricket for years."

She was silent.

The end was in sight. How disappointing that she was truly as empty-headed as she appeared. As they elegantly promenaded toward her family group, she squeezed his arm and said, "Sir, you must be wondering why I have been so quiet."

"I . . . hadn't noticed," he said, weakly.

She forced him to stop with her, and turned to him. "I was concerned to hear of your plans for the morrow. I do not think I can mistake your reason for coming to visit my brother."

It was his turn to remain silent, wondering what she intended to say. Did she really understand his intentions? And if she did, what business was it of hers?

"You intend to offer for Pamela," she said, bluntly, her eyes assessing him.

With the uncomfortable feeling that she likely knew to a farthing how much money he held in his vest pocket, he frowned. "It is possible. However, until I actually do, if such is my intention, it is no one's business but my own."

"I know that," she said, her tone brisk and impatient. "But before you propose, I think there is something you should know about Pamela."

Twelve

"And what would that be?" His voice was frosty and forbidding.

Rachel looked up into the earl's handsome face. She opened her mouth. And closed it again. Was it so bad, what she intended to tell him? It was only the truth. But it would surely change Lord Strongwycke's mind about his intentions, and perhaps Pamela had come to feel differently about things. What did she really know about her younger sister's emotions? They rarely talked anymore, she had been so caught up in her own life and the Season and the gay whirl of balls and parties.

It was what she had expected and wanted from this Season, but it left her feeling oddly empty.

But she had to say something; he was waiting. He was rather forbidding with that wintry expression, not at all the soft smile that he directed toward Pamela. "My sister has for many years . . ." She paused and bit her lip. To tell or not to tell? When the thought had come to her, it just seemed that this impossibly handsome, wealthy and well-titled earl ought to know that the girl he was going to ask to marry him had always been in love with their neighbor, Sir Colin Varens. But was she willing to divulge what might no longer be true, and were her own intentions truly just to save him from making a mistake? Or was there something else in her heart?

Was it . . . jealousy?

"I—I . . ." She stuttered to a halt, for the first time in years unsure of how to proceed.

"What is it, Miss Neville?" Strongwycke's attention was wholly fixed on her now, not like during their walk, when she could tell he was only bearing her company out of politeness.

"I . . . I . . ." Frozen into inaction, she faced facts. She was jealous of Pamela and the attentions of this handsome, well-born, rich nobleman. Jealous. Grass-green with envy. Of *Pamela!*

"Miss Neville, this is our waltz."

Lord Yarnell had approached them, and his words were uttered in a frosty tone. He was sensitive about appearances, and Rachel wondered whether her and Strongwycke's attitude, paused on the edge of the dance floor, had raised any gossip. She gave her beau her arm, and prettily apologized to him.

"Excuse us, Yarnell, but I crave one more word with your partner. Miss Neville, you were just about to say something about your sister," Strongwycke said.

Rachel took a deep breath, making a tremendous effort to conquer the feelings she had just discovered. "Pamela has for many years . . . been accustomed to riding astride across the countryside. I doubt if she will give it up when she marries," she said, with a haughty lift to her head. "I hope you intend to keep a good stable, sir, for she will be satisfied no other way." She turned with her partner and joined the swirling mass on the ballroom floor, leaving behind the earl, who stood staring after her with a frown on his face.

* * *

Moonlight flooded Pamela's tiny room on the family floor of the townhouse. One of the things she had hated about London in her only abbreviated Season was this house. It was ugly and cramped compared to their rambling house in Yorkshire. Haven Court was an ancient priory, dating from long before the Wars of the Roses, and was a tangle of long passages, enormous halls, and gargantuan windows facing the setting sun in the evening. *This* house, built in the early years of the previous century, was narrow and tall and dark, surrounded by other narrow, tall, and dark homes.

But this night the moon had found ingress; her room, overlooking the minuscule walled garden below, was bathed in opalescent moonlight that poured through the narrow window, and seemed almost a fairy bower, with the flowered wallpaper and fresh bouquet on her bedside table. She sat in bed, her knees up and clutched to her chest with her arms and the bedcovers pulled up to her chin. She couldn't sleep.

Wouldn't sleep. Maybe ever again.

Her first real kiss, and it had been Strongwycke, not Colin, like she always thought it would be. And yet she couldn't find it in her heart to regret the kiss. Once, when she was a child, she had held a butterfly to her face and the soft fan of its wings had been like the earl's first kiss, delicate, gentle.

But then the second. . . .

She took in a deep breath and let it out slowly, then pushed the bedcovers away from her. It was almost summer and the room felt warm for the first time, as if there was a fire in the fireplace. Her cheeks were flushed, and yet she was shivering.

Laying her flaming cheek on her knees, she wondered why he had kissed her. She had just been considering his compliment, when he told her there were all kinds of lovely, and that she was very pretty herself. She had been wondering if, once Yarnell declared himself as Rachel's suitor and Colin knew there was no hope for him with her, he could turn his affections to Pamela after being in love for so long with such an elegant, absolutely breathtaking lady as her elder sister.

And then Strongwycke had taken her in his arms and kissed her.

She touched her lips, remembering the warmth that had stolen through her, and how her heart had pounded. It had left her dazed, speechless. The rest of the evening had floated by in a delirious haze, and she had the feeling she made not a jot of sense to anyone for the rest of it.

Dexter had even teased her about it, calling it "spring fever."

But she did remember one thing. Strongwycke had said he was coming to visit Haven the next day. What was that about? Why would he . . . ?

As the answer crept into her brain, not in a flash, but first as a conjecture and then a likelihood and then finally a certainty, she felt cold all over. Gentlemen as upright as the earl didn't make love to girls unless their intentions were serious. Lord Strongwycke was going to ask for her hand in marriage!

Lady Haven was bubbling with anticipation. She hummed, and the lady never hummed, for her mother-in-law had once told her that she had the voice of a jackdaw, and she never attempted a tune after that.

"Lydia, what is that noise you are making?" The dowager, attracted—or repelled—by the noise, tapped into the drawing room as her daughter-in-law arranged a vase of new flowers that had arrived just that morning from Lord Yarnell.

"I am humming! I am happy, and so should you be for once in your miserable, over-long life. Haven engaged to be wed, Rachel almost betrothed to Lord Yarnell, and now this completely unexpected blessing!"

"For once we are in agreement on something. May it never happen again," the dowager said, as she lowered herself carefully to the seat of a hard chair. She frowned and shook her head, absently rubbing her aching knee. It had been giving her trouble ever since the moment she woke up, and that was never a good sign. "But I do not have a good feeling about it."

"How can you not?" Lady Haven stared at the other woman in amazement.

"My bones. They do not lie and they are saying all is not smooth yet. We should not count our fleet until all our ships have made it into port."

"You are just looking for trouble. You *always* look for trouble. Do not spoil this, you nasty old besom, or . . ."

"Do not be impertinent with me, Lydia," the dowager said, rallying at the delicious hint of an argument, "or I shall . . ."

Both were stopped by a tap at the outside door. There was the sound of greeting, and Lady Haven covered her mouth with her hand. "I wonder if

Strongwycke could not wait? Or perhaps Yarnell has finally decided to declare himself."

"And that is another thing, about this business with Yarnell," the dowager started, ready to voice her views on the marquess and his intentions. She did not like the man, and had begun to think that if Yarnell did marry Rachel, it would be the death of any hope of happiness for the girl.

She was interrupted, as Haven chose that moment to enter from the dining room. They were all to gather there that morning, as the dowager and Lady Haven had decided to have it out as to Haven and Jane's wedding date and site. They wanted the whole family there because jointly, they hoped to pressure Jane into marrying soon and in London. Haven's mother had even gone so far as to ask discreetly for the name of a baker who could do a bride cake quickly. She had made up her mind not to be deprived of the society wedding *she* had been denied many long years before.

The butler entered and bowed. "Sir," he said, looking to the viscount. "There is an acquaintance at the door, and he wishes to ask if it would be convenient for the family to receive unexpected company?"

"Who is it?" the dowager asked, querulously, perturbed at the disruption of their morning conference.

The door was pushed open just then, and in came Sir Colin Varens and his sister, Andromeda.

A tumult broke out. Haven clapped his friend on the back, truly happy to see him, and greeted Miss Andromeda Varens; now that he was betrothed he could afford to be kind to her once again as the old friend he treasured for their past amity. For a time he had avoided her company, as every meeting was awkward, with her trying desperately to ferret a proposal out of him. Now, safely engaged to Jane, he could afford to be her friend again.

Varens was loudly delivering messages from friends and Haven's estate manager, while Lady Haven was asking questions about planning for the local harvest fair that she would be taking control of the moment she was back in Yorkshire. Over it all the dowager plaintively asked for calm. She could not even hear herself think, she complained.

Rachel, drawn by the noise, entered, and calmly greeted the baronet and his sister. Lady Haven called for coffee and sat their old friends down, making them as comfortable as possible in the narrow drawing room.

"How did this come about, Colin?" Haven asked. He sat, uncomfortably dwarfing a chair not meant for a gentleman of his size.

The young baronet looked self-conscious, the dowager mused, examining his homely face. She was sure this was the trouble her old bones had portended, for she would not have chosen to have the fellow in London, just as Pamela was attracting a worthy suitor. But at least the fool would be as oblivious to her younger granddaughter's fine qualities as ever. That must aid in Pamela's decision. Putting the two side by side, Strongwycke and Varens, would surely defeat any lingering preference the girl could have for the stuffy gentleman.

So perhaps this was a streak of good fortune after all. She had to believe that the handsome, self-assured earl would win in any comparison.

Looking supremely conscious, the baronet, keeping his gaze away from Rachel, who sat with Andromeda on a settee near the fireplace, answered Haven. "We get to town so seldom, and Andy . . . uh,

Andromeda wanted to do some shopping. Oh, and we have some glad news that we wanted to deliver in person."

Jane entered that moment and joyfully greeted Varens and his sister. "Please," she said, once seated. "Don't let me interrupt."

"You will be happy about this too, Miss Dresden, for I believe she is a particular friend of hers. Mrs. Mary Cooper—your old friend, Haven, from childhood—is now Mrs. Latimer."

"Mrs. Latimer! Latimer the surgeon?" Haven said, sitting forward. "She married him? How did that come about?"

The dowager was not surprised at the amazement in her grandson's voice. Mary Cooper, a widow with a very young baby, hadn't seemed to be in the frame of mind for marriage when they left Yorkshire. She missed sorely her beloved husband, Jem, who had died before their baby, Molly, was born. She had been in mourning for well over a year.

"It is the most romantical story," Andromeda Varens said, clasping her hands together and sighing. Miss Varens, a tall, handsome woman of thirty-one years, still had the giddy romanticism of a seventeen-year-old. "Mrs. Cooper's babe was ill, and she came down to the village to stay with a friend, while the apothecary cared for Molly. Mr. Latimer heard about Molly and came to visit. The apothecary, foolish humbug that he is, was dosing poor little Molly in the most severe way with purgatives, and poor Mary was almost frantic, for the babe grew weaker daily. Mr. Latimer diagnosed a case of the croup, which, you know, can become quite serious if it is left untended. The baby becomes hoarse, you see, and then . . ."

"Andy!"

With that warning from her brother, she hurried through the story. "Without the enfeebling effect of the purgative, Molly improved," she finally said, "and Mr. Latimer—he is a widower, you know, and as good a man as this earth has seen—well, anyway, he confessed that he had fallen in love with Mary and begged her to marry him."

"Needed an efficient housekeeper for his own comfort, no doubt," the dowager grunted. "And a mother for his child."

"It was all done so quickly," Rachel marveled.

"What is to wait for once the two know their wishes? A benefactor"—here Varens shot a look at his sister—"purchased a license for them to marry quickly. They are wed, and Mary Cooper is now Mary Latimer. Latimer intends to adopt Molly as his own."

Jane said, slowly, "So, the cottage; she has left it?"

"Oh, yes. Latimer's cart was there two weeks ago and loaded up her spinning wheel and folderol. She left the keys with your housekeeper, Haven," Varens said. "The furnishings she said came with the cottage and should stay with the cottage." He stood. "We have more news to divulge, but we shan't stay too long with this unexpected visit. We have taken rooms at the Traveler's Inn, near the park, and I hope we may stand you all dinner there one night. They have an excellent cook."

Haven stood, too, and pounded his friend on the back. "We shall be overjoyed, Colin. Name the day."

"This next Wednesday, seven in the evening." There was general agreement. But still Varens didn't appear ready to leave. He shuffled, his homely face flushing pink. Then he took a deep breath, looked up with a determined expression. "Miss Neville, I wonder if I might have a word with you in private."

"Lord," the dowager whispered to her daughter-in-law. "The imbecile is going to propose to Rachel again."

Lady Haven groaned and rolled her eyes.

Rachel, with a self-sacrificing expression on her pretty face, preceded the baronet out of the room.

Thirteen

"Rachel, what's wrong?" Pamela, just coming down the stairs scrubbing her eyes—she had not gotten much sleep the night before, and so had slept later than usual—saw her older sister striding petulantly from the library.

"Ooh! I am so angry!" Rachel stopped and paced in the hall. "That country clod," she said pointing toward the half-open library door, "and his weird sister have arrived at the worst possible time! Ooh!" She stamped her foot. "And now we will have to acknowledge them as acquaintances, and they will expect to be introduced around town and will damage our reputation. What will Lord Yarnell think? And his family! His mother is *most* particular about the acquaintance they form, and for it to be known that we are on an intimate footing with such provincial types as Colin and Andy . . . I do not know what it will do to our social caché. And then . . . and *then* the fool has the temerity to propose yet *again!* As if I would ever, in a thousand years, consider his proposal. Does he have any idea how many gentlemen . . ."

But Pamela lost the rest of Rachel's tirade as she gazed toward the library door. Colin? In London?

Without thinking, she moved toward the door and pushed past it, uncertainly peering into the gloomy, dank depths. Rachel's quick footsteps could be heard as she raced up the stairs and away from the site of such humiliation. Pamela's eyes adjusted to the dimness and there, by the unlit fireplace, huddled a figure in an attitude of utter despair. She approached tentatively.

She should leave. No one should see such naked pain as was evident in the way he was hunched over, head bowed, face in his large, calloused hands. But she was his friend. Friends were there when you needed them. Friends didn't shy away from pain or hurt.

"Colin?"

Slowly, he lifted his face and gazed toward her, his eyes glazed with grief. "Pammy?"

"Oh, Colin," she said, tears clogging her voice. She rushed to his side and sat down beside him, forgetting everything but the anguish on his rugged, homely face. She put her slender arm over his shoulders, rubbing the bulky muscles under his countrified jacket. "Why do you keep doing this to yourself?" It wasn't the first time he had proposed to and been rejected by Rachel. "Why? She will never accept you, and you must know that by now!"

"I thought she might be glad to see me," he said, humbly. "Thought I might be a taste of home, and that would turn the tide, you see. Of course I knew a girl like her . . . she'd have her pick of London beaux. But I thought a face from home. . . ." He shook his head with a bitter twist to his lips. "Who am I fooling? I thought no such thing. But I *was* afraid she would have found someone already; if I got here in time, I thought, then I could do something, stop it, or . . ."

"Colin!"

He took a deep breath and straightened. "There is no illusion this time, though, is there? No doubt left." Another deep, gasping breath, and he seemed to rise above the pain, to shake it off. "It is final. I have been a fool, but she couldn't have been clearer. And then I overheard what she said to you out in the hallway. Am I to understand some lucky man has won her favor?"

"Lord Yarnell," Pamela admitted. "He hasn't proposed yet, but all expect him to, for he has been most particular in his attentions. But he isn't half the man you are! He is a puff, a fop, a man-milliner. All he thinks of are his clothes and his status. I detest him."

"He must have something, or Miss Neville wouldn't be smitten." He stood and adjusted his coat. "Ah, well, I shouldn't keep Andy waiting. You must come and see your friend, Andromeda. She is so looking forward to seeing you again, Pammy . . . er, Miss Pamela." He gazed at her for the first time, noting her dress, a pale yellow confection with ivory ribbons that glowed in the dim light from the hall. "Aren't you a sight!"

"You don't like it?"

"Of course I do; you look like a buttercup." His expression softened and he touched a silky ribbon, letting it slide through his fingers. "But you are still our little Pixie, for all your new sophistication."

Not the most comforting words she could have heard. Would she always be just "Pixie" to him, as she was to her brother? He put his arm around her shoulders in a casual, brotherly way and they strolled together out to the hallway, where Andromeda was waiting.

Pamela greeted her with a hug, grateful to see friends from home. She made an appointment with

Andromeda to go to the library, for that lady wanted to see what books she should purchase with the precious sum given to her by the reading society of their town. From thence, Andromeda explained, she was off to Ackermann's to purchase a wedding present for Mr. and Mrs. Latimer.

That, of course, required an explanation, and with Andromeda Varens's tendency toward circumlocution, it was another half hour before the brother and sister left.

With all of the excitement, the intended conference canvassing Haven and Jane's marriage didn't take place. Talk over lunch—Rachel didn't come down, petulantly complaining of a headache—was about the Varens's visit and Mary Cooper's marriage.

"Much better than she could have expected to do," Lady Haven said.

The dowager grunted, cutting into a delicate serving of plaice. "If you and I agree on one more subject, Lydia, I shall think I am going soft in the head."

"You long ago went soft in the head," Lady Haven retorted.

"Latimer is the fortunate one," Haven said, ignoring his mother and grandmother's usual bickering and motioning to the footman for more beef. "Mary is the most sensible, intelligent woman in the village. She will make him an excellent wife."

Pamela agreed. "He is lucky to get Mary and Molly. Don't you think so, Jane?"

Jane, chasing a piece of fish around her rose-patterned plate, said, "Hmm? Were you addressing me, Pamela?"

Patiently, she repeated her question.

"Oh, yes, most certainly."

Haven cast his fiancée a questioning look, but she

had gone back to her fish, even though she didn't eat another bite. He watched her for a long while, how she dully waved off her favorite dishes and finally sat back, with a distracted sigh.

Pamela took another roll and said, "I look forward to going shopping with Andy this afternoon. She is so much fun; always has the most interesting ideas!"

"You, young lady, are not going anywhere," her mother said.

"Why not?"

"Have you all forgotten?" she said, her voice lifting with annoyance. "Lord Strongwycke is coming this afternoon for an appointment with Haven! A very *important* appointment!"

"Pamela won't be present, Mother, and she need not stay in the house for that reason," he answered, testily, as Pamela colored to a brick red.

"It would be rude of her to not be here when his lordship wants to . . . you know!"

"Good Lord, I find myself in agreement with Lydia again," Grand said, in a disgruntled tone. "Take me to Bedlam. But Pamela, you *will* be here when Strongwycke arrives."

Pamela looked from one to the other, and then appealed to Haven. "I don't need to stay, do I?"

Jane looked up, alerted by something in her voice and finally paying attention to the conversation. Haven gave her a significant look, and then said to his sister, "No, you don't need to stay while Strongwycke and I meet. We'll be seeing him later at the theater if I am not mistaken. There is plenty of time."

"I agree," Jane said, joining the discussion. Diffidently she added, "Perhaps, if I might, I will go out with you and Miss Varens, if I would not be intruding."

Relief on her piquant face, Pamela nodded as she reached over and squeezed her hand. "You know you are welcome, Jane."

Strongwycke was actually whistling as he approached the Haven town home. He gave his stick and hat to the butler, as he said, "I believe I am expected."

The butler ushered him into the only bright room in the house, the second floor saloon. Haven had relocated his desk there because he said he couldn't abide the gloomy atmosphere of the library. His mother threatened daily to have it removed again, as it took up so much space.

The earl strode across the room, clasped Haven's hand warmly, and took the seat indicated. He examined the viscount. When they had met a few years before, Strongwycke had not yet met Dorothea and his sister was alive and well. All the pain of the future was unthought of. He and Haven had gotten along famously, leading to the all-night drinking and talking he had referred to upon first making his re-acquaintance.

And this would be his brother. It gave him a warm feeling inside, for he had never had a brother. Euphemia had been his only sibling.

Haven, who had just finished a letter, signed it and sealed it. He looked up. "I have just been writing to congratulate an old friend upon her marriage."

"A happy chore."

"Yes. Old friends—our nearest neighbors of consequence in Yorkshire—have come to London and brought the news with them. I don't suppose you have ever met Sir Colin Varens and his sister, Miss Andromeda Varens?"

"Can't say as I have," Strongwycke said, politely.

"They will be joining us this evening."

"I look forward to meeting them," he replied, moving restlessly in his chair. He wanted to get down to business. Once he made a decision, he liked to act upon it immediately. But there was something in Haven's tone that he couldn't quite understand, something particular about the Varens siblings? He shook his head. He didn't know them, and they meant nothing to him.

"You will like Colin. He is the most sensible man I know. On most subjects."

Strongwycke sensed a story to be told there, but had no patience to ask. "Haven," he said, leaning forward. He wasn't one to dither around a subject. "It cannot have escaped your attention that Miss Pamela and I have spent a great deal of time together since your arrival in London. What started as a mere acquaintance to benefit my niece has become something more."

"Go on," Haven said.

Frowning over the other man's tone, which seemed to wed reluctance with distaste, Strongwycke sat back and rested his elbows on the arms of his chair, and steepled his fingers. "I have become very fond of her."

"I can't imagine a person who would not be fond of my sister," Haven said.

"My fondness has become deeper, more personal. Matter of fact, I have come to love her most sincerely."

No response.

"I would like to ask for your permission to court her and to ask for her hand in marriage."

Haven didn't seem surprised, and indeed there was no reason he should be. Strongwycke had made it quite plain the evening before what his business was. It was possible Haven and Pamela had spoken of it, in fact. Pamela, of course, knew what was coming.

"Do you have reason to believe she will welcome your suit?"

Startled by the other man's cool tone, Strongwycke said, "I have every reason to believe she expects and anticipates my proposal, yes."

"You do?"

Strongwycke was taken aback by the doubt . . . more than doubt, the disbelief in the other man's voice. "See here, Haven, are you in possession of some knowledge you would like to share?" This was not how he had foreseen the meeting would go. He had thought that by now they would be sipping brandy and congratulating each other on their new status as brothers. He had pictured it all, how he would be invited to join the family at dinner, how he would take Pamela aside and ask the question, the congratulations of the family. . . .

And yet Haven seemed loath to believe he would be successful.

He didn't answer directly. "Pamela is very young yet," Haven said, moving things about on the desk. His thick thatch of sandy hair was askew, and he disarranged it more by running his fingers through it. "Not only in years, but in experience. This is her first real Season, you know. Last year she was only in London a month or so, and then had to come home."

"Haven, I understand your hesitance, but I have reason to believe Pamela truly cares for me—a private reason, a *good* one—else I wouldn't be approaching you about this."

The viscount looked startled, his hand arrested in the act of folding a bit of paper into triangles. "As her brother I have the right to ask, what private reason?"

Strongwycke began to feel some impatience with the other man. What was this all about? "You have the right to demand, but what is between Pamela and myself I feel should remain there until I have had an opportunity to talk to her. Is she home?"

"No . . . uh," the viscount looked uncomfortable. "She is out with the friends I spoke of."

"Did she not want to stay in this afternoon?" Strongwycke was frankly bewildered. Certainly he couldn't have made himself any clearer the night before. Did they think that earls dropped off trees like ripe plums? He hoped he wasn't vain, but he was yearly made aware that he was a very eligible gentleman by the number of scheming mamas and their daughters that he had to fend off during the Season. And beyond, for he had been besieged at house parties, Christmas events, and even hunting parties.

"No," Haven said, his voice stronger. "She particularly wanted to go out with Colin and his sister."

Strongwycke calmed himself. These were old friends, and she would be excited about seeing them, likely. He knew well how warm her heart and firm her friendship was, and he would not love her better for being more calculating. "I will speak with her tomorrow, then. Tonight won't be a good opportunity. I am to meet acquaintances at the theater, and will, perforce, have to spend part of my time with them." He stood and stuck out his hand. "Until tonight, then, Haven. And I hope soon to be able to call you brother."

Haven took his hand in a firm grip. "I appreciate your forbearance, Strongwycke," he said, his voice warmer than it had been. "You have no idea what it is like to exist in a household of contrary females."

The earl chuckled and headed for the door. "I shall take one off your hands, my friend."

His joke didn't appear to sit well with Haven; the viscount shrugged and his eyes clouded.

In the hallway, the correct butler had Strongwycke's hat and stick ready and opened the door for him. At that same moment, Pamela and a lady climbed the steps.

"Miss Pamela!" Strongwycke said. "How fortunate! I thought I would have to call on the morrow, but since you are just home, I would like to beg a moment of your time on an important matter."

"I—I . . . I am so sorry, Strongwycke, but I have promised my friend the rest of the afternoon, you know, and it wouldn't do to be rude! Would it?"

Taken aback by the unwonted nervousness of her voice and her stuttering speech, Strongwycke took a step back, letting them through the door past him, and said, "I will call tomorrow, then." He felt the other lady's avid gaze on him, but was too offset to stop and wait for an introduction. Putting his hat on his head, he said, "I will see you tonight, though, at the theater?"

"Yes, of course. Sir Colin and Miss Varens have agreed kindly to accompany us."

"I look forward to it then," Strongwycke said, struggling to regain his equanimity. "Until tonight."

Fourteen

"You are all so kind," Varens murmured to Pamela, as they sat in their box at the theater. "You and Haven and Miss Dresden. I feel as if I have been a fool." He glanced over at Rachel, sitting with Lord Yarnell; she whispered to him and giggled behind her fan at the various gaudily dressed dowagers in other boxes.

Pamela sighed, blissfully. It wasn't Colin's words that made her happy so much as the feeling she had that his eyes were finally open to Rachel's utter disdain of his suit. That had been the obstacle all those years to any chance for him to find another lady who might be a better wife to him, a more fit helpmeet. In other words, herself. "You weren't a fool," she whispered. "You were in love."

"Was I?"

There was bitterness in his voice still, and it made Pamela wary.

"Call it infatuation, instead," he murmured.

She relaxed.

"You are so very different, Pammy," he said, indicating her elegant dress and hairstyle. "I very much approve of the changes in you."

"I haven't truly changed," she started, but he was still speaking.

"While you were such a harum-scarum infant there was no chance of any gentleman finding you fit to take to wife. Now you would make any gentleman proud." Varens glanced around at the other boxes. "There is scarce a lady here who can hold a candle to you and . . . and your sister."

Crossly, Pamela felt that somehow, in Colin's view, she was still second-best to Rachel. When would he eliminate her from his speech? Andromeda demanded her attention at that moment. She was trying to make out the declension of a certain German word used in the opera they were viewing. Pamela shrugged and shook her head. What did she know of German nouns, verbs, or tenses?

Peevishly, she glanced around her box. Jane and Haven were having a whispered argument, Jane's face white and strained. Lady Haven was trying to speak to Lord Yarnell, but he was pretending not to hear her, and Andromeda and Colin were now speaking of something.

She sighed and surveyed the theater. In a distant box, Strongwycke was surrounded by a party of gentlemen. One of the fellows had a gaudy-looking female draped around his neck. The earl, though, was staring straight ahead, his brow furrowed.

Lord, but she was a coward. Strongwycke was going to ask her to marry him. She should have been brave enough to hear him out, at any rate. What was she afraid of, after all?

What she was afraid of was that she didn't know how to answer him.

What was she going to do? Haven just said it was up to her, but his tone wasn't encouraging. She supposed she should be thankful he wasn't pushing her to make a decision; many brothers wouldn't have let her have a say in the matter. Strongwycke was a catch, almost as much of one as Lord Yarnell. If her mother had her way, Pamela would be married to him by the month's end.

But if anything, Haven was too nonchalant. She was a bundle of indecision, and it frightened her. How could she be undecided? After all, she had only come to London to learn enough that Colin might find her more desirable as a wife. He liked lady-like women, dainty, delicate . . . like Rachel. She had learned how to appear so. In public she was demure, quiet, refined. But in private she still liked to run, like she had playing cricket with Strongwycke on the Richmond Park green just a week or so before.

And Strongwycke didn't seem to mind. That was the crux of her indecision, the reason she just couldn't say "no" outright and be done with it. It was so final. If she did say "no," wouldn't Strongwycke retreat from her? Wasn't that natural? And she would miss him sorely, for he was one person with whom she didn't need to be anything but herself. He didn't even mind that in the early morning she still rode astride, with a dirty old cap pulled down over her curls. No one would recognize her as Miss Pamela Neville, he said. So where was the harm? He never by word or gesture implied that she must change in any way. He told her she was pretty.

And he wanted to marry her.

She shivered. It was such an enormous decision, and one she had never expected to be faced with. It was much easier to not make it, to not say one way or the other just yet.

The evening passed. Strongwycke joined them for the last act, and invited them all to a ball that was to follow the opera, at the home of his acquaintance,

Lord Fingal. Lady Haven accepted for them all, and they proceeded there, with Strongwycke as their guide.

Colin met some acquaintance there that he had gone to school with many years before, and disappeared almost immediately into the card room. Rachel and Lord Yarnell joined a party of his friends, and that left Lady Haven, Jane, and Haven with Strongwycke and Pamela.

"Why do you two not dance?" Pamela's mother said, with a significant arch to her brow.

"You are so very wise, my lady," Strongwycke said, bowing. He held out his arm and tentatively said, "Would you care to waltz, Miss Pamela?"

Reluctantly, she nodded. They joined the swirling mass of lords and ladies, misters and misses. Once more, Pamela was swept away by the feel of Strongwycke's hand on her back guiding her through the bold steps. She released all reason and just enjoyed for that time.

But soon the music came to an end. The next dance was to be a galop, and the energetic music started almost immediately, even as sets were forming.

"Come for a walk with me," Strongwycke murmured, still holding her close to him. "We can't talk with this infernal noise going on." They had danced, during the waltz, to a remote corner of the ballroom, and the brilliant light of a thousand candles did not penetrate the gloom of the alcove.

"That noise, sir, is called music," Pamela answered. She wasn't sure she wanted to be alone with Strongwycke, who alarmed her now, not at what he might do, but at what she might feel. She had never experienced the sensation of floating across a ballroom floor as she had in his arms, and the memory of his brief but tantalizing kisses was frightening. At least with Colin there was the solid feel of certainty. Colin. Now there was a thought to bring her back down to earth. "I don't think we should go outside, my lord." Her voice, she was happy to note, was strong and even. She would stave off the inevitable for as long as possible while she sorted out her tumultuous feelings.

"I think we should," he murmured, his handsome light brown eyes holding hers in a gaze, not threatening, but knowledgeable.

"You do?" And now, just seconds later, she didn't recognize her own voice, so breathless did it sound. She seemed to tumble in one giddy second from certainty to wild anticipation. What was *wrong* with her?

Without another word he guided her through the floating curtains of the French doors onto the terrace, and down some steps into the dusky garden, where the scent of night stocks drifted and the heat from the ballroom dissipated, leaving her chilled and quivering.

"You are cold," he said, as they stopped on the stone pathway, his voice coming from somewhere above her ear.

She shivered again. The chill was even seeping through her slippers and freezing her toes. "I am." They would go in now. No gentleman of Strongwycke's caliber would keep a young lady outside to catch her death of the grippe.

Instead, though, his arms gathered her close to his chest, until she could feel the pounding of his heart against her cheek where it lay close to his superfine wool coat. She closed her eyes, wondering at the panic that flooded her body, the fear that was no fear of physical harm, that jolted her. She was no coward. What was wrong with her?

"Strong," she whispered, "what are we doing out here?"

In answer, he tilted her face up with one finger under her chin. His usually solemn expression was lit with a soft smile, one that lifted the corners of his mouth in a most appealing way. She could hardly see his shadowed eyes, but knew that they were examining her own, and was self-conscious. What would he see there? Could she hide how she trembled? How her very heart quivered at this moment? It was all so strange and new. If this was Colin. . . .

"I can't forget how your lips tasted. I need to taste them again." His voice was deep and filled with emotion.

When Strongwycke's lips touched hers, Pamela felt in that moment as if she had been jumping her mare, her heart raced and thudded so heavily. And then she forgot it all, forgot the garden, forgot the night, forgot everything except this new sensation, his mouth drawing on hers, suckling the tender flesh of her lower lip, his tongue tracing lightly the line of her upper lip.

This kiss lasted much longer than her only other experience. It was dizzying, stupefying, thrilling. Without conscious plan, her hands slid up over his coat and clasped behind his neck and she stood on tiptoe; anything to prolong this delicious sensation.

"Pamela," he whispered, at last. He rested his cheek against her hair. "My dear one, I have been wanting to do that all evening."

Strange and frightening sensations twisted through her. At the same time that she wanted to tear away and run, she wanted to pull his face down for another kiss.

"Pamela, my sweet, this is the moment I have been waiting for." He pushed her away a little and gazed into her face, his brown eyes dark in the dim light from the terrace. "Miss Pamela Neville, I have never met another lady like you. You put every other girl in London in the shade. Would you . . . will you consider marrying me?"

The moment had arrived, and so suddenly! There was no staving it off, no pretending he hadn't said what he had just said.

She stood, speechless for a minute, her heart pounding, almost sick with indecision. Yes or no? What should she say?

"Strong! . . . may I . . . may I think about it?"

Fifteen

"Think about it?"

She nodded, mute.

He sighed and held her for a moment. Then, putting his arm around her shoulders and guiding her back towards the terrace, he said, "Pamela, do you . . . do you like me?"

"Of course I do," she said, striking his chest with the flat of her hand. "You have become a very dear friend to me."

"Friend," he said, bleakly. He said not another word as they walked the pathway and mounted the steps of the terrace.

He stopped her before they went in, turned her to face him, gazing at her in the better light shed by the open doors. "Once I made the mistake of not saying how I felt. Because of that, Dorothea didn't know what she meant to me, and I lost her. Because of you, I have come to be grateful that she had the good sense to marry where her heart led her. And to release me to find my true love." Steadily, he stared into her eyes and pushed back one curling tendril from her forehead. "Pamela, I love you. Very much."

Filled with awe at his admission, Pamela was silent and looked away toward a potted yew tree, not able to meet his eyes. He loved her. How could that be?

Was he sure? The precious admission filled her with such fear, she didn't know quite how to respond. "How do you know?" she said, in a small voice. She touched the folds of his cravat and adjusted his pearl stickpin.

He chuckled and traced her downy cheek with the back of his gloved hand, then lifted her face with one finger under her chin. "As always, that is a surprisingly sensible question, in light of my mistaken infatuation with Dorothea. I can see how you would need to know."

She was silent. That was not at all why she was asking the question; she was asking to seek information for her own needs. How did one know if one was in love? How did *he* know? But let him think what he would. She was rapidly becoming confused and needed some time and calm to think.

"It isn't that I can't imagine my life going ahead now without you in it," he continued, his tone contemplative. "But I don't *want* to imagine it. I have been in London too long. I want to go back to Shadow Manor, and I want you by my side." He grasped her shoulders and ducked a little, so he could look her in the eye. "You are so unexpected, like a cleansing breeze that has wiped away all the cobwebs from my heart. I am not a flowery or a sentimental man, but you have just made me make a speech. I *love* you."

She stayed silent, confused by the warring emotions within her. It was all so new. She had never expected Strongwycke to fall in love with her, never even thought of him and marriage in the same breath.

What was she going to do?

"I had better get you back inside," he said, guiding

her toward the doors. "It is getting even colder, and we have already been gone too long."

Inside, he left her, asking her to give his apologies to her family, but he must spend some time with Lord Fingal, his mentor. He said not another word about marriage, but asked if she would like to ride the next morning with him and Belinda. She gladly accepted the invitation, wishing that they could just forget all about the kisses and the proposal.

And yet, that was not possible now. Everything had changed, and they could not go back, only forward. But forward to what?

Strongwycke strode away, holding firmly in check his emotions. It had taken all of his considerable self-control to appear calm and composed, when what he really wanted to do was shake her. But no, that wasn't quite accurate. Not shake her; he wanted to kiss her again, wanted to *show* her how she felt, give her no room for doubt.

But that was not the way, and he knew it. She must know in her heart it was the right thing to do, not just be swept away with the considerable attraction that was between them. Again he had misread a lady. He had thought she was ready, that she knew her heart as well as he did his own. She had even seemed to be sending him the subtle message that she welcomed his suit.

Joining his colleagues, he went with them to the library for cigars and port, and let his mind roam as Fingal held forth on some subject or another.

She was too damned young, he thought, throwing himself into a deep club chair in a corner where he would be ignored. He let the other men's voices roll around him, the murmur soothing to his raw nerves, like waves washing ashore. Maybe Haven was right after all. She was young in experience, and just not ready for everything that marriage meant. He had the feeling that Pamela's education in the ways of the world had been neglected while Lady Haven lavished all her attention on the elder Miss Neville. And yet, some of that was the very thing that he loved about Pamela. She was not practiced, nor had her natural inclinations been ruthlessly beaten out of her. She was free-spirited. There was an honesty in her soul, and so much of society was fraudulent and cold, practiced and calculated.

She was just Pamela, and he loved her for her innocence and freshness. But she did not seem ready to marry, and certainly not marry him. Morosely, he contemplated the possibilities; perhaps it was just that while he had fallen in love with her, she remained heart-whole.

With the memory of their kisses in the garden on his lips, he could not believe that. She felt *something* for him. He wondered if, like a tiny ember, he could fan that "something" and raise it into a flame.

She had asked for time. He stubbed out his cigar and took a swig of port. All right, it was not an unfair request. This was an important decision for both of them. He would give her one week.

"Rachel?" Pamela, in her nightrail, had just slithered down the dark hallway to her sister's room and peeked in.

"What is it?" Rachel was still sitting at her dressing table, her glossy hair being brushed for the requisite number of times. She sent the maid away with a wave of her hand, and continued on with her nightly routine, one that she followed even at Haven Court, with lanolin cream on her cheeks and elbows and knees and a close inspection of every line and crease on her young face.

Pamela knew—had heard a hundred times—that this was the year, this was Rachel's opportunity to find the husband she had so long wanted. She had specific goals in mind. Her husband must be titled, handsome, wealthy, well-thought of in society, and with no female relatives living at home. He had to be without obvious vice, meaning Rachel did not intend to tolerate a husband who gambled, was a drunkard or lecher, nor would she allow near her any man who would not or could not dress in the style Beau Brummel had made *de rigueur.*

"Rach, how do you know when it is right . . . when the right man has asked for your hand?"

Her pale eyes wide, Rachel stopped preening and gazed at her younger sister's reflected image in the big mirror over her dressing table. "Has . . . something happened?"

"Strongwycke asked me to marry him."

Rachel's eyebrows raised a whit, but if she was shocked, her placid face held no other sign. "What did you say in answer?"

"I asked him for a little time."

"And he agreed?"

Shrugging, Pamela sank into a chair near her sister's dressing table. "He didn't *disagree.* Not in so many words." Moodily, she stared at her own hands, so rough and brown compared to Rachel's perfect, pale ones. A man like Strongwycke, who could surely have his pick of ladies of the *ton,* had asked *her* to marry him. It made no sense! Unless what he said was true.

"Rach, he told me he *loves* me!" She watched her sister's face, but for once could not read the emotions that flitted over it. Some dismissed Rachel Neville as single-minded, but Pamela still remembered long nights talking, when they had shared a room and snuggled under the covers, giggling and chattering until the early hours. In their youth they had presented a united front, and had engaged in all manner of antics to drive their parents mad. At the height of their bad behavior, Grand had even voluntarily moved to the dower house for a few years, stating that undisciplined children were the devil's handiwork. And they were wild and carefree children, little bounded by rules or regulations, with a father who was under his wife's thumb and a mother who was inconsistent and erratic in her discipline.

All of that had changed when their father died. Rachel had withdrawn, and by the time she came out of her misery, their powerful bond was shattered, changed. As they were growing up and Rachel was becoming a young lady, they were placed in separate rooms and their relationship was forever altered. They never regained that intimacy, but Pamela still remembered it fondly and would forever see within her prissy older sister the harum-scarum girl with the tangled masses of chestnut curls, who danced across the moors in wild abandon. Somewhere, buried deep in her heart, the old Rachel still lived, Pamela just knew it.

"He told you he loves you."

Pamela nodded, watching her sister moving her vanity set into exact positions on her dressing table. Even when others damned Rachel as cold and calculating, Pamela still believed in her sister's benevolence and sweetness. Someday someone else would see it, too. Unless she spoiled herself forever by marrying that detestable bore, Yarnell.

Rachel turned away and resumed her beauty routine, but then stopped, bit her lip, and turned back to her younger sister with an unreadable expression on her lovely face. Again she said, "He told you he loves you."

Frowning, Pamela said, "Yes. You have probably been told that innumerable times, but it is the first time a gentleman has said anything like that to me."

There was no answer. Rachel applied some cream to her arms and rubbed it into her hands.

"Rach, how do you feel . . . that is, have you ever . . ." How to put this into words? It was all so confusing and new. Until now she had only ever yearned for Colin to stop moping about Rachel and notice *her*. In her whole blinkered existence she had never once thought another gentleman might want to marry her. "Have you ever felt all tingly when a gentleman kisses you?"

The cream pot dropped. Rachel turned on her seat and gazed down at Pamela. "What have you been doing?"

"Strongwycke kissed me. In the garden last night. And the other night, before he said he was coming to visit Haven the next day."

"Good Lord, Pammy. Have you no common sense? It would be the ruination of your reputation if anyone saw you acting so . . . so immodestly!" She shook her head.

Tears welled up in Pamela's eyes, and then the strangest thing in the world happened. Rachel flitted from her stool and wrapped her arms around her younger sister. "Pammy," she whispered in the old tone, the tone of a girl who loved her little sister.

"Don't cry, dear! You have to decide what you want. Whatever you do, don't hold on to the past. Do what will make you happy, but don't take forever about it." She put her hands on her sister's shoulders and stared into her eyes. "Opportunity only comes to visit once in a long while. Seize your future! If Strongwycke can make you happy, then marry him! If he cannot, then say 'no' and be done with it. But be careful and do not let anyone push you into a marriage you do not want. You deserve someone who will love you and cherish you as they ought."

At that same moment, Jane was peeking out her door, looking both ways up and down the hall. She had spent a miserable hour trying to settle herself to sleep in the drafty, gloomy room she had been assigned, but was more awake than ever. She could not go on this way any longer.

She softly closed the door behind her and tiptoed down the room, past the murmur of voices in Rachel's chamber and past the silence of Lady Haven's room. Heart pounding, she tapped on the next door and heard the heavy footsteps within. Haven opened the door, his sky-blue eyes widening at the sight of his fiancée shivering in the hallway. "Get in here!" he said, grabbing her arm and pulling her inside. He gazed up and down the hall, before closing the door. "No one saw you?"

"Of course not," she whispered.

Haven wrapped his arms around Jane and pulled her against him. "To what do I owe this unexpected pleasure?" he asked, his tone gentle.

"Gerry, I don't want to fight," she said, laying her face against his chest. Their quarrel earlier had left her feeling frightened and miserable. Despite knowing he loved her, she still felt vulnerable, as if that love could be tainted by their quarrels.

"I don't want to argue either, my dearest love."

He couldn't even remember what the tiff was about now, but he had the feeling that their increasingly frequent arguments were the result of the tension between them, the ongoing battle over when and where they would wed.

"Haven, kiss me?" she said, her voice trembling. She closed her eyes and raised her face to him, waiting.

He obliged most happily, losing himself in the softness of her lips, the fragrance of her flowing hair and the voluptuousness of her body under his hands. His own state of semi-undress, his jacket off, cravat gone, shirt open, made their naughty meeting more enticing. She discovered the open "V" of his shirt, and touched his skin, her small hand cold. The familiar pulse of arousal pounded through him.

He picked her up and laid her down on his massive canopied bed, joining her and consuming her mouth in kiss after delicious kiss. Gazing down at her, her dark wavy locks spread out over his pillow, he knew that the next time they kissed, he would not want to stop, not that he ever did. He stroked her hair, threading his fingers through it. "You are in a very dangerous position, my lady and wife-to-be." He let his hand drift down, skimming her cheek, her neck, down to her bosom. She was clad only in a filmy nightrail, and he hungrily dug his fingers in, grasping a great handful of soft material. For their wedding night, he thought he would buy her a dozen such nightgowns, just so he could tear them from her and devour her as he wanted.

The erotic thought made him almost double over with pounding need.

"I trust your integrity as a gentleman, sir," she said, gazing up at him.

Damn. That was not a good thing; it placed a heavy burden of behavior on him, the restriction of behaving as a gentleman ought, when all he wanted to do was ravish her . . . with her consent, of course. She moved sinuously, and he groaned. Tempted beyond endurance, he bent his head to kiss her again, and they lost several more minutes as he plundered her moist mouth and moved against her plump thigh. Panting, he stopped and buried his head in the bedclothes. If she expected him to behave as a gentleman ought, then she would have to stop doing what she did so well, tempting him beyond endurance.

He was going to go quite mad. He lifted his face again to gaze down at her.

Lacing her fingers through his hair, Jane said, "Let us just run away, Haven, back north, to Yorkshire. Mary's old cottage is empty; we could stay there, live there for a while. No one would even know we were in Yorkshire! We can be married on the way and make an adventure of it."

So, that was what this was about. As unfair as he knew he was being, when he was trying to manipulate her into marrying in London, a flare of anger coursed through him. "Good God, Jane!" He grunted and pushed away, standing and pacing by the bed. "I cannot abandon my responsibilities here. Pamela needs me. I will not have our mother, or anyone, push her into a marriage with Strongwycke against her will."

Frustrated, Jane slipped off the bed and straightened her disarranged nightrail. "Haven, you speak as if you are the only one who has Pamela's best interests at heart. Do you think your grandmother would let anyone push her favorite grandchild in a way she did not want?"

"But she is old and Mother is determined . . ."

"Your grandmother is the most stubborn, hard-headed woman I have ever met. Your mother is no match for her when it comes down to it, and we both know it."

"But my love, I am the head of the family . . ."

Jane sat down, defeated. "I know, I know." She buried her face in her hands, and then dropped them in defeat. Taking a deep, calming breath, she said, "I know. And you're right. I am merely being selfish. I have never been so in my whole life, but I want to be your wife more than anything in this world."

"Then marry me here, and we can . . ." He indicated the bed with a sly wink.

"No," she said, standing and moving toward the door. She turned, the doorknob in her hand. "I am standing my ground. I have never done so before and I am frightened, Gerry, afraid that you will lose a little of the affection you feel for me. But I *will* stand my ground. I want to be married in Yorkshire and spend our first night as man and wife in our cottage. And if it is not built, then Mary's cottage will do just fine. But I want my wedding night as I want it."

"So you want your own way and will not bend?"

"Not this time." There was a finality to her words that left no room for argument. She opened the door, looked both ways up and down the hall, and skittered to her own room.

* * *

The morning was gloomy and rain threatened, the sky a deep bruised color. But Pamela took the chance that Strongwycke and Belinda would not be deterred by the threat, and she sneaked out the door to the stable, and, cap jammed low, trotted on Tassie along the quiet streets, with only the vendors' barrows and drays as competition. Hyde Park was misty, the grass jeweled with droplets of water and a fog rising off the Serpentine.

As the fog thickened, she wondered if she would find her friends there, and was relieved when she saw them standing by the old tree that was their meeting place.

"Hallo, Pete," Belinda shouted, using her jocular name for Pamela when she was riding breeches.

"Hallo, Bob," Pamela cried, retorting in kind.

For Strongwycke had broken down and done the unthinkable, allowing his niece the luxury of breeches and riding astride on these early morning rides. He had protested at first, and it was against his better judgment, but he had turned out to be softer than Belinda would ever have imagined, especially when her own pleas were joined by those of Miss Pamela Neville.

"You are both mad, but I am more so than both put together," the earl said, glancing around. "To wink at such behavior . . ."

Pamela chuckled and Tassie whickered. "But sir, you are just letting a couple of stable boys run your horses, in't that so, Bob? 'Is lor'ship, e's a right proper toff, an' 'e carn't be bovered wiv racin' the steppers 'imself."

Strongwycke laughed out loud, and Pamela lost the ability to breathe for a second as she gazed at him, eyes wide. How *fine* his laughter sounded! And what a man he was, to allow her and his niece to fracture all the rules in such a way. Where would one ever find another man like him?

Where, indeed? And yet she was willing to keep him dangling like a trout because she could not be decisive.

To forget her bafflement, she challenged Belinda to a race, and they took off in the mist, trotting over a green rise and down a long sward, the pounding of their horses' hooves the only sound. But when they came to a halt, she reluctantly gazed around her and said, panting, "The mist is far too thick; we mustn't gallop again. I would have neither of us hurt, nor would I endanger the beasts."

Belinda trusted her friend's perspicacity where riding was concerned and agreed for once to be cautious. When it came to horses, no one knew more than Pamela, she had been heard to say recently, and so they trotted at a sedate pace back to where Strongwycke would be waiting, after his own canter about the lake.

"Do you like my uncle?" Belinda asked, as their horses fell into step side by side.

"Of course I do!" Pamela said, watching the fog eddy and swirl. "He is a very good sort of fellow."

"But I mean in another way," the girl said, pulling her cap off and letting her hair stream down. She shook her heavy mane back, pushing it out of her eyes. "Do you *like* him?"

"Whatever brought that into your mind?" Pamela said, irritated. She could not escape it, it seemed, this constant reminder of the question that lingered between her and Strongwycke.

"It's just that . . . well, he is always talking about you, and asking what I think of you. And I overheard him talking to his solicitor the other day about marriage settlements. I just . . . wondered. If you did marry him, I should like it very much."

It became chillingly real in that moment. Until then, marriage had been some hazy, indefinite idea Pamela had thought of in relation to Colin. She would live at Corleigh, ride his horses, be sister to Andromeda, and live out her life in Yorkshire as Colin's wife.

But marriage meant so much more. It was a contract. There would be negotiations on her behalf for marriage settlements, pin money to agree upon, future children to make arrangements for.

Children!

Strongwycke came out of the mist in that moment, powerful and tall on his fractious mount, his tousled hair blowing in the breeze.

Children. A husband. And she would be a wife and mother, expected to perform those functions with aplomb. Expected to. . . .

"I have to go, Belinda." She raised her voice. "Goodbye, Strongwycke, I will see you later. Get home before the rain starts." She wheeled Tassie around and bolted.

Sixteen

For two days it rained. Pamela didn't see Strong-wycke alone and she wasn't sure if that was a good thing or a bad. She felt strange around him now, like she couldn't quite be herself, though his behavior was as impeccably natural as always. He was invited for tea and joined them at the theater, and always he treated her with kindness and consideration.

But there was a glow in his eyes, and a knowing smile on his lips. It worried her.

Their family group included Andromeda and Colin almost all the time now, and Colin seemed to seek out her company more and more. They spoke of Corleigh, and his plans for its future. They talked about Mary and her marriage, and the baby, Molly. Their relationship was cordial and friendly. It should have been the happiest time of her life.

She was miserable.

It was afternoon and they were having tea in the drawing room, minus Jane and Haven, who were out visiting. Lord Yarnell was there, so Rachel was fully occupied. Pamela had to believe that her sister knew what was best for herself with regard to Lord Yarnell, since she had given sensible advice about the Strong-wycke proposal. Advice Pamela was not sure how to take, yet. But as a brother-in-law the stuffy marquess left much room for improvement.

Andromeda was divulging all the latest gossip from home to Grand—nobody was more interested in the minutiae of life than Miss Varens—and Lady Haven was divided between asking Colin questions about their home parish and deferring to Lord Strongwycke about everything else.

Pamela, primped and prodded into acceptable dress, meaning, this time, one her mother liked, sat stiffly staring out at the drizzle as it coursed down the window in rivulets. Lady Haven monopolized Lord Strongwycke's time, finally, archly talking of how perfect a specimen of proper behavior Pamela had become. The earl managed to keep a straight face, though he must have seen how the subject of the long and detailed conversation was squirming at hearing herself spoken of so openly, her past misbehavior canvassed and her present perfect conduct lauded. And so Pamela kept her gaze turned to the window.

Colin, under the guise of stretching his legs, came and sat beside her, putting one large, knobby hand on the back of her chair. "You look so lovely sitting here, Pammy, rather wistful. You would rather be home, I would wager."

Gratefully, she said, "Yes. How well you know me, Colin."

"I suppose it is wrong in us to call each other by our first names when we are in company like this. But we are still old friends, are we not?"

"Of course we are," she said, eagerly, letting her posture relax. "I have always liked you."

"And I, you," he said, covering one of her hands where it rested on the table between them.

She pinkened, discomposed by his earnest tone.

His eyes were illuminated from within by a strange new light, and she didn't know how to respond, never having seen him thus except when he was speaking to Rachel.

"I might go so far as to say, I can't think of another lady, even including your fair sister, who suits me so well as a friend and . . . and perhaps more." He stared down at their joined hands and then looked up, searching her face.

Pamela, caught off balance, didn't reply.

"What I am trying to say and making such a mull of is, Pammy, dear girl, would you do me the honor of marrying me?"

The sapskull was asking her to marry him in company, where she couldn't even respond properly? Pamela restrained herself from telling him what an idiot he was, that everyone, even the most bacon-brained feather-wits, knew that a lady liked to be asked privately, so she could respond in an appropriate manner. A girl should be asked in a moonlit garden and kissed until she was light-headed.

Like Strongwycke had proposed.

Her mother had the earl still in her clutches, and he was beginning to look a little desperate. He glanced over at her with a pleading look, but Pamela's mind was racing too much to give him anything but a blank look.

Marry Colin?

"Colin, I . . ."

It should come easy. She had imagined this day, longed for it, despaired of this ever happening. And now he had asked her to marry him. If she said "yes," she could be married and back to Yorkshire within the month.

It should be simplicity itself.

So why would the words not come out of her mouth?

"I know this has come as a surprise to you, my dear." Colin patted her hand as if he was a kindly uncle. "If you would like to think about it for a few days, I completely understand."

A more unloverlike speech she couldn't imagine, but she was grateful, for once, for his avuncular manner and nodded.

"We shall leave it at that, then, and I will speak to Haven when he comes in."

She nodded once more, and that was it. That was the end of the great proposal for which she had waited her whole girlhood. He moved away to make general conversation with his sister and Grand. When Haven and Jane came in, scattering raindrops on the rug as they shed pelisses and hats, Colin rose and asked for a moment with Haven alone, and they disappeared off down the dark hallway. Jane frowned after them.

Pamela sat, not able to let her agitation show, longing to be alone and to vent her feelings with a good long run or gallop or scream. And yet she must sit, hands demurely folded, feet together on the faded rug.

Jane, ever perceptive, sat down by her, shielding her from the rest of the company. "Sweetheart, you look ready to jump out of your skin. What is wrong?"

"Oh, Jane," she said, in an agonized whisper. "I think I am in love with two men."

"It is a ridiculous situation," Jane said to Haven, watching him as he paced, head down, in the tiny, cramped library. She sat curled up on the cracked leather sofa. She had told him of Pamela's heart-rend-ing declaration, and the whispered conversation that followed. The girl was confused, it seemed to Jane, be-tween what she had always thought she wanted, and what appealed to her now. But Jane wasn't going to be the one to try to steer her toward the earl, just because she thought he was the right man for her. No one should interfere so in another's autonomy.

"It wouldn't have been thus if you and Grand didn't scheme to confuse the poor girl by pushing Strongwycke on her at every opportunity."

Jane kept a firm check on her anger. He was ac-cusing her simply because he had his own ideas of what Pamela needed. He wanted to keep his favorite sister nearby; if she married Colin they would always be near. "And how were we to know that Colin would come to his senses and realize that Pamela was a far better match for him than Rachel?" she pointed out. "I still am not convinced that he really cares for Pammy in the right way, as a lover and husband should. In fact, I don't think he has even *told* Pamela that he loves her."

Haven stopped and gazed down at Jane. "You don't know him like I do. He is thoroughly disillusioned with Rachel, and can see that Pamela is by far the su-perior match for him. He said everything that was decent and proper in asking permission to court her. He loves her." He dropped down to the seat next to Jane, and she slid toward him as his weight settled.

"Did he say so?" she asked, her tone challenging. "And how did he come to that amazing new knowl-edge, that Pammy is the girl he should marry and spend the rest of his life with? Because she gets along with Andromeda better than Rachel does, and likes to ride his horses? Haven, you know it needs more than that to make a good marriage."

Did he? Did he have any idea himself? He looked over at the infuriating woman he wanted so badly to wed. He had thought, when they became engaged, that she was a complaisant and prettily behaved woman. And she was for the most part, except for this streak of stubbornness about their actual wedding.

"What *does* it take to make a good marriage?" he asked.

"Love," she said, looking tenderly into his eyes. She slid closer, until her leg was pressed against his thigh, and pushed back his thick, unruly mat of hair. "No matter how much you and I quarrel, I still know I love you and want to be your wife."

"So do I. Want you to be my wife, I mean," he growled, pulling her onto his lap.

The next few minutes were lost, but Jane pulled away and, flustered, straightened her bodice and patted at her hair. "But it takes more than love, Gerry. It takes, I think, a similarity of vision. You and I want the same things, mostly. Haven Court, and children, and family. And our little cottage." She slyly smiled at him. "You do still want our cottage, don't you? To be utterly alone at night, so no one can hear us." She moved back so that her thigh was touching his again, her hand on his leg, rubbing in small circles. She whispered into his ear, "No one can hear me cry out . . ."

Haven, his face red, clenched his fists. "Jane," he said. "If you mean to tease me so . . ."

She touched his ear, her finger tracing the line of it and gently trailing down his neck. He pulled her back toward him, and another few minutes were lost as they kissed and touched.

"Jane, enough!" he finally said, burying his face in

her neck and letting out a hot sigh. "I can't, especially as things stand now, leave London. Pamela's future and happiness are far too important for me to abandon her now. I want you so very badly I ache throughout my body. You have me fevered with anticipation. I spend most nights pacing, knowing you are just down the hall and I can't go to you. If you will not marry me here, in London, then please, we must stop doing this. It is torture."

His words were like an arrow piercing her. She lifted his head and framed his handsome, broad face in her hands. In the gloom of the dank room his eyes were still such a brilliant blue that they reminded her of the Yorkshire sky over the moors. It wasn't her birthplace; she had been reared in the tranquillity of the south of England. But the wildness of Yorkshire appealed to her, thrilled her, and she had fallen in love with it, just as she had fallen deeply, irrevocably in love with the master of Haven Court.

Those gorgeous blue eyes were shadowed with worry right now, though, and had dark circles under them, attesting to his sleepless nights. She brushed back his hair and kissed his forehead.

Was any need of hers worth making him miserable? Life was short. How many couples, during the war, had missed their short chance at love and life because they decided to wait until the fellow came back? And then he never came back.

The future was too precious to take so lightly. One should never put off happiness in an uncertain world.

"I will," she said, suddenly, knowing that whatever happened, she was making the right decision. She loved him. Did it matter, ultimately, where they married? "I will marry you wherever you want, here in London, Yorkshire, Gretna Green; wherever and whenever you want me, there will I be." She moved into his arms and kissed him long and lovingly.

Grand was dissatisfied. She cast a disdainful look at Rachel, now placidly stitching in the weak light from the window, and at Pamela, listening to—or appearing to listen to—her mother. Why did the present look, to her, like a pale wash of life as she remembered living it?

Were the colors so much more vivid when she was twenty? Or was it she who had had all the life washed out of her, like color from sun-faded silk?

But everything was so easy for these youngsters, she thought, eyeing her grandchildren. When she had been a girl, travel had been perilous and arduous. Now the mail coach traveled at astonishing speeds, and anyone with the money could travel the length of their great country and beyond in ease and comfort.

And when she was young, all of her decisions had been made for her, up to and including her wedding, when she was just fifteen. It had been up to her to deal with the unpleasant as well as the pleasant consequences after that day, to try to make the best of a life she hadn't chosen. She was such an innocent that when she had gone to the marriage bed, it was with the idea that kisses and nothing more would be expected of her. She was in for a rude awakening, and for a long time had been horrified at the unpleasantness of a woman's lot in life. Once she had borne her husband a son, things got easier. She had even learned to enjoy some things. And her husband had become astonishingly kind once she had decided she deserved better treatment. It had taken months and had been a wild and raucous time of arguments and demands, misery and silence, but she had taught her husband not to take her lightly, and to treat her with respect.

And that he would get no sexual favors if he did not. He was not the husband of her choosing, but in the end she had loved him deeply, and had intensely mourned his passing.

The present day was so very different. Her granddaughters would choose even their own husbands. For all their mother's badgering and pushing, they would ultimately not be made to do anything they didn't want to, and they knew it.

Strangely, out of the female inhabitants of the house the one she respected most was Jane, soon to be her granddaughter. The girl had a stubborn steak, and she liked that. From running away from her Aunt Mortimer to avoid being bullied into a marriage she did not want, to putting her foot down and refusing to cave in to their demands that she and Haven marry in London. Now *that* was backbone! All the more so because she could see that the girl was used to giving in, was complaisant to a fault in the normal course of things. How much effort had it taken to defy them all?

The object of her thoughts came into the saloon at that moment, arm in arm with Haven. She had very much the look of a girl who had been kissed and maybe more, and Haven the look of a man struggling to regain his composure.

"Everyone," he said, his voice husky with suppressed emotion. "I have an announcement to make. Jane has finally, after much cajoling, agreed to be married here in London, next week."

Lady Haven leaped up with glad cries, and

Pamela joined them. Even Rachel approached the family circle.

"Humph," the dowager said. "Weak as the rest of 'em," she grunted, to no one in particular. "No backbone after all."

"What did you say, Grand?" Jane separated herself from the group—Haven was at the center of his sisters and mother—and knelt by the old lady.

"So, as vacillating as the rest of 'em, eh?" the dowager said, glaring at her. "What happened, did he put his hand down your bodice and you squealed and gave in?"

Jane flushed at the old woman's broad speech. She cast a glance back at Haven, who beamed at his sisters and mother as he listened to their ideas for his nuptials. She looked squarely back at the old lady and said, "It is none of your business, ma'am, where his hand has been. But we are both unhappy with the way things are. We want more of each other, and it doesn't matter where it is."

"More of each other." She snorted. "Namby-pamby euphemism for a poke and a cuddle. Don't know what's stopping you. Don't have to be married for that. Get in a family way; then he'll do whatever you want, just to marry you. Even take you back north."

Shaking her head, Jane eyed the old woman with affectionate exasperation. "I just refuse to make him unhappy. It seems to me that he has far too many harrying females in his life," she said, dryly. "I will not be one more."

Serious, for once, the dowager said, "My dear, you will set the tone for your entire marriage this way. You have set a dangerous precedent; Lydia has gotten her way. Oh, I know I wanted this too, for my own selfish reasons. I want great-grandchildren before I die. Unlikely now. But Lydia just wants to show off for society. She was robbed of a big wedding herself because . . . because of my interference, and she has never forgotten it."

Jane sat down next to her and took one of the old lady's veined, knobby hands in her own smooth, supple one. "Go on, Grand."

The woman's eyes were like a Yorkshire lake, deep and blue, but with a wet sheen to them. It was like she was looking at a misty painting of the past coming to life as her expression altered, subtly. "Lydia was lovely when she was a girl. Strong-minded, but not so fretful as she is now. It was an arranged marriage, of course. Most were then. But the dearest wish of her heart was to be married in London, extravagantly. My son would have agreed—he was a very agreeable lad—but I insisted that they be married in our own home, Haven Court. Gave a long speech about how the Haven dignity demanded it; nonsense, all of it. Just didn't want to go anywhere right then. My husband had only been dead six months. I could not leave the grave behind; it haunted me. And so my son gave in."

Jane squeezed her hand. "And you think now that Lydia is doing the same to Haven that you did to your son and Lady Haven."

"Isn't it?"

Jane thought about it. She didn't want to get married in London. She wanted a wedding in the tiny parish church in Lesleydale, with Mary Latimer—Mary Cooper that was—and Molly there, and a quick retreat to their cottage-to-be for their first night as husband and wife.

But more than that, she just wanted to be Haven's wife. And she knew that though she had accused him on many occasions of not being willing to stand up to his mother—he hated turmoil and would purchase peace at almost any cost—*this* time, he truly was staying in London for Pamela's sake. And *this* time, Jane understood. The girl's plaintive wail that she was afraid she was in love with two men still echoed in her brain. She knew in her heart that she wouldn't abandon Pamela at this crucial time, either.

What would it be like to be so torn and not know what was right? The girl had two equally valuable proposals, from two meritorious men. Strongwycke had much to recommend him, and Jane thought that Pamela had a great chance at happiness with the earl. But Colin was her first love, and she had steadfastly loved him for years.

No one but Pamela could make the ultimate decision, but Jane would not desert her any more than Haven would, in this time of doubt.

"I think," Jane finally said, "that Lady Haven will think she is the winner here. And you may be right; that will bode ill for future contentious issues. But Grand, I love him so much! I would marry him in a public inn on the road to hell, if that was where we had to go."

Grand chuckled. "All right. I will not call you a weakling. However, be sure to get some concession in return for giving in. Never, *ever* in negotiation, sell yourself cheaply."

"I am not a ripe plum, my lady, to be bartered."

"I think Haven finds you a very ripe plum indeed," Grand said, with a wink. "and I am surprised that he has not sampled the wares yet."

Having the last word and discomfiting Jane delighted the dowager, and she was in high good humor the rest of the day.

Seventeen

Two more days had passed in this state of indecision, Pamela reflected, as she sat in the drawing room while they received guests. Both Strongwycke and Colin had gone to church with the Haven family the day before, and they had sat on either side of her, unaware that they were vying for the same prize, if prize she could consider herself. It seemed that Strongwycke saw Colin as just an old family friend, and the baronet saw the earl as . . . Pamela wasn't sure, but he didn't seem in the least threatened. For some girls it would have been heaven, having two beaux. Two men wanted to marry her, two worthy gentlemen, each with much to recommend him.

But Pamela was finding it impossible to choose. Sometimes one would hold sway in her mind, and then the other. Colin, after all, was the man she had always thought to marry, if she had the opportunity. He was intelligent, a worthy landlord, a prime horseman, a good friend, and the owner of the sweetest piece of land in Yorkshire; Corleigh was as much home to her as Haven Court. Her life would change very little, at least at first.

Until the children started coming. But then she would have Andromeda, and a better aunt to her future offspring she couldn't imagine.

Children! It always came back to that, didn't it? *Can I imagine having children with this man?* she thought, staring over at Colin. Or *any* man?

Clad in an unfashionable suit and dusty boots, he sat with Lady Haven and Andromeda, and some society lady whose name Pamela couldn't remember. He wasn't a good-looking man in society's terms; his face was strong-boned and his nose hooked. And he had no idea of how to dress, nor did she think he really cared about the figure he cut. But he had a friendly face when he smiled. And he was a very good man, kind to his tenants, hard-working, religious in a subdued fashion, and intelligent without having the least pretension to being a scholar. And his sister was funny and smart and good company, not boring like Rachel had become in the last few years. Life would be pleasant at Corleigh.

She would be close to home and Haven, Jane, and Grand.

But . . . Colin hadn't even asked her to dance once since he had arrived in London because he didn't like to dance. She did, she had found, very *much*. Should he not have danced with her at least once or twice because *she* liked it? And he hadn't even thought of kissing her yet; he would probably have been shocked by the idea. How could she compare the two men properly if she hadn't kissed one of them?

Because that was where Strongwycke really pulled ahead in the tight race. The two men were neck and neck up until then, but Strongwycke. . . . She shivered whenever she thought of his kisses, but there was an element of— what was it about the way he made her feel? Alarmed? Feverish? Yes, that was it. He made her feel feverish.

That was no reason to choose him as a husband, though, was it?

But to be fair, everything else she had learned of him in the past weeks was admirable. He was good company, and a more caring friend and uncle one couldn't find. He, like Colin, was an excellent horseman, and talked often of beautiful Shadow Manor, his home in the Lakes District. And she liked Belinda very much, finding in the girl a younger sister, something she had always longed for but had never had. If she married Strongwycke she thought she could be a good influence on her and a friend. To all of this, his fine points and goodness, was added the fact that she already knew that she cared deeply for him.

And he had told her he loved her. Surely that was important?

One very powerful factor in his favor was that Strongwycke, unlike Colin, didn't mind her frantic outbursts. He smiled at her whimsies and indulged her to a shocking degree. He even seemed to appreciate that she was different from other tonnish ladies.

Yes, there was definitely that.

She sent Colin a glowering look, which he didn't see because he was engaged in idle chit-chat. But she had reason to be very angry with him at that moment. Just that morning, the weather having finally cleared, she had been heading toward her normal morning gallop in Hyde Park, hoping to meet up with Belinda and Strongwycke there. Haven and Jane knew about it and abetted her fraud, perpetrated on her mother, that she slept late some mornings. Lady Haven approved of that; she thought it denoted the delicacy of a lady to sleep late after a ball.

But just that morning, in the park, as she raced to meet Belinda and Strongwycke, who should she run into, out for an early ride, but Colin? She sighed and looked away. He had given her a verbal dressing down, and had insisted on accompanying her back to the townhouse. Not content with ruining her morning, he had ensured that all future pleasurable morning jaunts were at an end; he had told Lady Haven what she was about, riding in breeches in public! He and Pamela's mother were equally shocked, and so that was that; her glorious morning rides were now forbidden to her. It was intolerably high-handed of him.

For some reason she hadn't been able to bring herself to reveal to Colin or her mother that she usually met Strong and Belinda there. Lady Haven might begin to doubt the earl's suitability as a friend if she found out he winked at her outrageous behavior. It occurred to Pamela at that moment that her friends wouldn't yet know why she hadn't shown up that morning.

Bother. What to do?

The topic of conversation was, inevitably, Jane and Haven's wedding, set for a week and a half away. Since all parties had expressed the desire to see the marriage take place in a church, Lady Haven had decided that it would be held at Holy Trinity or St. John, Smith Square; both were grand enough to suit her idea of where the Viscount, Lord Haven should be wed, and yet neither could bring down the accusation of ostentation on such undeserving heads.

"For I have a horror of appearing pretentious, you

know," Lady Haven said, airily, to the unnamed society lady.

"Only of appearing so," Grand, ensconced in her comfortable chair, muttered.

"And it shall, after all, be a private affair."

"Though she has verbally, to my knowledge, issued one-thousand-three-hundred-and-forty-two invitations." Again, Grand's muttered aside.

They were interrupted in this fascinating conversation by the butler announcing Lord Strongwycke and Miss Belinda de Launcey.

Pamela started and then bounced out of her chair. A chance to explain! The earl and his niece came in, Belinda dressed in a becoming white dress and pink spencer. It wasn't strictly acceptable for a girl Belinda's age to make morning calls during the Season, but Pamela had urged it as a way of helping the girl see how polite behavior would help in society. It would save the girl much grief if she could learn early what Pamela had struggled with for years, as a result of being largely ignored by her mother in favor of the more beautiful Rachel.

Strongwycke smiled over at her, as he introduced his niece to the company. The girl was soon claimed by Jane and Andromeda, who exclaimed nicely over her lovely dress. Belinda, on her best behavior, became almost pretty, even given her unformed, youthful look.

Haven signaled to Pamela and she approached her brother.

"I won't ask if you have made a decision between your two suitors yet," he murmured, taking her hand. "But I think you ought to tell each gentleman of the other's proposal."

"Must I?"

He nodded. "It is only fair, Pammy. You should start with Lord Strongwycke." He cleared his throat. "Pamela, have you shown his lordship our garden yet?"

"Garden?" She paused. "Oh, yes, the garden." It was a straggly, tiny, light-starved patch of ground, but she saw what her brother wanted. And then, she supposed, she must show Colin the garden. This was all far too complicated.

"Unless you wish me to do it, as your guardian?" he added kindly, *sotto voce*.

No, anything but that, she thought. For some reason, Haven didn't seem at ease with Strongwycke and would make a mull of it, certainly. The earl, smiling, came forward and offered his arm.

Once they were outside, the light breeze riffling Pamela's hair, she guided him to a sunny corner—the only sunny corner in the high-walled garden—as she explained her absence that morning. She bemoaned her inability in future to go for their morning gallops, but he was philosophical, saying only that he supposed they had been lucky until then. He slyly hinted that in future, with an understanding husband, morning rides would become a reality once more. He had assumed something had prevented her attendance on them that morning, he said, and hadn't been alarmed.

And that was another thing in his favor, Pamela thought. He believed her to be competent, intelligent, able to take care of herself. She had been treated as a child for so long, and especially by her indulgent older brother, that she had continued to act as a child, she now realized. Would she slip back into that role with Colin, who often, as kind as he was, treated her as if she was mentally deficient?

With the earl she felt . . . like a woman. It was disconcerting in a way.

In the sunny corner a stone bench stood, and she sat down, tucking her hands beneath her legs. If it were Colin, he would have told her to sit like a lady, but the earl said nothing, and took a seat beside her.

"I must admit I take this as an encouraging sign," he said, watching her face with hope in his expression. "The fact that your brother so pointedly sent us outside."

She winced, not having thought how this would look to him. "I do have something to tell you, but it isn't about . . . about your proposal. Exactly."

"Oh. All right." He studied her face. "Not anything too good, if I am right."

"Nothing b-bad," she said. She shifted and fidgeted with the rose ribbons of her dress. "You have met Sir Colin Varens and his sister, Andromeda."

"Yes. We have all spent much time together in the last few days. Too much time, if it is not ungracious in me to wish I had you to myself a little more."

"S-sir Colin has done me the honor of offering me his hand in marriage as well," she said, in a rush.

There was silence for a moment, and she glanced sideways. He was still silent, and looked off over the garden wall, squinting in the sunlight.

"You wouldn't even be telling me this if you weren't seriously considering his proposal."

His voice was flat and uninflected, but Pamela thought she detected hurt and something else. Anger? Or just pique?

"You must understand, Strong, that I have known Colin since I was a little girl . . ."

"And yet until he and his sister showed up in London, I had never heard you mention their names."

"I didn't think them relevant to . . . to us. To our friendship. Colin has forever been in love with Rachel, but he finally got it through his thick skull that she was never going to marry him, and so . . ."

"And so you will be content to be second best. Satisfied with being compared forever with your lovely, perfect, prideful sister."

It was so exactly what she worried about with Colin's proposal, that she remained silent.

"Ah, it *has* occurred to you that you are second best with him."

"It isn't like that. Rachel was his first love, and . . ."

"Tell me, how long did it take for him to so conveniently fall *out* of love with her and *in* love with you enough to propose?" His voice was tight with anger.

"You are being unreasonable, Strongwycke. Totally unreasonable. And I won't speak to you when you are thus." She stood, to go back inside.

"Pamela, I apologize." He caught at her hand but she pulled it away. "Please, don't go back in."

She turned back and waited. His face was turned away again.

When he finally spoke, his voice had lost the angry edge. "I will admit that my pride has been hurt. If I understand correctly, you are actually considering marriage to a gentleman who never thought of marrying you until he was finally rejected by the love of his life. And this after I offered my hand . . . and my heart. Have you considered, my dear, that it took him only a couple of days after his final rejection by your heartless sister for him to decide that if he couldn't have her, he will take her sister, a pale imitation of the real thing?"

"That is cruel," Pamela said, trembling.

"But truthful." He stood and closed the space between them with two steps. He grasped her shoulders. "My dear, don't let familiarity tip the balance toward Sir Colin. I am sure he is very worthy, but . . ." He broke off and pulled her closer. "But I love you," he whispered. He kissed her then, with the sun touching their faces gently, the spring breeze tangling their hair together and her skirts fluttering and wrapping around his legs.

She searched his face when he released her. His handsome face was not as familiar as Colin's, but wasn't it as dear to her? Should she say "yes" this minute and trust that her fear of the unknown would dissolve, that she could make a life for them both and for Belinda too, without regretting her other choice? He said he loved her. Colin had never said that. She didn't even expect him to. Was that wrong?

He kissed her again, his lips gentle, searching, asking but not demanding. She lost track of time, of space. When he released her, his smile was gentle, genuine.

She could say "yes." This moment could become her treasured memory of a proposal accepted, a romantic recollection of the warm spring breeze and the green scent of grass growing. "Strongwycke, you are so kind to me. I think . . ."

But the moment was broken as Belinda bounced out the back door. "Uncle, we must go."

"Belinda," he said, looking over his shoulder at his niece. "Go away. I am . . . I am busy."

With a saucy tilt to her head, she put her hands on her hips and said, "The carriage is waiting out the front door, and you told me that one must never overstay one's welcome." Her dark eyes flashed. "Wasn't that what you said was proper? Fifteen minutes to half an hour? It has already been almost an hour since we arrived, and we must go on to Lady Milsham's."

"You see what I must suffer through," Strongwycke said, his good humor almost fully restored by the kiss. "She is already lecturing *me* on proper etiquette. This is your doing, Miss Pamela!"

As they walked arm in arm back to the house, he whispered, though, "I am impatient, my dear. Please, don't make your deliberation a long one. And choose me. I promise you, it is the right thing to do."

Pamela sighed happily and squeezed his arm. The next time they were alone. . . .

They entered the house and strolled the long dark passageway to the front rooms, and then Strongwycke, with Belinda on his arm, exited the front doors and down the steps.

Haven, as they watched the carriage pull away, put his arm around Pamela's shoulders. "Well? How did it go."

"Oh, Haven!" She leaned her head against his arm. "I think he is the one!"

Her brother took a deep breath. "Don't discount Colin so easily. At least give him equal thought and consideration. And you must tell him about Strongwycke."

Pamela nodded and glanced over to where Colin was studiously ignoring Lord Yarnell, who seemed to have become a permanent fixture of their drawing room without ever proposing to Rachel, who was in daily—nay, *hourly*—expectation of his offer.

"Colin, old friend," Haven said. "Would you take Pamela on an errand? She seems to want something from the milliner, and better for you than me to go."

Andromeda stood to accompany them, but Jane,

catching a look from her fiancé, said, hastily, as she put one hand on the other woman's arm, "Miss Varens, we have not yet spoken fully about the lady school for the poor children in Lesleydale. I am most interested and would like to become a patron. In fact, we must discuss what books to purchase while we are in London. I rely on your good sense for this."

Willingly, that lady sat down as Pamela said, "We shall only be a half hour, Andy, then I will return your brother to you."

They were in Colin's light gig and on their way, when he turned and said, "Now, what is this all about? I know Haven wouldn't send me on an errand to the milliner with you. An unlikelier pair for that he could not have picked. What have you to tell me?"

Pamela opened her mouth and then closed it again. It was within her power, that moment, to tell him that she politely declined his kind offer of marriage. Then the decision would be made and she could go on with life.

It was the right thing to do. "Yes, Colin, I have something very important to tell you. May we ride through the park?"

He skillfully wielded his whip over the heads of his team, and they sped away, toward the relative quiet of the park.

Eighteen

The park was green and lovely in the afternoon sun, the gardens burgeoning, bursting with life brought forth by the heavy rains of the last few days. Pamela waited until they were on the path toward the heart of the park, and then said, "Colin, I am very honored . . ."

"First, Pamela, please . . . I know I shouldn't interrupt you; it is a bad habit of mine, and one that I will attempt to break myself of. But I just wanted to say that asking you to marry me . . ." He struggled with his words, and finally went on. He gestured around him. "It is like today; I feel as if I have finally come into the sunshine after years of dwelling in the gloom. I've been so very blind, when all along the perfect lady for me has been under my long nose."

He was going to make it more difficult, Pamela thought, panic welling up within her. She didn't want to hurt him. What was she going to say now?

He guided his gig toward a quieter path, slowed to let the horses walk along the crowded thoroughfare, and frowned down at his bony hands, gloveless on the ribbons. "I feel I need to explain. I suppose it seems rash, this sudden interest in you, when all along I have been so enamored of your sister."

Pamela nodded to a lady of her acquaintance. She

had perfected that aura of serenity that had never been hers, but beneath her placid exterior her mind was furiously working. Was this not Strongwycke's objection to Colin's proposal? What would he say? She stayed silent, determined to at least hear him out.

Colin's hands were steady on the reins as he guided them among the many carriages, gigs and phaetons during that busy time of day. "Andy is in alt, you know, at the thought of you coming to live at Corleigh. Hugged me," he chuckled. "When I told her I had asked you to marry me she actually hugged me. Said I was finally showing some sense."

Touched, Pamela merely said, "She and Rachel never did see eye to eye on anything."

He snorted. "Your understatement is duly noted."

Neither of them spoke for a few minutes, until he finally guided the gig out of the morass and into the open, where there was room to let the horses go a bit. He found a quiet path. "Ah, now I can breathe. Detest London crowds. Bunch of cow-handed amateurs. Where was I?"

"You were explaining," Pamela said, "how your interest shifted so quickly from Rachel to me." She couldn't believe she was being so cool. This was Colin. Colin! The object of all her dreams, the man she had longed to marry since she was thirteen, old enough to think of such things.

"Yes." He shifted and looked uncomfortable. "I don't want you to think this is just . . . that you are second-best in any way."

Pamela was shocked into silence. It was what Strongwycke had said, what she had feared.

"But . . ." He struggled with his explanation. Words were never his strong suit; he had always been one more for action, though he had done his best at poetry and flowery speeches for Rachel's sake. "It was like my eyes were sealed with wax. Rachel is . . . she is beautiful."

There was a wistful tone to his voice, and she felt her anger build.

"Not that you aren't!" He glanced sideways at her. "What a remarkable transformation London has made in you. I think . . . I think I had just got in the habit of believing myself in love with Rachel, and it didn't allow me to see that right before me was the perfect young lady for me."

Pamela sighed. She couldn't stay angry at Colin even when he acted in a high-handed manner. Her best interests were always in his heart, or at least she thought they were. He was no poet, but she knew that his feelings ran far deeper than his words. And yet still, there was that nagging doubt. He spoke of what was right for him, but what about what was right for herself?

"You are well-born—I know you could marry better than me," he said, humbly, glancing swiftly in her direction and then away again. "I'm not a grand catch, and I know it. Even if I didn't, it has been duly driven home by seeing that prig, Yarnell, every day. Damn, how can she stand him? His accent, his clothes . . . and the man smells like a whorehouse!" He flushed a bright red and looked at her in alarm. "Pammy, I'm so sorry. I should never have used that word around you! I am just so used to you, so comfortable in your presence, I suppose. My apologies." He reverted to the subject at hand, Lord Yarnell. "And yet, he is truly a better marital prospect than I. And I know *you* could do better in the material sense, Pammy, than to marry me."

Reminded of her ostensible reason for being on this drive, Pamela realized she still had that unpleasant duty ahead. It might confirm for Colin how worthy she was, though, that an *earl* wanted her hand! Strongwycke, after all, was almost as well titled as Yarnell! Immediately after the thought occurred to her, she was ashamed. She wasn't in competition with Rachel as to who could attract the better suitor, and she didn't think of Strongwycke as an earl, but just as her friend.

"But more than that," Colin went on. "You unite a happy combination of characteristics I would want in a wife. You love the country as much as I. And horses. We think alike on those subjects. So I would never have to worry about you fussing to come to London."

"Colin," Pamela began. He was headed down a dangerous road, for it truly sounded as if what he liked about her was how little trouble she would be.

"No, let me finish!" he said, holding up one hand as the other held the reins in a relaxed grip. "How do you like this team, by the way! Sweet goers, eh? I bought them two days ago."

"I don't think . . ."

"No, like I said, let me finish. I keep getting off the subject at hand."

Crossly, she thought that was another thing; Strongwycke always listened to her and let her finish what she would say. Colin *said* he must learn to stop interrupting her, but then he kept interrupting her! If he kept talking, she would have her decision confirmed by the end of the ride.

"Anyway, the country, Andromeda . . . where was I? Oh, yes, and . . ." He flushed and turned his steady, honest gaze on her. "I never noticed how

sweet you are, like one of those garden fairies m'
mother used to believe in and paint pictures of. Do
you remember? She used to use you and Rachel as
models because Andromeda was too tall; she always
loved you both. But *you* . . . she always did say you
were so small and perfect and . . . pretty. Very, very
pretty." He cleared his throat and looked off over the
Serpentine as they crossed the bridge.

Pamela sighed. Just as she had been sure he was
never going to say anything truly nice to her. . . .

"But you see, I can *see* you at Corleigh, in the stables, in the garden, roaming the moors." His tone
was earnest and full of sensibility. He was wont to call
himself nothing but a farmer, and his speech was
generally blunt to a fault, but in truth Colin was in
danger of having too romantic a heart. He liked to
set his ladies firmly up on a pedestal, the better to
worship them. "You belong at Corleigh, Pammy; you
belong to the hills and the forests."

Pamela couldn't speak, for her voice would be
clogged with tears. It was the very picture she had
had for years, since just after her thirteenth birthday,
when someone asked her what her wish would be if
she had one. Made in secret, it was that she and
Colin would marry someday, and roam Corleigh's
hills and valleys together. The dear old dream revived in her breast, and she felt that perhaps, just
perhaps, she ought to tell Colin "yes" immediately. It
would make so many people happy! Colin, Haven,
Jane, Andromeda . . . and herself?

Was she sure? Hadn't she decided just an hour ago
that Strongwycke was the one?

"And we would have children to build Corleigh up
for. Pammy, I have so many plans! I . . ."

Pamela lost his next words as the idea of children

with Colin penetrated her brain. Children. With Colin? She knew what that meant; she was a country girl, and mating—human and animal—was no mystery. But with *Colin?* Colin who had never even kissed her yet? Would she like that? Would she shiver when he kissed her like she did in Strongwycke's arms?

"Colin, kiss me!" she said, suddenly, as they drove through a shady grove of trees.

"What?"

"I said, kiss me!" She moved closer to him.

"Pammy, not here! Not now!"

"Then where, and when?"

"Somewhere else," he said, his voice brusque. He clicked to the team and the horses sped up. "Good God! In the middle of a public park?"

"But . . ."

"Pammy, behave yourself."

She sighed and moved impatiently. How was she going to ever decide? She had thought her mind was made up, but clearly she was still just as undecided as ever.

"Colin, haven't you wondered why Haven sent us out together?"

He shrugged. "Give us some time together, I suppose."

"No, Colin, I have . . . I have another proposal of marriage to consider. Before yours."

He pulled the horses to a halt. "You have another . . ." He frowned. "From whom?"

The disbelief in his voice hurt. She pulled herself up with all the dignity in her, and said, "From the Earl of Strongwycke!"

"Strongwycke? That fellow who was there, at your house? And who has been hanging around like a teat on a bull?" He clapped one hand over his mouth. "Pardon, Pammy; my mouth runs away with me sometimes!" Then he sat in silence for a minute, the reins relaxed in his hands, staring off toward the far shore of the lake. "Why does *he* want to marry you?"

Pamela was about to answer angrily, but Colin interrupted, once again. "Ah, I suppose the fellow wants a mother for the child. Is she really his niece?"

"Yes, you great dunderhead! She is his niece, and he isn't looking for a mother for her. Good Lord, I am only six or seven years older than she!"

"I am sorry, I didn't mean it to sound as it did. I mean," he stuttered, "I didn't mean it to sound like the fellow couldn't want to marry you for other reasons, but I mean to say, an earl? What do you know about being a countess?"

That struck her dumb. What *did* she know about being a countess? There was so much more to this marriage business than she had ever thought.

"So," Colin said, his dark brows drawn low over his eyes. "I have competition for your hand. Never expected that."

He glanced sideways and saw her bristle. "There I go again. God, Pammy you know I can't make pretty speeches; don't go all 'hedgehog' on me. How can I compete with a fellow like that? He's an earl! Money, power, position," he said gloomily. "Good lookin' sod too. An' me as homely as an old boot."

Her anger softened but did not disappear completely in the face of his self-deprecation.

He clicked and set the horses in motion again. "So, have you made up your mind yet?"

"No," she replied, curtly.

"D'you like him?"

"Yes."

There was silence on the way home. When they approached the house he cleared his throat. "I . . . I won't come in, Pammy . . . uh, I suppose I shouldn't call you that, should I? But Miss Pamela sounds so damned formal. Could you send Andy out?"

The dejection in his voice touched Pamela's tender heart, and she laid one hand on his arm. "Colin, you know that whatever my decision is, it won't be made based on who has the most acres or the higher title. Or who is better looking, for heaven's sake."

Gratefully he looked into her eyes and said, "Yes, there is that. You aren't a mercenary girl. Or shallow. Thank you for that. For reminding me."

She squeezed his arm and hopped down. At the top of the steps, as the butler opened the door, she looked back. Colin waved and tried to smile.

"Will we see you tonight, Colin?" she called out. "At the Parkhurst ball?"

He took a deep breath and sat straighter. "Yes. Yes, you will. Andy and I will be there."

The ballroom was heated and overcrowded. Why did people do this, Pamela wondered, invite more people than their rooms could possibly accommodate? She understood the principle. A tight squeeze was a good thing; it meant you were well-thought of. But still!

She was with her mother and Grand, who had deigned to join them this evening, and Haven and Jane. Rachel had joined Yarnell's family group, his irritable-looking mother, and his haughty aunt. The marquess's younger brother had headed for the card room the moment they arrived.

Dexter, sweating and irritable, joined her after dancing with another girl. "Gad, but it's warm. 'Nuff to put a fellow off dancin' for good." He nodded pleasantly to the others, but spoke only to Pamela.

"You are just peeved because Miss Milton is now engaged and won't dance with you," Pamela said, naming a diamond who had just formed a very advantageous alliance.

"Don't care if she is engaged. Still can dance, can't she?"

"Ah, but her fiancé is Wellington's godson, or some such . . . or Nelson's or Prinny's," Pamela replied, mischievously. "Nobody is quite sure whose godson he is, for the rumors have it all three ways. But still very highly placed. She is out of your sphere now, old boy."

"I much prefer you, anyway," he said. "You wouldn't care to marry me, would you?"

She laughed, and he looked hurt. "Come, Dex, you aren't ready to put your neck in parson's noose, and you know it. Much better for you to wait four years and marry Belinda."

"Belinda? Old Strongwycke's niece? That infant?"

"She won't be an infant then, dolt. In four years she will be seventeen and you will be twenty-three or so. And you will *not* refer to his lordship as 'old Strongwycke.'"

"Ah yes, respect our elders, and all that."

Pamela thought for a moment, and then said, "Do you think he is all that old?"

"He's thirty!"

"But he doesn't *seem* old to me."

"Damned . . . er, I mean rather sedate, though. Solemn chap."

Pamela considered that. Dexter hadn't seen the

earl with his head thrown back in the early morning sun, laughing about something she had said or done. She had thought him solemn too, but then gradually had realized that he was somewhat reticent, and that recent events in his life had caused him to withdraw more. But in her company he seemed to crawl out of that self-imposed shell.

Was that because he loved her? He had openly told her he did, and that frightened her more than anything. What a responsibility being loved was, for it gave you the power to make the other person happy or sad!

She hadn't sought that power, did not want it.

Colin, on the other hand, though he said he was fond of her, hadn't said he loved her yet. Why hadn't he? Shouldn't he?

She needed advice.

"You can't say he is solemn," she said, ending the argument, "when you have played cricket with him for hours at Richmond."

"That is true. All right, he is perfection itself." Dexter looked at her, his eyes widening. "Don't say . . . has the old boy proposed to you?"

"What if he has?"

"Bully for you, Miss Pamela," he said, with a mocking bow. "Good catch, he is. My mama says so, and if she thought he would once look at my pimply sister . . ."

She smacked his arm. "Don't be cruel to your sisters, dolt."

He saluted. "Yes, ma'am. Or should I say, 'my lady'?"

"Neither. Go away, Dex," she said, irritated suddenly by his foolery.

Jane moved close to her in that moment. "Pamela,

I thought I should warn you; both your suitors have arrived and both are . . ."

"Good evening, ladies," Strongwycke said.

"H'lo all," Colin said.

Both men stopped and stared at each other.

"Coming this way," Jane finished, weakly.

"Oh, Lord, what a mull I am making of this. What shall I do, Jane?" she whispered, clutching her sister-to-be's arm.

Lady Haven that moment summoned Strongwycke, and Colin triumphantly moved toward Pamela. The earl kept casting glances their way, but he was held by Lady Haven's powerful grip as she loudly asked him, with his niece of course, to attend the wedding of her son, Haven, and his fiancée, Miss Dresden.

"One-thousand-three-hundred-and-forty-four," Grand muttered.

"Miss Pamela," Colin said, formally. "Would you care to dance?"

And so they danced. If Pamela expected a country dance to make her choice simpler, it did not do the trick. Colin wasn't as competent as Strongwycke, but there was much laughter in him, and she enjoyed herself.

Strongwycke claimed her for the next, but he was quiet, not so easy as he had been, she thought. It made her wonder, what was she doing? She had come to London to make herself a fit lady for Colin, only to find that she wasn't so unfit as she had thought. She still longed for the country, but there was pleasure to be had in London, too. Balls were not torture chambers, and afternoon teas had their share of joy in gossip and pretty dresses.

And so whatever she had done worked, for now

Colin found her a suitable wife. As long as she didn't gallop at dawn astride her mare, Tassie. So she had accomplished her goal. Why did she now feel so confused and wretched, then?

As the dance ended, Strongwycke said, "Will you walk in the garden with me, Miss Pamela?"

"Yes . . . , uh, no. No. I can't."

His brown eyes warm with understanding, he murmured, "Don't you trust yourself with me?"

"It's not that," she said. *Or was it?*

He took her arm and they started the promenade back to her family group. "What is it, then?"

"I don't think" she said, slowly, "until I have made my decision, that we should be alone in . . . in that way."

"Would you deny me every means of promoting my suit?"

"But I do not think that my decision should be made just because I l-like your kisses!"

"At least you admit it." As he returned her to Jane's company, he bowed and said, "I will respect your wishes, Miss Pamela. May I call tomorrow and take you—with Belinda, of course—for a drive in the park?"

"Certainly, sir," she said, with dignity. When he left, she bit her lip and said, "Jane, I desperately need your advice."

"I won't advise you on whom to marry," Jane said. "But we can talk about anything and everything."

"Thank you," Pamela said.

Strongwycke didn't approach Pamela for a while. He had been badly shaken that afternoon by the revelation that he had a competitor for Pamela Neville's hand. He had managed to maintain a light demeanor with her so far, but wasn't sure how long that would last. In his abstraction, he didn't notice when a well-dressed couple approached him.

"Strong," said a familiar voice.

He looked up. "Dorothea!"

It was, indeed, Dorothea and her husband.

"Strong, may I make known to you my husband, Lord Dalhousie?"

The two men shook hands, coolly.

"Actually, we have met, my love," Dalhousie said. "How is old Lord Fingal, Strongwycke?"

"As always. Likes the sound of his own voice."

"Would you get me a cool drink?" Dorothea asked her husband. "I am feeling a little warm."

He looked concerned, rubbed her shoulder, and said, "Anything for you." But as he left, he cast a few worried looks over his shoulder.

"So, he knows you and I were betrothed." Strongwycke still couldn't keep a tinge of the old bitterness out of his voice.

"Of course he does. Do you not remember the gossip in the paper when I released you? I did not come out of it looking very good."

"I looked quite the fool myself." He glanced across the ballroom. "It seems I am destined to always be second best."

She followed his gaze. "Miss Pamela Neville. What a lovely girl, Strong, so unstudied and sweet. Have you . . . are you affianced?"

He shook his head. "I have asked, but the lady is undecided," he said. "Again I have a competitor. And he has the advantage of being an old family friend, and, I fear, favored by the lady's brother and guardian."

"Strong, I am so sorry about the way things ended," Dorothea said. She put out one hand and touched his sleeve. "If I had known how you felt . . . but you have always been so reticent."

He looked down at her hand and frowned. "That is what I have attempted to mend with Miss Pamela, but it seems to have made little difference."

"You have told her how you feel? Do you love her?"

He paused. "Yes . . . yes I do. And yes, I have told her. But I don't think I really understood it until now." He gazed into Dorothea's eyes and listened, for once, to his heart. No, he didn't love her any more. He truly was healed, and Pamela had done what a year of bitterness could not.

As Dalhousie made his way back with a glass of punch, Dorothea hurriedly said, "If you love her, fight for her, Strong. You deserve to win this time. She is young, as I was, but I think she is ready to love you. Make her know her heart. Do not play fair."

Dalhousie joined them and handed the glass to his wife. She thanked him prettily and they strolled off.

Do not play fair.

Strong looked across the ballroom to where Sir Colin Varens and his sister stood with the Haven family group, laughing and talking like the old friends they were. All right, if he had to plant himself in their drawing room, he would make the push. She would learn her own heart, and she would choose him.

He took a deep breath and started toward them. He wouldn't leave her alone to make the wrong decision. He would not play fair.

Nineteen

Haven, working at his desk in the gloomy library—his mother had forced him to move the big walnut desk back there, saying the sitting room was reserved for wedding planning—gave up finally and buried his face in his hands. It was no good. He couldn't think. As he worked, conning over accounts sent south by his land steward, all he saw was Jane's pale, unhappy face before him. Knowing she despised London, he had forced her to come and stay. She had given in with good grace, seeing that Rachel and Pamela needed their opportunity to find a husband. But then he, with the aid of his grandmother and mother, had cajoled and wheedled her into agreeing to a society marriage, the one thing they had both agreed they didn't want. And all because he wanted her: wanted to love her, wanted to be with her, wanted to marry her without further delay.

All along he had told himself it was just that; he loved her and wanted to marry her and what did it matter when or how? Wasn't sooner better? After all, once they were wed and together she would be glad.

Wouldn't she?

But what did he want for his marriage? He had decided many years before that he would never conduct his like his parents', where one party made all the demands and the other was expected to capitulate or suffer. In their case, it was his mother who made the demands and his father who was expected to acquiesce. Jane had only given in because she loved him and wouldn't see him unhappy. She would sacrifice her own wishes for him, and knowing it, he had taken base advantage. Was that any way to begin their married life?

He jumped up from his chair and paced the length of the room. It took only two good strides.

Was he going to let others determine the tenor of his marriage?

No. By God, he and Jane would do things the way they wanted to do them, and he would honor the promises he had made to her. He strode out the door and went in search of his wife-to-be. Not in the drawing room, nor in the dining room, nor upstairs in the morning saloon. It wasn't a big house. Where could she be? Still in her chamber?

His blood stirred at the thought of accosting her in her bedchamber, her silky hair spilled out over the white linen sheets, but he put the thought away from him. It might be many more weeks before he could be with her, and he would need to be circumspect in the meantime if he was to keep his sanity. They would have their Lesleydale wedding, but it wouldn't be until he had settled his sisters' future. Finally, *finally* he would do things right. He descended the stairs to the hall, and asked a passing maid if she had seen Miss Dresden up yet this morning.

Before the girl could open her mouth, though, the front door opened and his mother, with Rachel and Jane in tow, bustled into the hallway. Servants, well-trained, arrived to remove hats and gloves and spencers, and to carry packages and messages.

Rachel mounted the stairs, murmuring something about getting ready for a morning call from Lord Yarnell.

"We have spoken with the vicar of St. John's, Smith Square, and he has agreed that he will perform the ceremony," Lady Haven said to her son, stooping for her maid to remove her bonnet, which required the careful extrication of pins and fasteners. "Valenciana, the confectioner, has agreed to my price—miserable Spaniard didn't want to, but I forced him into it—and will provide the breakfast. And I have hired on extra help. You will be appalled at the price I paid just to have the rugs cleaned in time, but it is necessary if we are to have guests for the wedding breakfast." She strode down the hall, talking as she went. "I have a man coming to repair the glass in the library window—we will need that room cleaned and aired to use for a smoking room for the gentlemen at the breakfast—and the drapers are coming to measure for the new drawing room curtains. I hope they do not take all day about it, for I have an appointment at one with the. . . ." Her strident voice drifted up into the dark recesses of the upper staircase as the lady disappeared.

Jane, her face pale in the dim hallway, was wide-eyed and staring. She blinked, but didn't move.

"My dear . . . are you all right?" Haven took her by the shoulders and stared into her eyes.

She nodded, mutely, but there were tears in her dove-gray eyes.

He folded her in his embrace. What had he done? Why had he put his own lusty yearning and his mother's wishes above his dearest love's needs? "We won't do it," he muttered, holding her close and rubbing her shoulders. "We won't let her take over our lives this way, I promise." He held her away from him and stared into her eyes. "Jenny, listen to me. We shall call the whole thing off and go north to be married as soon as this business with Pamela and Rachel is settled. Until then you are to do exactly as you like. But we will be married in Lesleydale, I swear it."

"Oh, Gerry, can we?" She buried her face in his chest and nuzzled. "Your . . . your mother has made arrangements with caterers, ordered yards and yards of material, bought new linens for the tables, planned parties and . . . *can* we wait? Can we wait until we go home? Is it possible?"

He sighed, deeply. "My love, we can and we will. I am still master of my own home, though I haven't acted as such for a very long time. If ever. But that will change, I promise you."

I must decide, Pamela thought, sitting in the back garden. There was no sun so early in the day. The tall townhouse cast a long shadow, and every corner of the garden was gloomy and damp. With the toe of her half-boot, she pushed a wet leaf over and watched a beetle scuttle away.

I must decide.

Why was it so difficult?

The night before was a perfect example of why it was so difficult, she reflected, thinking back. Strongwycke, always charming and gentle, had been especially gallant, complimentary . . . she had found it a trifle wearing after a while. And Colin, too, was on his best behavior and had even danced with her a second time. The two men had quarreled over the supper dance, so she had crossly awarded it to Dexter. Then both men had been there as she left, guiding her to her carriage and handing her in, one on either side. It had been a ludicrous scene, but it had brought home her predicament.

She had to decide, and soon.

What would she have done if Colin hadn't made his offer? She tried to turn her mind back to the days before his startling proposal; it was difficult. Things had changed so much in the last week or so. But she remembered how confounded she had been by Strongwycke's proposal. It had taken her a couple of days to become accustomed to looking at him as a suitor, and not just a dear friend. And then Colin had arrived, just as she had begun to think Strongwycke might make a very good sort of husband for a girl like her. It had confused her all over again, especially when he started to treat her like a lady instead of as a child. It was the fulfillment of all her girlhood dreams, and how could she turn her back on that? Would it not be fickle to refuse him now, when she had sworn upon countless full moons that all she wanted in life was to marry Colin?

Jane's advice, in their late night talk after the ball when the rest of the household was asleep, was to go where her heart urged her, but oh! Where was *that*?

The back door opened and Rachel, dressed in a lovely dark blue spencer over a celestial blue day gown, stepped out, a disdainful look on her face. She approached her sister.

"What a miserable garden," she said, looking around as she walked daintily down the damp path, assiduously avoiding any muck or gravel.

Pamela, sitting on the stone bench, shrugged. "It is London. There is no room here, and the house is badly situated. No sun."

Pacing up and down the walk, Rachel finally

turned to her younger sister and said, "I have been told that Colin has proposed to you."

"M-hmm."

"What did you tell him?"

"I haven't said anything yet. I haven't made up my mind." Pamela heard the defiance in her own voice; she expected Rachel to take her to task, and she wasn't disappointed.

"What is there to think about? You have an earl on the string!" Rachel came and sat beside her sister. "You actually have to think between the two men? Strongwycke has," she said, enumerating on her gloved fingers, "a better title, more money, a larger estate, and no spinster sister living with him. Belinda, after all, will be married and out of the house in a few short years, whereas Andromeda is likely to live with Colin for the rest of her natural life. It should be an easy decision, even for you!"

"Rach, you say that because you have never liked Colin that way."

"But you still have that idiotic infant-worship for him. You should get over it."

Pamela gazed at her sister curiously. "What is it, Rach? Why are you in such a taking?" She was used to her sister's vitriolic manner, but today Rachel was agitated, too, as tightly coiled as a spring.

Her manners would never have revealed that to anyone who didn't know her well, but Pamela could see it in her stiffness and blank eyes. She was rigid with tension, and yet, her hands folded on her lap and her back perfectly straight, she appeared to be absolutely calm.

Rachel glanced over at her sister, was about to say something, stopped, but then launched into speech after all. "I know you all think I have been cruel to

Colin. He is a good friend; I know that. I will always value the times we had as children, how kind he was to us, what fun we had together." Her voice had softened as she spoke of their youth. "But," she continued, her voice hardening, "you have no idea of how annoying it is to be worshipped, to be gazed at as if one is a goddess, a perfect idol. You all think I take it for granted, but it isn't that at all. I am far from perfect, but Colin always treated me as if I was porcelain. It was *incredibly* annoying. It was like having a dog around, panting, gazing with big, adoring eyes . . . I hated it! I felt like kicking him."

Pamela was about to answer, but Rachel held up one hand. "No, I know," she said. "Ungrateful of me, but there it is. And Andromeda detests me. I know she does. She thinks I have been cruel to her brother, and I understand that. If anyone treated Haven as cavalierly as I treat Colin, I would hate them too. But what else was I to do? He left me no choice but cruelty. I have been trying for years to get him to leave me alone, but he *insisted* on proposing constantly. It was unbelievably irritating. Nothing I said or did made a jot of difference. I *could* have kicked him and he would have treasured the bruise!"

"I never thought of it that way, I guess," Pamela murmured, nodding. "I suppose I can see how annoying it would be if you could not get someone to take you at your word."

Rachel turned on the bench and took her sister's hand, pleading, "Don't marry Colin just to stay close to Haven Court. For heaven's sake, I am marrying to get away from there, from Mother and Grand and all of their interference!"

"But Mother and you . . ."

"Mother thinks she knows what is best for me. But

only I know what is best for me. It is just lucky that our intentions coincide this time, or there would be a battle."

"Yarnell?"

Rachel nodded. "Yarnell."

"Has he proposed yet?"

"I think he is going to today," Rachel said, releasing Pamela's hand. She bit her lip and twisted her hands together. "I *hope* he is going to today. I have met his mother and aunt, and they approve. So I think he is going to ask Haven today."

"Good luck, Rach," Pamela said. "I . . . I wish you all the best."

"Thank you. And you too."

"Why Yarnell?" Pamela said after a moment of silence between them.

"He is a marquess," Rachel said. "And he is handsome, and he has been very kind to me. He will make a good husband." She looked away for a moment, and then looked back, with a frankness in her expression not always there. "And he early showed his preference. My looks will not last forever. Despite what Jane may say, they are my best attribute. I have good breeding and a decent dowry, but so do a thousand girls in London. I am beautiful, though. More beautiful than most, though not all."

Her voice was cool, with an analytical tone. It made Pamela sad, but she couldn't really say why. Rachel and she had never seen things the same way. This was no different.

A maid trotted up the garden path and curtseyed before the girls. "Miss Neville, Lady Haven said for you to come in, as Lord Yarnell and Lord Haven be closeted together, after which 'is lordship—Lord Yarnell, not the master—says he wants to see you alone, an' your ma . . . er, Lady Haven said as how that was all right."

Pamela saw Rachel pale and she reached over and squeezed her sister's hand. There could only be one thing Yarnell and Haven would have to discuss, for they weren't overly friendly with each other.

"Then it is true," Rachel said, turning and hugging her younger sister. "Today is the day I will become engaged."

"Are you sure about this?"

Hands trembling, Rachel straightened her dress as she stood, smoothing out imaginary wrinkles. "I am sure."

Remembering Major Sir Henry Waring's proposal, and how Rachel had refused him, Pamela wondered what was different about Yarnell. "Why Yarnell?" she asked again.

Rachel looked down at the gravel walk, and said, in a low tone, "You will never understand. Nor will Jane. She is the kind of woman *every* man loves and wants to marry. And *everyone* likes you, Pammy, because you are so . . . so friendly and good-natured." She reached out and touched her sister's curls, a tremulous smile on her lips. "Yarnell likes me exactly as I am. I do not have to pretend with him to be someone I am not. Colin thought I was perfection in every way. Major Waring thought I was kindhearted because he saw me pet the head of an infant once." She rolled her eyes. "I only did that because the mother was Lady Bolingham, a great hostess. Yarnell knows what I am and who I am, and he wants to marry me." She shrugged simply, elegantly. "I may never find anyone else who will."

She squared her shoulders, turned, and regally sailed back toward the house.

After Rachel was gone, Pamela thought about her words for a long time before going in. Was she right? Was that the only way to happiness, to marry someone who accepted you for who and what you were, with no unreal expectations? And how could she apply that to her own decision?

Strongwycke certainly didn't seem to expect anything from her but to be herself. She had remarked on that very fact many times. But Colin knew her better, knew her far longer.

As confused as ever, she went back into the house, to the drawing room, which was tumultuous with celebration. Yarnell had been accepted, and after a brief time with his prospective in-laws, drinking champagne and unbending enough to be congratulated by all, he took Rachel home with him to break the news to his mother. Lady Haven was ecstatic, restlessly pacing the length of the room, imagining glory to come. Rachel was brilliant, Rachel was her own darling daughter. There had never been such a great marriage as this would be. She began to speak of the marriage settlements, how much pin money her daughter could expect, what her dress allowance would be, the exciting question of whether Yarnell would buy a new carriage to celebrate his wedding or not.

Haven, disgusted with his mother's talk, finally said, "That is enough for now about the wedding, Mother. Let Rachel and her beau enjoy the engagement before you plan their wedding and every detail about it for them. And speaking of weddings, I guess this is as good a time as any, Mother, to tell you a decision Jane and I have made." He put his arm around his fiancée, pulled her close, and said, "We have decided after all not to be married in London, but to wait until the Season is over and, as in our original plan, be married in Lesleydale." He could feel Jane tremble, and knew she was preparing for the reaction.

There was dead silence for one second, and then. . . .

"You will do no such thing." It was Grand, not Lady Haven who spoke first. The old lady rose, majestically, and tapped over to them, leaning heavily on her cane.

"Do not be preposterous," Lady Haven said, a heartbeat after her mother-in-law. "You cannot change your mind now."

"How awful" the dowager said, dryly. "Lydia and I agree again. However," she continued, "I suspect our reasons are not the same."

"You won't change my mind on this," Haven warned, his blue eyes dark. He glanced from one to the other of the dominant women in his life. How often had he given in to their demands? How many times had he had to balance what his grandmother said against what his mother said, trying to keep peace between them? No more. It was his life. His and Jane's.

Lady Haven began to sputter, and said, "You cannot do this, not after I have gone to so much trouble, and not after I have bullied Valenciana into doing the breakfast. I have already ordered a cake! I will not be humiliated in this way!"

"As I thought, our reasons are not the same." The old woman approached her grandson and looked up at him, her blue eyes meeting his. She looked from him to Jane and back again. "I admit I wanted you to be married in London. I am proud of my grandson, and to see him and his marriage celebrated as it ought to be, would be a grand day for a noble and exalted name. However, if you had remained firm, I would not have pressed you harder. But now you have made the commitment. *Now* you have spoken not just for yourselves, but for all Havens and for your sisters' good name in this town and for your children."

"What has our private decision to do with that?" Haven said, between gritted teeth.

"It has been announced, talked of, admitted to by yourselves in company. Your mother has made arrangements, hired people. What do you think the gossip-mongers will make of a postponed wedding?"

Haven shrugged.

"They will think we aren't sure, or that there is some trouble, or . . . or that there is some scandal in my family. Or yours." Jane's voice was calm, accepting. She met Grand's eyes, and something passed between the two women, some understanding. The dowager nodded.

"Do you think we care about that?" Haven asked his grandmother.

"No. Not a fig," the dowager said. "Nor should you." Her voice changed, became harder. "But ask Rachel and Lord Yarnell." She met her grandson's eyes, cold blue striking cold blue. "He is as haughty a fellow as I have ever seen, but this is a very good marriage for Rachel. Better than I thought she would do. A *marquess*. Do you truly wish to embarrass his family? You have seen them; they are a stiff-rumped, proud lot. Do you want to give them any cause to back out?"

"Of all the convoluted, twisted, tortuous reasons . . ." Haven was angry and could hardly get the words out.

"But she is right," Jane said. She turned and laid

one hand flat on his chest. "Gerry, I have been in society long enough to know what these people are like. They *will* twist it somehow. It may not result in any permanent damage, but it will cause talk, and talk is unpleasant. We can't risk damaging Rachel's chances at a happy marriage."

"So let us hear no more about it," Lady Haven said, brusquely. "Enough of that, now. We have weddings to plan, and if my youngest daughter will decide on which of her suitors will be the lucky gentleman, I shall be a happy woman."

She looked around, but Pamela had crept away during the commotion, and was hidden somewhere, no doubt contemplating her own uncertain future.

"Unlikely," Grand said, lowering herself carefully into a heavy chair. "Extremely unlikely that you will ever be happy, Lydia."

Twenty

Strongwycke paced the length of the drawing room of the Haven London residence, waiting for Pamela to come down. He hadn't slept the night before, and his mood, usually temperate and mild, had degraded to foul and edgy. He didn't know what was wrong with him, except that the night before, at yet another ball, he and Varens had done the same idiotic dance, each competing for Pamela's favor, and only succeeding in falling all over each other and making fools of themselves. He hoped he wasn't a prig, but he didn't like feeling foolish. That one young lady should have him so wrapped around her finger had given him pause for thought, but he saw no way past it. He had fallen in love with Miss Pamela Neville, as maddening as she was, and he would be satisfied with no other end than that she would marry him.

A tap-tap-tap in the hallway indicated he wouldn't be alone for much longer, and he did his best to put on a genial expression. His success could be judged by the dowager's first words upon greeting him.

"Ah, Strongwycke," she said, as she entered and headed for the most comfortable chair. She eyed him as she passed. "Look like the devil has you by the tail this morning. What is wrong with you?"

"I beg your pardon, my lady?"

"Don't poker up on me, boy. I can sense a foul mood, even if my eyes aren't what they used to be. Going to give my granddaughter a good spanking? Eh?"

Shocked to his core, the earl took a seat and forced his rigid frame to relax. "I cannot understand what you are saying, ma'am."

The dowager muttered under her breath. "Trouble with you young folks is you are not lusty enough. Wait for this, wait for that. Can't understand it myself." In a louder voice, she asked, "What's to wait for? Pamela needs a fellow to show her what she is missing by dallying as she is. If you are not man enough for the chore, maybe Varens is, though I doubt it. Don't like the long-nosed baby baronet, myself."

Strongwycke, completely at sea, remained silent.

Sighing deeply, the dowager stared blearily at the earl. "You are a good-looking man. Even I can see that. Pamela is a girl like any other. Have you even *tried* to use your physical attributes—and they are more than adequate; I may be old, but I am not yet past appreciating male flesh—to do a little convincing? *Make* her come around?"

"I . . . I don't think I know what you are talking about, my lady." He was beginning to, though, and if he was right in what he thought she was saying, he was shocked.

She frowned over at him for a moment, and then cackled, slapping her knee. "You think I am advocating force, you great ninny! As if I would recommend you take my granddaughter that way! I would kill you if you did that." Her voice was dead cold when she levied the threat. "No, you blistering idiot. I am saying, kiss her until she is weak, then ask her again to marry you. Make her lose her senses and take advantage of the moment, or are men in this day and age not capable of a little seduction?"

Pamela's voice in the hall called out to her maid to bring something down, and Strongwycke said, hurriedly, "Madam, whatever you are saying, I want Miss Pamela to make her decision while she is clear-headed. I want her to want *me*, not just be . . . be seduced into marriage. I love her too much to trick her with any chicanery or damnable knavery."

"Then you do not understand Pamela in the slightest." The old woman shook her head. "I am afraid she is letting old loyalties, old feelings, old sentiments blind her." Her voice wavered, finally, after being so strong. "I just hope she makes the right choice."

"Regardless, it will be *her* choice," Strongwycke said. He stood as Pamela came into the room.

"Strongwycke, can we stop at Colin's hotel for a moment? I told Andy I would give her this book to read."

She was dressed in her green riding habit, with gold frogging, and she wore a jaunty shako on her auburn-tinged curls. She was utterly adorable, her freckles sprinkled like cinnamon over her nose and cheeks, and his foul temper melted away like a Gunter's ice in August. "Your wish is my command," he said, smiling down at her.

The dowager snorted. "Maybe it should be the other way around," she said.

"What did you say, Grand?" Pamela stooped and kissed the old woman's cheek.

"Wasn't talking to you, child. Was talking to your beau."

"Oh."

"Off with the both of you. I have thinking to do." Strongwycke guided her out of the room, but stopped and gazed back in at the old woman. She returned his look, but said nothing more.

Outside, he helped Pamela up onto Tassie, and said, "Your grandmother . . . is she getting a little odd?"

"Grand? *Getting* odd? Good Lord, she's always been odd. I love her, but most of the time I don't understand her."

"Good. I thought I was the only one."

The day was warm, and the traffic heavy. They didn't speak, too busy guiding their mounts through the streets toward the Traveller's Inn on a short street off Park Lane, near their destination.

"Belinda has taken a strong liking to Miss Varens," Strongwycke finally said, as they approached the inn. "Didn't stop talking about her the other day, after our visit."

"I have always liked Andy . . . and I shouldn't call her that. I don't think she likes it, but I picked it up from Colin." As they stopped in front of the inn, Pamela took the book out of a bag she had tied to her saddle.

A footman approached and took the book and the note for Miss Andromeda Varens. Strongwycke and Pamela turned on the narrow street and circled the block, finding their way back to the entrance to the park. It was the busy time of day, unfortunately, and so they spent the next hour greeting acquaintances, riding short distances, stopping as a jam occurred, and greeting more acquaintances.

As an opportunity for wooing, it left much to be desired, Strongwycke thought, impatiently, as

Pamela spoke to a gentleman on horseback, an acquaintance of her friend Dexter's. His horse sidled impatiently, and the fellow trotted off, only to be replaced by another. She had many friends among the young gentlemen of the *ton*. Pamela had freely confessed to him her freakish behavior of the previous Season. She had learned, she said, that while indulging every whim of her own had led to some great larks and some lasting memories, it had resulted in too much trouble for other family members. If they had stayed much longer, she would have ended up in serious trouble, she thought, and would have shamed the Haven name. It had sobered her somewhat. She had no wish to bring notoriety to their name in that manner.

Finally breaking free of the crowd, they were able to canter. She was a marvelous horsewoman, Strongwycke thought, watching her guide Tassie with just a flick of the reins; rigged out as every young lady ought to be and elegantly riding sidesaddle, or riding astride, dressed in clinging breeches and a baggy lawn shirt, she was born to gallop. In that moment, an image of her at Shadow Manor, riding over the hills, filling his home with laughter and love, overwhelmed him; a new sense of purpose surged through his veins.

He trotted ahead of her and led her to a tree near the lake, then dismounted and helped her down.

"Why are we stopping?" she asked.

"We need to talk," he said, firmly. "Will you walk with me?"

They looped the horses' reins over a low branch, and Strongwycke took her arm. The day had been delightful, so far, Pamela thought, as they strolled down closer to the Serpentine into the shade of an old, gnarled tree. While there were others around, she could almost pretend that there was no necessary decision looming, that she could go on this way, with both Strongwycke and Colin paying court, enjoying both their company and London and the Season in a way one short year before she wouldn't have believed possible.

"Pamela," Strongwycke said. "We can't go on this way forever. I gave you a week, and that is over."

"I know, Strong," Pamela said, her heart sinking as she was faced yet again with that nasty necessity to make a decision between two men she loved. "But it is my whole *life* we are speaking of. I just need a little more time."

"It is *my* life, too! When we first started spending time together, I never got the feeling that there was anyone else in your heart, no one else in your mind. I thought we had an understanding," Strongwycke said, tapping his riding crop against his boot.

"That was before . . . you don't understand," Pamela said, her stomach twisting at the unhappiness she saw on his face. How could this be happening to her? She had never expected to have any man want to marry her and now there were two! She turned her face and stared at the light glinting off the Serpentine. For once the infernal miasma that seemed to insidiously seep through London streets was absent, and the air sparkled with unusual brilliance. Others were in the park and were walking, talking, laughing. And yet here she was, facing an angry gentleman whom she would much rather be kissing than quarreling with. She looked back into his brown eyes, the dark brows furrowed down over them. "I have known Colin since I was a little girl, and our attachment is an old one, existing . . ."

"Existing in your own mind, for most of those years, it seems to me," he interrupted, moving toward her, holding her with his powerful gaze.

She had seen Gerry with a beetle once, pinning it to a mounting board for some odd science project. It had squirmed and its legs had waved as it struggled in its death throes. She had cried, and Gerry had told her to stop being a baby. At this moment she understood how the beetle had felt, impaled, unable to escape, and with a pain in the region of the heart. She hated the suffering she saw in Strongwycke's eyes, but she still didn't know if she could trust what was between them to last her whole life. She had cared for Colin for many years now, so was it not logical to suppose she would go on caring for him?

But he hadn't kissed her yet, and Strong had.

And was going to again.

He took her shoulders and pushed her against the thick and twisted trunk of the ancient tree under which they shaded, and pinned her there. Like the beetle, she twisted, and then stopped.

"Pamela, don't make me wait," he muttered, and his lips closed over hers.

Her fingers dug into the fabric of his riding jacket, and then relaxed as she felt a languor steal over her.

He was doing it again. Kissing away her doubts, filling her with an oddly painful desire. The sun peeked through the leaves of the tree and touched her face, and the warmth stole through her. The feeling of the rough bark at her back receded, the fear of discovery in such a compromising position fled, and soon, there was nothing in her mind but him, how good he smelled, how good he felt.

How much she loved him.

But he released her all too soon. With a brooding expression, he gazed down into her eyes. "If you say you are going to marry that long-beaked, stuffy 'baby-baronet,' as your grandmother calls Varens, I will leave London immediately."

"Leave?" she squeaked. Never see him again? Never kiss him. . . .

"I won't stay to watch you being squired about town by him, engaged to him. I will not be a good loser, I warn you, Pamela."

This wasn't the mild, easy-going Strongwycke she had come to know. There was almost anger in his eyes, and her heart thudded.

"I won't be played like a trout on a line, my dear. You either love me or you don't. You can't have both of us; you must make a choice and make it soon."

He was trembling, she realized, and that was why his hands were shaking. But he took her in his arms again, locking her tightly within his embrace. "I love you. But if you have the bad taste to prefer that . . . that odious country clod to me, I will know it wasn't meant to be. I will expect your decision by tomorrow night."

"Th-that is my birthday party," she said. Now, instead of enjoying getting ready for her party, she would be worried about the decision she was facing. It wasn't fair!

"I know. If you can't decide on the night you turn twenty, you will never know." He lowered his face again, and as the sunlight touched them, and with everything else fading away, he kissed her again, putting all of his need and pain and desire into it. "I love you, Pamela," he whispered.

* * *

Grand, in her chair in the withdrawing room, waited. She heard the door, and the butler, and a voice. It was the voice she had been waiting for.

The door opened and he came in. "My lady," he said, bowing politely.

"Varens," she said. "Have a seat."

"I got a message that I was to come here immediately." He sat down on the edge of a chair. "Has something happened? Or has Pammy made up her mind?"

"Pamela is out with Strongwycke. No, she has not made up her mind, and she never will as long as you confuse her with your call to home."

"What do you mean?" He frowned and fiddled with the tassel on his boot top.

Grand stared out the window at the scene of carriages and horses and drays passing by. She must word this carefully, because it was vitally important that the young man she had known all his life should understand. She did not want to hurt him, but he must see what he was about. "I mean simply this. Do you really love my granddaughter, or is she merely a convenient replacement for Rachel, who is lost to you forever?"

He stood. "I would never use Pammy that way. My feelings for her . . ."

"Are the feelings of a big brother."

"What do you know of that?"

"I know. Varens, I have known you since you were a baby." She turned her basilisk glare on him and her lip curled. "You have never shown a moment of interest in her other than as a brother. You still love Rachel and if you do not face that you will make the biggest mistake of your life and drag that poor child into it, too. And ever after you will live just miles away, and hear of Rachel, and know of her children, and be faced across the breakfast table every morning with her pale, washed out, shrunken shadow."

"That is a despicable invention, my lady." He stood, trembling and agitated, and walked toward the door to leave. But at the last moment he whirled and glared at the old lady. "You know nothing of my feelings for Pammy."

"Good God," the dowager said in disgust. "You even use Haven's pet name for her, just as if she were your own little sister."

"It . . . it is an endearment."

"It is an abomination. It makes a baby of her." She rose slowly, aided by her cane, and faced Varens. "Men have it so easy," she said, staring into his eyes. "You make your own choices, live your own lives, stay in your own home, even. When I was a girl, I lived in Kent, and I loved my home. I loved the ocean, and I loved . . . I loved a boy there. Or thought I did. But my parents arranged a marriage for me, and sent me to live in Yorkshire when I was just fifteen. Fifteen! It might as well have been the end of the earth, to me at that age."

Varens frowned. "And I would protect Pammy . . . Pamela, from that same pain."

"But it *saved* me," she said, rapping her cane sharply on the floor. "Saved me from making a grave error. I loved the boy because I loved our simple lives together, running in the meadow, fishing, riding bareback across the fields. He was not right for me, though. He turned out to be a bad lot." She straightened. "We all become women and men, Varens, and we must face facts and make our choices and live with the consequences."

"You make it sound so dreary," Varens said, his

face set in hard lines. "Ma'am, I would not be rude to you for the world, but . . ." He stopped, old habits of courtliness restraining him.

"No, speak your mind," the dowager said. She watched the baronet's face, interested despite herself in the flashes of emotion, of anger and determination. Was he more than she had thought? Was there more to him than his simpering, cloying, unrequited affection for Rachel would seem to indicate?

"I would give Pammy the freedom to live her life as she always has, to race across the meadows on Tassie, to . . ."

"You, sir, are a liar!" Her cane banged the floor.

He stopped, taken aback by the old woman's thundering voice.

"You," she continued, more quietly, "have been trying for years to mold her into the image of Rachel, to constrict her, to bind her. You tattled on her harmless jaunts in London, riding in the early morning. She would meet Strongwycke there, you know, and he did not force her to mend her ways." Ah, yes, that needle had found its mark; she could see it on his homely face. "You poke and prod her into some perfect image you have in your mind," she said, following up, jab after jab, blow after blow. "Why do you not just admit it? She will never measure up, in your mind, to the perfection that is Rachel!" The final uppercut.

"I don't . . ." Varens paused. He took a deep breath and walked to the window, staring with a blank gaze. When he turned back, he said, "I do that, don't I? Try to make her into something she is not."

"You do."

"But I love Pammy."

"You love her as the little sister you would like to have. Andromeda is your elder, and in a way has dominated you for much of your lives. She is a strong woman, despite her foolish eccentricities. You have always envied Haven his little sister." It was new to the dowager, too, this understanding of his feelings for Pamela.

"I have to give her up, don't I?" His voice quavered and thickened. "I have to give them both up."

"Yes." The dowager's voice was kinder. She put out one hand to the man she had never been able to like, finding in his pain a thing to pity. She took his knobby hand in her own arthritic one. "For your own sake, as well as for theirs. Pamela will not die if she marries the earl and moves to the Lakes District. It will be the making of her. She will finally be a woman. You all must let her go, you and Haven especially."

"I think I will go now." He kissed her hand and released her. "I don't want to be here when Pamela comes in. I need . . . I need time to think."

As he walked out, the dowager sagged down into a chair, drained by the effort she had put forth. She was asleep there when a maid came in to dust the room.

Twenty-one

Yet another ball. The London Season was interminable, it seemed. Strongwycke joined Pamela's family, gazing at her openly until she blushed, with the knowledge of their intimacy that afternoon. Lady Haven graciously greeted him, then rushed off to see Lord Yarnell's mother and aunt, who had just arrived. The dowager winked at him, to his surprise, and Miss Jane Dresden smiled kindly, as always.

It was only her brother who was not fond of him. And that was because he clearly preferred the suit of his long-time friend and neighbor Sir Colin Varens, who joined them that minute with his sister on his arm. Strongwycke glared at him, but the fellow only returned the look with a mild gaze and a nod.

How puzzling! Didn't the fellow feel the least bit of animosity toward him? They both wanted Pamela, and certainly in worldly terms his was the better offer. And in the past few days they had been falling all over each other in the competition for the young lady's favor. But perhaps Varens had reason to be too secure to be threatened. Strongwycke frowned at the unwelcome turn of his own thoughts. It was possible, even *likely*, that Haven had given him some assurance that he would do everything in his power to see that his sister wed the baronet. And Pamela, sincerely attached to her home and her brother and the baronet, might have already decided in his favor.

Perhaps that was the explanation for the new ease in the baronet's manner toward him. It gave him a pang to even contemplate that.

By the next night he would know. Or even sooner, if she had already made her decision. In that one panicked minute, he wished he could take back his arrogant demand of that afternoon. She could take as long as she wanted, if she just didn't hastily decide on her old friend, Sir Colin.

"May I claim the first dance?" Varens was saying to Pamela.

She glanced toward Strongwycke, but prettily accepted.

They walked away before he realized that he had wanted to secure the next dance and the supper dance. It would have to wait until the fellow brought her back. To pass the time, he asked Miss Dresden to dance.

They sailed around the floor together, making desultory conversation. But then, after a moment apart, he blurted out, "Why does Lord Haven dislike me?"

Panting just a little from the exertion of the very lively steps, she said, "He doesn't dislike you, my lord, he just . . . Haven has gotten it into his head that Colin and Pamela are meant to be together."

"And you don't agree?"

"It doesn't really matter if I agree or not, but no, I think that Colin— I think the change from Rachel to Pamela was far too quick to be true love. I think he is mistaking friendship for love."

"What says Haven to that?"

"He believes that Colin was in love with Pamela all

along and just didn't know it." She shook her head. "I think the root of it all is that he just doesn't want to lose his little sister. He is especially close to Pamela, and worries about her. I think he is reluctant to let her go, to admit that she is grown, now, into a young lady. And she has; she has become a woman in the last while, I believe."

"So you don't think there is anything personal?"

"I know there is nothing personal. He admits quite freely that you are a splendid fellow. But you live so far away."

"I do? We are only a hundred miles apart. Or less! We can see each other every month, if she wants that."

"He would see her almost every day if she married Colin."

"But that is no way to decide on a husband!" he protested.

She shrugged.

And what more could he say? He understood Haven's dilemma. He had dearly loved his own sister, and missed her fiercely when she married and moved away. And yet, she had had her own life, and married where she loved. Did Haven not want the same for his little sister?

The music came to an end, and Strongwycke took his companion's arm and began to take her back to Haven's party. As he did, he cast his gaze around, just in time to see Varens and Pamela slip out through the doors onto the terrace. *Dammit*, he fumed. The fellow was taking base advantage. He wouldn't go down without a fight. Until she had actually accepted one of them, it wasn't too late.

He made polite noises as he left Miss Dresden with the Haven party, and then threaded through the crowd and the lines forming for the next dance, to the doors that opened onto the terrace. He would *not* give up without a fight.

He stepped out. The night was moonlit, made for romance, lightly perfumed with a pleasant breeze. It should have been him taking Pamela out to the garden!

Where were they?

There were couples. The night was warm, and flambeaux lit the terrace itself to add respectability to the courtship rituals that were even now taking place. A whispered word, a murmured response, a hand pressed earnestly, a long, yearning look between lovers.

Strongwycke strolled, trying not to look desperate, trying to control the flare of fear that roiled in his stomach. Where *was* she?

He stepped off the terrace, having satisfied himself that not one of the couples was Varens and Pamela. The garden was laid out with stone pathways that wound through formal rose gardens and wilder patches where shaggy hollyhocks and Canterbury bells grew stately and tall. A small willow drooped, and he spied a couple behind it, but one look at the red hair of the gentleman and he knew it was not Varens.

But yes, there; he would recognize the slight form of Pamela even from a distance as a couple strolled down a distant path. The two disappeared around a bend, the baronet's arm protectively around her waist. How would he approach them; what would he say?

What would he see?

He moved forward, relying on his wits to provide an answer in time. Through the dusky gloom, his step more uncertain as the light from the brilliant ballroom and the flambeaux dimmed with distance, he advanced.

And then he heard their voices, and they guided him onward.

". . . so search your heart Pammy, and see if I am right," Varens was saying earnestly, emotion throbbing through his voice. "You *know* I am right. You *must* know. If it is real, then admit it! Which of us can you not live without?"

"Colin . . . you . . . you are right," she said, her voice filled with wonder. "How could I have been so blind?"

As Strongwycke moved forward, he could see Varens take her in his arms. He couldn't approach. His feet, as if welded to the spot, would allow him neither to approach, nor to depart.

"We have both been blind, my dear, for a very long time," he said, gently, caressing her curls.

"I think . . . I think I just didn't want to hurt anyone," Pamela said, her voice breathy with emotion. She rested her forehead on his shoulder.

"But you must be true to yourself. Admit it, you have known from the start." Varens's tone was husky with suppressed feeling. He put one finger under her chin and turned her face up.

Her own voice thick with tears, she said, "You are right, of course. I have never known how deeply I could love until now, until you have shown me what real love is."

"You will make a good wife. I love you very much, Pammy." Varens took her in his arms, bending to kiss her.

Strongwycke turned away, released from his spot by the knowledge that all hope was gone. A sour taste flooded his mouth and he wanted to retch, his stomach convulsing. He had never felt such pain in his life, or not since Euphemia died. It was done. There was nothing he could do now. As long as she had accepted neither of them, there was a chance for him, but now she was betrothed and he must, in honor step aside. The pain was searing, but his control was rigid. He walked away, across the grass, up the steps, over the terrace. He entered the glaring, overheated ballroom, crossed it without a word to anyone, and tripped up the steps to the cloakroom, his tread becoming more weary, as if his path was through oatmeal.

"Strongwycke, where are you going?" Haven said, stepping out of the card room.

"Well, you have got your wish, sir," he said, bitterly. "Pamela has accepted your good friend, Varens. I wish them all the happiness in the world."

He left the house, stepping out the door and into the London night.

Haven, trying hard to fight back a grin, approached Jane. "I have good news," he whispered, taking her arm. They slipped into an alcove, and he let his baser urges get the better of him for a moment, kissing her breathless.

"If that is your good news, Gerry," she said, clinging to his arms, "I think I would like to hear more." She reached up to pull his mouth down to hers.

"Ah, my dear one, don't tempt me or I will carry you off to a private room and ravish you. However, I was just celebrating. It is all finally settled. Pammy has made her choice."

Wary, Jane said, "She has? How do you know?"

"Just saw Strongwycke leaving. Gloomy sod. Apparently, Pamela told him she has accepted Varens's offer!"

"Oh."

"Jane, I know you were, for some incomprehensible reason, pulling for Strongwycke, but she has chosen Colin. Be happy for her!"

"Oh, I will be. I like Sir Colin, truly. Look! They are back with the family," she said, peeking around him at the family grouping. "Hush," she said, pulling Haven after her. "I suppose we must pretend like we don't know what has happened until they make an official announcement."

"Hard to do," he said, rubbing his hands together. "But I suppose I can manage."

Andromeda was nodding at something her brother had just said, and Lady Haven was talking earnestly to Pamela. Trying his best not to look conscious, Haven, Jane on his arm, joined them.

"So," he said, airily. "What is everyone speaking of?"

"A matter of the greatest import," Lady Haven said.

"Ah, then Jane and I should be included in this important discussion, shouldn't we?"

"Absolutely," she said. "For you are vitally concerned. Pamela has just told us that she and Varens were out in the garden talking."

"Yes?" Haven lifted his eyebrows in what he hoped was a questioning fashion. His mother was much more sanguine about this than he would have thought possible, given that her youngest would be rejecting an earl for a baronet. It was a credit to her true motherly instincts, buried, but showing occasionally. Jane squeezed his arm, and he tried to calm himself. But this was an announcement that he sincerely believed would bring such satisfaction to all the family! Two young people, so sincerely attached; how could it fail to produce much joy?

"Yes," Pamela said. "We were in the garden, and as we were coming in we heard Count Mallienne say that the Lombard Theater has just burned to the ground! Imagine that! They say it was the gaslights."

Haven stood, open-mouthed, waiting.

"We were all to go there Saturday night. Remember?" Lady Haven said, staring at her son, misinterpreting his gaping puzzlement.

Pamela was swept away by Dexter that moment, and no announcement was forthcoming. Haven didn't know what to think, and Jane advised silence. What if they were waiting to announce it for some occasion? Perhaps Pamela's birthday party the next night. That made sense to Haven, and so he stayed silent. But it wasn't easy.

Late in the night, Pamela rose, unable to sleep. She had expected to feel differently this moment, but then she had expected that she would have been able to speak to Strongwycke that night. After Colin and she talked, it all became so much clearer. She was grateful to her old friend. He had become, he said, suddenly wiser. He didn't elaborate, but she felt there was more there to be discovered.

He truly felt that what was between them was friendship, he said. Though that was not the worst basis of marriage, there should be more. If she could say in her heart that she didn't feel that "more" for Strongwycke, then she should make her decision accordingly. But if there was something more, beyond mere feelings of amity with the earl, then she should meet her future boldly, and not let anyone stop her.

She should take his offer. As for himself, he withdrew his offer of marriage. He loved her as a sister, but she deserved so much more in a suitor, deserved someone who could love her as a woman ought to be loved. He knew that now.

And it was true. Looking at Colin in the gloom, she had seen the same good friend she had always seen. And nothing more.

He kissed her as a friend, and it was a revelation, holding none of the fierce longing and sweet desire she felt when Strongwycke kissed her. If only he had kissed her earlier! She would have known immediately.

She had been anxious to return to the ballroom, bursting with her desire to see Strongwycke, to talk to him. To tell him she didn't need to wait until the next night. She had made her decision. Fear was still present, but now she had her feelings for Colin in their proper place. She would always love him as another brother, a boon companion, the old friend of her childhood. But she had become a woman in the meantime, and that woman responded to the earl, to his touch, to his kiss.

To his desire for her, which sparked an answering yearning in her own blood. Her face flamed and she shoved her feet into slippers and padded down the dark stairs and through the quiet hall. She couldn't stay still. She was restless with unresolved needs. If it were not so wrong, she would have mounted Tassie and gone to his London house that moment. Of course she couldn't do that. It was unthinkable to visit a gentleman at his home without the company of others, and in the middle of the night! Even she knew that, and wouldn't cross that boundary between acceptable and unacceptable again in London.

There was a light flickering in the library, and with the horrible news of that theater fire on her mind, she pushed open the door and entered, to find her brother by the fire, port glass in hand, reading. "Oh, Gerry, it is only you!"

"Pammy! Come in. What are you doing up?"

"I can't sleep."

"Too excited?"

His knowing look alarmed her. What did he know? How much *should* he know, as her guardian? Did he know the way Strongwycke kissed her, and how she felt about him when he did? She certainly hoped not. He wouldn't understand. Though come to think of it, the way she had seen him with Jane, perhaps he would understand only too well.

She shrugged and curled up in a vast leather chair near the fire. Looking at his bluff profile, she hesitated, but then said, "You and Jane long to be married, don't you?"

"Yes."

"Then why don't you just do it? Get married and go back up to Yorkshire?"

He stretched back in his chair. "We have to go through this elaborate London marriage now, Pammy. We are bound to it."

"Why?"

He grimaced. "It has been explained to me at length, and even Jane concurs. Knowing how much she would rather marry in Lesleydale, I must believe she knows what she is talking about. Apparently, if we put it off and wait until we go North at the end of the Season, all of London will gossip and think there is something wrong between us. We can give them no reason for that, not with Rachel's wedding to the sensitive Lord Yarnell coming up. And your own, now."

"Who knows when that will be," she said, gloomily, thinking that the way her mother was, it could take forever, all of the planning. "But that only holds if you wait to get married. Rachel's wedding isn't until July. You two could get married, go North, spend time in your little cottage and on the estate alone, and *still* come back down to London in time."

"You know, that is true." He sat back in his chair and stared at the ceiling. "It is only postponement that will cause gossip. If we marry right away the worst the old cats will think is that we had to rush it. A bit of a scandal, but an understandable one. And one easily disproved by time."

Pamela grinned at the dawning joy in her brother's voice. "So do it! Go, get married. Jane is miserable here in London, and you are, too. With any luck you will have a little one started by the time you have to come back for Rachel's wedding."

"You are as bad as your grandmother," he said reprovingly, staring at her.

She snorted. "I have seen the way you two look at each other. It won't be for want of trying if you do not have a little one nine months exactly from your wedding day."

"Watch your mouth, young lady. I shall have to warn Colin about your broad speech, learned from Grand. As if he doesn't know you well enough, I suppose."

"Why would you have to warn Colin?"

"Just a manner of speaking, Pammy. He will be responsible for you from now on, after all."

They gazed at each other in the flickering firelight.

Haven laughed and broke the silence. "I am terrible at keeping a secret. I saw Strongwycke on his way out of the ball tonight. He told me you had finally decided on Colin. Seemed pretty broken up about it, I must say. I almost felt sorry for him."

Pamela uncoiled and braced herself with her hands on the arms of the chair. "How did he . . . where did he get that idea?"

"You didn't tell him?"

"Tell him what? There is nothing to tell. I mean, it isn't true. Colin told me he was taking his proposal back, that we shouldn't suit after all, and that he had been an idiot and a base coward."

"What?"

Pamela, trembling, told him all, that Colin had taken her outside to tell her the truths he had come to understand. That he loved her like a sister. That they would only ever be friends. And that, while there were worse bases for marriage, he thought that she had someone who truly loved her. If she loved him, she should be bold and seize her future, and not hide behind the past.

"I have searched my own heart," Pamela said, clutching her hands to her chest. "I think I have known all along that I love Strong—no, I *have* known all along that I love him—but I have been so afraid to take the chance, to be bold. I know that is unlike me, but marrying him is taking such a different path from the one I thought I would take. I love him so much; I will go anywhere, do anything, for him."

"But Strongwycke distinctly said . . ."

"I don't understand." Pamela leaped to her feet and grasped her curls in both hands. "Good God, he said he would leave town if I told him 'no'! But I didn't tell him 'no'! I was going to tell him 'yes'! I went to look for him, but I was told he left the ball. Why . . . ?" She stared with wide, frightened eyes at her brother.

Haven stood and took his sister's shoulders. "Pammy, calm down. Good God, if I'd known you really preferred the fellow . . . I will go in the morning and find out what is wrong, how he got the wrong idea."

"Thank you, Gerry," she said, tears stinging her eyes. "Bother, how did this go so wrong? I . . . I am going up to bed now."

"Pammy," Haven roared, stomping through the house, leaving the front door open on the scene of the usual morning bustle of the street. Jane came running down the stairs, having been closeted with Pamela.

"What have you found out?" she asked, breathless.

"He is gone. Left. He and Belinda have headed North, just a half hour ago. The knocker is down and the servants are putting Holland covers on everything. His housekeeper said the agent has been told to lease the house for the rest of the Season if he can, because the earl won't be back to London this year."

"Gone? But why?"

"I can only think . . ."

"What is going on?" Lady Haven glided down the hallway, just as Pamela joined them, jumping down the last two steps.

"Pammy, go get your shawl. We are going to get to the bottom of this. He only left a half hour ago, so there is still time to catch him. I know which way he went."

"Where *who* went?" Lady Haven squawked.

"Gerry," Jane said, clutching at his arm. "May I go with you?"

"Better than that," he said, grinning down at her. "*Much* better."

"What is going *on*?" Lady Haven said.

Her son ignored her. He took Jane in his arms and said, "How would you like to get married? Today. On our way north to Yorkshire." He pulled a stiff document out of his pocket and waved it in front of her. "I have the license."

"Gerry," she gasped. "Could we?"

"Only if you can pack a bag in ten minutes, for that is when I am taking Pamela to find her own true love before he is all the way back in the Lakes District, the idiot. I intend to drop Pamela off with Strongwycke, and then you and I shall head North. Home. And we will stay in Mary's old cottage our first night as man and wife, just as you wanted."

The dowager, tapping out into the hall from her tiny room off the hall, gleefully said, "That is the way! Carry her off!"

"Mother-in-law, this cannot be!" Lady Haven said, her voice raised, hysterically. "I have planned a wedding, and the invitations are at the printers, and the confectioner . . ."

"Ninny! We are at last disagreeing again, Lydia. I feel twenty years younger for it. Your son is finally proving he is a man with blood in his veins, not water. Spend all your fuss on Rachel's wedding and leave the others alone."

And so, despite Lady Haven's tears, Haven, Jane, and Pamela were in the carriage and on the road out of London within the half hour.

Twenty-two

Belinda, a pout on her face, said, "Why are we going back up North so suddenly, though? I thought you and Miss Pamela were in love . . ."

"Enough!" Strongwycke said, harshly, swaying with the motion of the carriage. He glared out the window at the passing scenery, unwilling to let his niece see the hurt and anger in his eyes. The child had enough to deal with, without that.

Belinda was silent for just a moment, but then spoke again. "But Miss Varens promised to take me to the theater one afternoon and introduce me to some of the people she has met. She is such an interesting lady, Uncle, and says I have the dramatic flare of a great actress!" Belinda made an eloquent motion with her arm, almost knocking Strongwycke's hat off.

"Watch what you are about!" he said, ducking his head. "Miss Varens should keep her opinions to herself, for no well-raised young lady would even think about the stage!" Strongwycke determinedly turned his face to look out the window of the carriage.

Belinda went back to talking to her governess, Miss Linton, who had been hired to live with them at Shadow Manor. She resolutely ignored her bad-tempered uncle, and if she secretly wondered if his ire were connected with Miss Pamela, she could hurt no one with her private thoughts.

Strongwycke mulled over the events of the last few days. Perhaps he would be thought a poor sport, leaving London without even congratulating the "happy couple," but he couldn't stomach the thought. The sight of Pamela in the baronet's arms still burned, making his stomach ache and his head hurt. Was it like this when Dorothea deserted him? He remembered anger and hurt, but not quite this burning anguish. He supposed he really thought Pamela loved him back, had felt it in her kisses. He had been more circumspect with Dorothea, and hadn't expected her to return his ardor. Pamela's sweet enticement had been an awakening of sorts, a lesson in the loveliness of new passion. To know she had shared kisses with Varens, and that the other man's were apparently preferable. . . .

He gradually became aware of the sound of another carriage thundering up behind them, and he glanced out, to see that it had pulled up even. The road was dry and dusty, and a cloud surrounded the carriage, so he couldn't see who was inside, if anyone.

But what was the idiot driver doing? The road was narrow, and if the fellow was passing, why did he not just get on with it?

He could hear shouting above the clatter of hooves and harnesses, and his carriage driver slowed, gradually, as the other carriage pulled ahead. Strongwycke settled back in his seat, but to his puzzlement, his carriage rocked to a complete halt, with the other in front doing the same.

Perhaps the other driver had noted something wrong with their rig, he thought. "Stay here, Belinda, Miss Linton. I am going to find out what is wrong."

He clambered out of the carriage and started toward the other vehicle, noting that the occupant of the other carriage was doing the same. It was a young lad . . . no, it was . . .

He whirled, and started back to his own carriage. "Strong, wait!"

He stopped, and Pamela raced up to him, her slim, breeches-clad figure dancing across the dusty road. She grabbed his arm.

"Strong, you must listen to me." Her tone was urgent, her gray-green eyes pleading.

He took a deep breath and ground his teeth. "I am sorry I didn't wait in London to do this, but I suppose I must offer my congratulations on your upcoming wedding to . . ."

"I am not marrying Colin! Where did you get that idiotic idea?"

"I heard you! Him! *And* you! And I saw you kissing in the garden at the ball last night. You can't deny it."

"But I am not marrying him! It was just the opposite."

Pamela cocked her head and waved, looking behind Strongwycke, and he turned to see his niece with her head stuck out the window of the carriage. "Belinda, sit inside with Miss Linton and behave!" he shouted.

"But I want to say goodbye to Miss Pam . . ."

"Sit!" His voice echoed in the quiet countryside like a gunshot. A hare leaped from the hedgerow and scurried across the field in dismay.

And now two heads stuck out of *Pamela's* carriage. It was Haven and Miss Jane Dresden.

"I do not appreciate being part of a farce, Miss Pamela," he ground out, his fist clenched at his side. "So if you will just turn around . . ."

Pamela threw her arms around his neck, catching him off balance, and kissed him. He pushed her away, saying, "I don't know what game this is, but . . ."

Haven waved jauntily and shouted back, "Right, then! Good to see you two getting along. We shall be back in one month. If you aren't married by then, we'll come to your wedding! Onwards, driver!" The carriage pulled off, leaving a dusty Pamela standing on the road, staring up at Strongwycke.

"Have you all gone quite mad?" Strongwycke started down the road, picking up speed as he saw that the carriage really was leaving. "Hey, Haven! Haven!" he shouted as he ran after them. "You can't leave your sister here . . ." But he already knew he wouldn't be heard above the hooves and creaking of the carriage. He stopped and stood, staring off after it.

"I told him that if we kissed," Pamela said, loud enough for him to hear, "he was to go ahead and leave, because it was all right. You would take me back to London with you." She paused. "Or wherever."

Strongwycke looked back at Pamela. She stood in the middle of the road, arms crossed, staring at him defiantly.

"You are mad." He started back towards his own carriage, having to pass her to get there.

"Perhaps, but I love you," she said, as he moved around her.

He stopped. Turning and staring into her huge eyes, trying to see what kind of cruel hoax she was playing, he said, "What did you say?"

"I love you. Will you marry me?"

"Don't joke in that manner, Pamela." His voice sounded hollow.

A bird swooped over head and called out to its

mate. She moved toward him and went down on one knee on the dusty road, taking his hand in hers. "I never joke when making a proposal. Will you marry me?"

He jerked his hand away. "What is this about?" His voice was deadly calm in the brilliant sunlit day.

"I love you. I have for ages, but—I was frightened." She stood and dusted off one knee and shrugged, sheepishly. "Colin seemed safe. He didn't make me feel all scary inside, all jumpy and nervous and twitchy, like you do. I didn't know what to think, you see. I have thought I was in love with Colin for a long time, but it was just . . . well, it was just hero-worship, I think. The hero-worship of a little girl for a gallant and good-natured friend."

Strongwycke, hope dawning, said, "Is that true? Then why were you kissing him in the garden?"

"He had just helped me see that I already knew what I should do, I was just running scared from it. That kiss was no different than if he was my brother. Couldn't you tell? If you saw it, it should have been obvious to you, for it was no more than the merest brush of our lips. If I had had a doubt left in my mind, that kiss would have told me."

Strongwycke thought back. The moment they had embraced, he had turned away, sick at heart, not wanting to see anymore. He narrowed his eyes and gazed down at her. "What did he say to cause this sudden self-knowledge? Did he reject you? Is that what did it? I will be second-best to no one."

Pamela moved closer to him and put her arms back around his neck. "Strong, I *love* you. But it frightened me, because I knew you loved me, too. It . . . it is a fearsome responsibility being loved, knowing you are responsible for the other person's happiness. I was afraid. A coward. I never want to fail you, because I want you to be happy always, you are so precious to me, and what if I can't make you happy?"

Strongwycke saw the doubt in her eyes, the fear, and his heart melted. He pulled her close and took a deep breath. "My love, you aren't responsible for my happiness; that is up to me. If anything, I want to make *you* happy. I want to fill all of your days with joy."

"You can," she said, tenderly, laying one hand on his cheek. "Just love me."

Her simple words broke down the last barriers, the cold wall he was trying to erect to protect his battered heart. He lowered his face, stared into her large, gray-green eyes, and then kissed her, deep and long.

They were interrupted by a whooping sound. It was Belinda, who had erupted from the carriage and was doing a mad dance in the middle of the dirt road as her governess, leaning out of the carriage, begged her to calm down, the poor woman's eyes wide with consternation.

"They're going to get married," Belinda cried, jumping up and down, her gown flaring and belling around her. "They are going to get married! Whoop!"

"Are we? You haven't said 'yes' yet." Pamela looked up at Strongwycke.

"We are going to do this, at least, properly," the earl said. He went down on one knee on the dusty road, as Belinda danced and sang a strange song behind them. "Miss Pamela Neville, will you do me the honor of being my bride, knowing you will have to deal with that strange creature who is making such a racket, yonder?"

Pamela, breeches and all, perched demurely on

his knee and framed his face within her two hands. "My lord, I would be honored and delighted to be your bride, and confine yon creature in some sort of shackles at our wedding so she can't scare the other attendees."

He laughed out loud at that, and said, "Then I now pronounce us betrothed. But you won't make me wait too long, will you?"

She shivered deliciously. "I won't. Make you wait, I mean."

A carriage pulled up and stopped. "I say," the passenger said, leaning out. "You folks are not in any trouble are you?"

"Oh, I think I am," Pamela said, dreamily, looking up, into a kindly elderly gentleman's face. "We are going to be married you see, and I shall have to take in hand that mad creature behind us, but I will be so busy with my husband, whom I will love very much . . ."

Before she could finish, the carriage rolled away, and the passenger was muttering, "Very strange people. Very, *very* strange!"

I have grown up, Pamela thought, surveying the attendees at her wedding breakfast in the dining room of Haven House a bare two weeks later. She wore a pale green, flowing gown with a circlet of ivory roses around her auburn curls, and a necklace of matched, flawless pearls given to her by her grandmother, the pearls that woman had worn on her wedding day sixty-five years earlier. *I have grown up finally, and it isn't so bad to be a lady and a woman, both.* She caught a warm glance from her husband, handsome and commanding in black, and blushed. *Especially a woman,* she amended.

She and Strongwycke were going to start out that very day toward Shadow Manor, by way of Haven Court to pay a wedding visit on her brother and his new wife, who were comfortably ensconced in Mary Cooper, now Mary Latimer's, former cottage, while their own was being built. At her own request, Belinda was going to stay in London with Miss Varens, with whom she had formed a strong bond of friendship, and Colin, who had, with surprising vigor, thrown himself into the London life he had used to despise.

Surveying each of her family members in turn, and winking broadly at Grand, who looked regal in azure satin and diamonds, Pamela hoped, mostly, that Rachel, calmly sitting beside her betrothed, Lord Yarnell, would find at least a fraction of her own happiness with the frosty marquess. But sadly, she doubted it. Rachel had her reasons, Pamela thought, but Yarnell was still stiff as a poker and humorless. She could not like her brother-in-law to be.

"Happy?" Strongwycke whispered, taking her hand in his and stripping off her glove.

"I'm very happy," she said, looking up at his dear face.

"I propose a toast," Colin said, standing. He smiled down the long table at the newlyweds. "Here is to long life, long love, and hope for the future."

"Here, here," someone said.

"And here is to intelligent choices," Grand said. "And good-looking husbands and warm beds."

Pamela threw back her head and laughed, gasping as Strongwycke boldly pinched her bottom. As always, Grand got the last scandalous word.

Or, not quite the last word.

"Kiss the bride, Strongwycke," Colin hollered, winking at the dowager.

"Yes, kiss her! Give her something to think about!"

Yes, Grand truly did always have to have the last word.

Pamela glared at her grandmother, wondering if she had always been so bawdy, but then, as Strongwycke obediently took her into his arms and kissed her long and deep, the others melted away and she was lost again, lost in her future, and all the joy that was still to come.

ABOUT THE AUTHOR

Donna Simpson lives with her family in Canada. She is currently working on her next Zebra regency romance, RACHEL'S CHANGE OF HEART, to be published in May 2003. Donna loves to hear from readers and you may write to her c/o Zebra Books. Please include a self-addressed stamped envelope if you wish a reply.